TEEN
HYDE

HIGH SCHOOL HORROR

TEEN HYDE

CHANDLER BAKER

FEIWEL AND FRIENDS
NEW YORK

A FEIWEL AND FRIENDS BOOK
An imprint of Macmillan Publishing Group, LLC

HIGH SCHOOL HORROR: TEEN HYDE. Copyright © 2017 by DiGa LLC.
All rights reserved. Printed in the United States of America by
LSC Communications US, LLC (Lakeside Classic), Harrisonburg, Virginia.
For information, address Feiwel and Friends, 175 Fifth Avenue, New York, N.Y. 10010.

Our books may be purchased in bulk for promotional, educational, or business use. Please
contact your local bookseller or the Macmillan Corporate and Premium Sales Department
at (800) 221-7945 ext. 5442 or by e-mail at MacmillanSpecialMarkets@macmillan.com.

Library of Congress Cataloging-in-Publication Data is available.
ISBN 978-1-250-05875-1 (hardcover) / ISBN 978-1-250-11769-4 (ebook)

Book design by Eileen Savage

Feiwel and Friends logo designed by Filomena Tuosto

First Edition—2017

1   3   5   7   9   10   8   6   4   2

fiercereads.com

For my mom, my role model

ONE

Cassidy

Mix. Mingle. *Try* to look like you're having fun," Paisley had said before disappearing into the crowded kitchen.

She'd abandoned me in record time, even for her, and I was left standing in a sea of half-drunk people with the vague feeling that I had some totally off-putting and incurable disease, like smallpox. Honestly, people might have preferred that. At least with smallpox they could host a fund-raiser. As far as I knew, there were no bake sales for the chronically sad.

I stuffed my hands into the back pockets of the dark-wash skinny jeans Paisley had insisted I put on instead of the old faded pairs I'd grown accustomed to wearing. It was either concede to the jeans or let my best friend wrestle me into a miniskirt and I most definitely wasn't ready for anything as flashy as a miniskirt. I scanned the room, trying to remember whose house this was anyway. Whoever it was, I didn't envy them. There were too many nice things combined with too many people. It was a parental disaster waiting to happen.

I meandered farther inside, being careful not to make eye contact with anyone. These people sure did like plaid. I stepped over a set of tartan throw pillows that had been pitched to the ground to make room for a group of girls to smash in together, one girl's legs thrown over those of her two friends, a casual message to the rest of the room: *We* are best friends. I knew because I used to speak that language fluently. But now I sought out somewhere to hide in plain sight. I found it in the living room, next to a piano, a furniture piece with enough heft to create a more comfortable, less populated perimeter. I picked up an unlit candle sitting on top, brought it to my nose, and sniffed in the scent of wild sea grass. Okay, so I had to turn it over and check the label. I had no idea how wild sea grass smelled. I had a theory about candles, actually. I was convinced that the world's candlemakers only manufactured, like, three different fragrances—fruity, fresh, and baking ingredient—all the other supposed "perfumes" were just marketing disguises designed to make us feel like we were purchasing something worth fifteen bucks.

I glanced over my shoulder. Nearby there was another group of girls huddled together that looked vaguely familiar—maybe sophomores—but none of them looked as if they wanted to discuss my candle conspiracies. That was honestly too bad. I might have been into that conversation.

I gingerly set the jar down on the piano and picked up a gold frame. In the photograph a smiling man and woman wore fedoras and held frozen drinks with little umbrellas in front of a glimmering pool. They looked so happy it made my joints ache. Paisley would probably scold me for snooping around their belongings. Hell, I would probably scold me. The old me would anyway. I sighed and replaced the frame.

A couple of the younger girls that I'd noticed earlier were casting furtive glances in my direction and whispering to each other. They were pretty, with long hair that fell past their shoulder blades and necklaces that matched their shoes. I stood there in no-man's-land, letting them whisper and stare. Even with my not-so-invisible cloak of doom and gloom, as captain of the cheerleading squad, I was still popular enough to be intimidating, although now with all the rumors about me—face it, many of them true—I was probably a little scary, too. Hence the whispering. I doubted any of them would have the guts to come right up and talk to me. Good, let them be scared, I figured.

I'd been at the party for twenty minutes and so far I'd managed not to talk to a single person since walking through the door. I felt weirdly proud of this. Like maybe I should keep it that way. An entire party without opening my mouth to speak. Or to make out with boys.

Getting drunk and kissing definitely fell within the realm of old me.

I squeezed past the group of girls and noticed as they fell silent the moment I came close. *Subtle, ladies*, I wanted to say. Only I didn't because I was anti-conversation. Anti-party. Anti-everything.

Instead, I observed. I glided out of the living room, feeling like a ghost of my former self, and into the kitchen. The back doors opened onto a patio where my classmates were spilling out into the night. I spotted Paisley's blond bob, bowed forward in concentration over a game of flip cup taking place on the breakfast table. Beside her, two girls from our cheerleading squad, the Oilerettes—Ashley and Erica—hailed her on with whoops and squeals.

I jumped at the feeling of a cold hand tugging on my elbow. "I heard a rumor you were here."

I jerked around to see Ava. Startled, my mouth fell open, but no words came out. I just blinked at her. She was a fellow junior on the Oilerettes, who'd made the squad for the first time this semester. Ava had a penchant for adding a personal flair to her clothes. She'd cut the neck opening of a black T-shirt, so that it now hung casually off one shoulder, blending with the shiny strands of her jet-black tresses.

I tightened my lips into something that I hoped resembled a smile.

"Sorry. Didn't mean to scare you." She looked me over. "Geez, it's a party, Cassidy." She playfully grabbed me by the shoulders and shook me as though she could shake free whatever piece had broken in the past few weeks. "You look more like you're at somebody's funeral." Her hands slid from my shoulder and she pinched the bridge of her nose. "Right. Sorry. God, bad choice of words."

In case anyone was wondering, it wasn't kosher to mention the words *death, funeral, dead, dying,* or *kill* in front of me. Not after my boyfriend, Adam, accidentally killed Paisley's on-again, off-again romance, Knox, just as I was being crowned Homecoming queen. Or after Adam had likely suffered a similarly gruesome fate at the hands of Hollow Pines's resident serial killer. Of course, all of this occurred once Adam had very publicly cheated on me with a high school nobody, so perhaps even the word "boyfriend" was generous.

Not that this wouldn't be enough to make anyone's greatest hits album for Worst Year Ever, but those parts of the story that people knew, the ones that made them whisper and look at me funny and apologize for making a stupid offhand comment that even I knew they didn't mean, those parts didn't amount to half of it.

I had a gaping hole in my chest so wide I found it shocking that the whole world couldn't see right through it. And the stone-cold truth was that Adam wasn't the one who put it there.

I caught myself staring off into space. Or rather, I caught my reflection in the dark circles of Ava's eyes, which were busy searching my face for signs of life. *Sorry, no signs here*, I wanted to tell her, only it felt like it'd take an exorbitant amount of effort, so I didn't bother.

I was actually relieved when Ashley bounced away from the game of flip cup to join us. Her cheeks were flushed with an early buzz. I remembered the feeling I got after the first few drinks, when my blood felt warm and gooey in my veins, every muscle in me relaxed and I loved everyone that I met. *Especially* the boys that I met. Those were the days when I didn't see any harm in a little kissing. But I knew now that the warm, gooey feeling was the same one that left girls with gaping holes in their chests.

"The Billys are on their way with wine coolers," Ashley said, referring to the guys on the football team, William, Billy Ray, and just Billy. I'd kissed William twice and Billy Ray once last year. Paisley had made fun of me for being easy, but in my personal canon of ethics I wasn't easy as long as I kept all contact above the waistline.

Still, I wished I could take it all back now.

Ava leaned closer to Ashley. "Paisley showed me those pictures of that sophomore, by the way. I'm actually mortified for her. First, she was stupid enough to send pictures to William in her underwear and, second, she wears cotton instead of lace."

With Ava and Ashley occupied, I took my opportunity to leave. I shrugged and pointed over my shoulder in a vague direction that could have meant I was getting a drink or going to the restroom. Ashley gave a quick smile and waved her fingers.

The restroom. Now there was an idea. I could kill at least fifteen minutes in a bathroom. Completely alone. I'd committed to an hour at the party. Enough to make the skinny jeans worthwhile.

I trudged along a carpeted hallway that looked as if it should lead to a bathroom and quickly ran up against the back of the line. Even better. I could probably kill twenty minutes now.

I waited, taking dutiful steps forward every time someone else shut the door behind them. I thought coming to a party would help, but looking back, I wasn't sure what. My mood? My outlook on life? My solitude? The invisible gaping wound festering in my chest? Those felt like lofty goals for a house party.

It'll be good for you, I replayed my friends' words in my head and sighed. *Give it a chance.*

I was finally the next person in line. No one had tried to talk to me the whole time I'd been standing here. A small part of me was put out by this. The old me would have chatted to people in line. Actually, the old me would have never ventured to the bathroom alone. Paisley and I would have gone into the bathroom arm in arm and taken turns fixing our hair while the other one peed.

The door opened and a skinny boy wearing a starched fishing shirt and holding a red plastic cup exited. I slipped in and closed the door shut behind me. Someone had left the hand towel off its hook and a bottle of shower gel had been knocked off the edge of the tub, but other than that, the bathroom looked relatively clean for mid-party.

I turned and pushed the button on the lock. It didn't stick. I tried again, only to find that the door didn't lock at all. *Great.* I blew hair from my eyes. Well, at least there was a line. People had seen me walk in, so I should have a modicum of privacy.

Moving away from the door, I decided to kill time by snooping through the owners' belongings. I still had no idea whose home we were destroying. I slid open the first row of drawers beneath the countertop. Blue goo oozed from a toothpaste bottle onto a dirty hand mirror. This bathroom must belong to a boy.

I found an electric razor resting in the second drawer and eyed it with interest. I turned it over, testing the weight in my palm. I'd never used one before. I eyed my long brown hair. The old me would never have left the house without styling it into loose curls to frame my face. Now, it was plastered on either side of my head. I leaned toward the mirror and swept a handful of hair away from my ear to see where I'd begin shaving. If I did begin shaving, that was. Which I wouldn't because that was crazy. Wasn't it?

My fingers felt twitchy, trigger-happy.

I hadn't been completely honest. Yes, there was the old me, the one with the wavy curls and miniskirts, the toned abs and the long list of doting boys. But then there was the old-old me. That version was a chubby girl who was good at math. That version had been invisible. Nobody even knew her name.

I switched on the electric razor and felt it vibrate in my hand.

When my family moved from Phoenix, I'd done some quick

mental math and concluded that life in a small Texas town like Hollow Pines would be a whole lot easier as the girl with abs and miniskirts. But now, I wasn't so sure. My calculations may have been off.

My heart pounded as I brought the razor closer to my scalp. I could go back to that girl. If that was what I wanted, all it would take was a few swipes of the razor and then Cassidy Hyde, Homecoming queen, would be gone. I licked my lips, my mind buzzing with concentration, when out of the corner of my eye, I spotted a gleam of silver in the open drawer.

I lowered the razor and took out a pair of scissors. These were better. *Baby steps*, I told myself. I pulled one of the front pieces of hair out in front of my nose, opened the blades, and held them at eye level.

My hands shook when suddenly the door burst open. Startled, I snapped the handles together and heard the short snip of the blades.

"Someone's in here," I yelled. A lock of my hair drifted down like a feather to lay lifeless on the countertop. My throat squeezed tight. I hadn't meant to speak.

Anger roiled inside me as I whirled to see Liam Buckley pressing his back to the door.

His lips spread into a crooked grin. "Hey, Cass."

"Hey, yourself," I said. There was no holding back the words now that Liam and I were sharing a twenty-five square foot space. "You weren't even next in line."

He lifted his eyebrows. Liam dwarfed me at well over six feet tall. He had eyes as green as emeralds, tan skin, and brown hair streaked with natural shades of golden blond so beautiful you'd swear he paid for them at the salon. "Sorry, had to piss like a racehorse," he said, pushing up the cuffs of his sleeves. His rumpled shirt was half untucked, giving him the casually privileged air of a prep school kid. "You mind?"

Before I could answer, he crossed the room, unfastening his belt as he did so.

My mouth fell open and my cheeks went blisteringly hot. Just before I heard the sound of his urine hitting the toilet bowl, I managed to spin back around and aim my eyes anywhere but the mirror.

"What is *wrong* with you?" I said.

His steady stream didn't falter. "Bunch of freshmen and sophomores in the line so I jumped it." Liam was a year older than me, a senior starter on the Hollow Pines basketball team. "Plus I needed someplace private."

This entire scenario was officially mortifying. The only problem was that the person for whom it should be mortifying was *him*.

I listened to the zip of his fly and then the toilet flushed. I glanced up into the mirror. At least he'd remembered to put the seat down. Liam was grinning at me as he approached the sink. I instinctively scooted over to make room. Last year I would have died from joy to be stuck in a room with Liam Buckley.

He turned the faucet and stuck his hands underneath the running water. So, not a total barbarian.

"What are you doing in here anyway?" His gaze flitted to the scissors and the lock of hair. "Joining witness protection, Cass?"

I blinked. "What are you doing calling me 'Cass'? You hardly even know me." I recognized the voice of the girl with the gaping wound in her chest, the one that didn't care to be sharing a room with Liam Buckley but instead would prefer to be left alone.

The left corner of his mouth curved up, puckering the skin

below his eye to reveal a small scar that had been hidden there. "Easy," he said, shutting off the faucet and shaking his hands dry. Drops of water speckled the mirror.

I chewed the inside of my cheek.

He turned away from the sink and rested the back of his jeans against the countertop. So, what, he was just going to *stay* now? He shoved a hand into his pocket. I watched him, reluctantly curious, out of the corner of my eye. He fished out a small, ziplock bag with a dozen or so pale yellow pills inside.

"I don't normally do this," he said, popping open the top of the bag. "But you look like you could use it." He turned his chin over his shoulder and nodded at the abandoned scissors and the lock of my hair. "Before you commit a crime against fashion or whatever."

"I'm not—" I began to protest.

"Seriously." His green eyes bore into me. "You need to stop. You have really nice hair."

My mouth snapped shut. Part of me wanted to laugh at how ridiculous this all was.

"Hold out your hand," he ordered and, for some reason, I obeyed. He placed a single pill in my palm.

"What is it?" I couldn't even feel the weight of it in my hand.

He selected another one for himself and closed the ziplock bag. "This," he said, pinching the round pill between thumb and forefinger, "is Sunshine. I don't tell just everyone I have this stuff, you know." His smile was easy, his shoulders relaxed, like he's showing me a rare quarter from his collection.

"What's it do?" The minuscule button of a pill looked too tiny to do much of anything.

"It makes you feel like . . . sunshine. Like it's the middle of the summer and you're having the best day ever. Like everything is golden."

I'd been to my share of parties and I was no stranger to alcohol, but I'd never so much as smoked a joint. I turned the pill over and stared at the identical back. I felt drawn in by the cheery yellow color of it. I thought of myself and of the gaping hole in my chest and wondered what I could possibly have to lose.

Just then, someone pounded the door. "Open up," a girl yelled. "There are people waiting."

"One second," Liam yelled. "That's our cue." He held up his pill as if we were clinking glasses. "Cheers." He set the dose of Sunshine onto his tongue, cocked back his head, and swallowed.

Without another thought, I did the same. My mouth was dry and the pill stuck to my throat on its way down, but I managed and, once it was gone, I stuck out my tongue to show that I'd really taken it.

He squeezed my shoulder. "That's my girl." And even though only minutes ago, I'd scolded him for calling me "Cass," this time, I made no smart remark. "Now, shall we go enjoy our night?" he asked.

I stared at the scissors and the dead hair and nodded, still skeptical that the word *enjoy* could apply to me. But my solitude had ended the moment Liam had barged in, so what else was there to do? The pounding on the door had picked back up. Liam casually opened it to greet a red-faced girl preparing to knock her fist against the wood again. "It's all yours." He winked.

The color drained from her face when she saw that it was Liam. "Sorry," she mumbled before ducking between us into the bathroom.

Paisley was waiting third in line, next to Ava. She stood up straighter when she noticed me. "Um, *hello*?" Paisley snagged my elbow as I was following Liam back down the hallway. "I guess somebody's feeling more like themselves." She eyed me from head to toe. "You're hooking up with *Buckley*?" She shared a look with Ava that I couldn't read.

I tensed. "No, it's not like that—"

Paisley smirked, bringing the rim of a wine cooler to her lips. "Right. It never is, Cassidy. Just remember, being easy keeps them breezy, know what I mean?" I did know, but then again, I wasn't looking for a boyfriend. Every boy in Hollow Pines could blow away in the wind for all I cared. "At least get to your fourth drink before you let him under your shirt, 'kay?" She patted me on the head.

Ava rolled her eyes and pushed Paisley gently with her shoulder. "Oh, shut up, Paize. Let her enjoy her night. This is the twenty-first century. Go get yours, girl." She offered me a thumbs-up.

I cocked my head, studying my pair of friends. In the time we'd stood talking, my cheeks had grown warm. Liam was disappearing down the hall. I thought vaguely that I'd like to catch up with him. Paisley snapped her fingers in front of my nose, bringing me back. I knew I should be annoyed with her, but instead, I felt my mouth stretching into a grin.

"Thanks, Paisley," I said. "You . . . look really pretty tonight, you know that?" And I was surprised at how sincere I sounded. It was true, though. A faint glow seemed to radiate from her blond hair. Her skin had a fairylike shimmer emanating from it. I squeezed her hand, feeling a rush of tenderness for my friend. "Isn't this night great?" I said.

Paisley's expression was a confused mix between a grin and a frown. "Yeah," she said. "I mean, I guess so."

There was a swelling in my chest, like a rising balloon, and it seemed to be plugging up the gaping hole that had been there moments earlier. "Okay, well, I'm going to go catch up with Liam. I'll see you guys there? Come dance with us!" I didn't know how I knew that Liam and I would be dancing. But it felt logical. I waved and trotted down the hall in the direction Liam had gone.

I smiled as I passed kids that I only sort of recognized from school. They smiled back. The interaction felt good. It felt right. My veins hummed with a molten warmth so pleasant that I felt as though I'd just had a weeklong spa trip.

I returned to the living room where less than an hour ago I'd sulked in the corner. There I spotted the back of Liam's head, peeking out over the crowded space. I threaded my way through the throng of people, politely excusing myself as we bumped elbows or hips. From the kitchen a nineties boy band song blared through the speakers. The beat matched the thumping in my chest. I remembered this song from car rides with my mom when I was younger. It was one of my favorites.

I tapped Liam on the shoulder. He was chatting with one of the sophomore girls that had been sneaking glances at me with her friends earlier in the night. When Liam looked down to see me standing there, his face seemed to break open with delight.

"Hey, you," he said.

I matched his smile watt for watt. "Wanna dance?" I asked. "I love this song."

He cocked his head to listen and then began bobbing along to the melody. He offered me his hand and twirled me in place. Laughter gurgled up from deep inside me, spilling out into the room. I couldn't believe how long it'd been since I'd laughed.

Liam and I threw our bodies into the music. Others joined us and before long, a circle had formed to watch the pair of us. I didn't take myself too seriously when I danced and neither did Liam. I brought out all my dad's dorky dance moves—the lawn mower, the running man, even the sprinkler. Tears sparkled in my eyes from all of the merriment. I'd forgotten how much I loved dancing, not for cheerleading, but for the fun of it.

Liam leaned close to my ear. His breath tickled and he smelled like coconut shampoo. "You're the most fun girl at this party."

And I believed him. Because all of a sudden it was as if the clouds had lifted and there I still was, shining again.

TWO

Marcy

An eerie green glow was cast by a neon sign in the shape of a pair of boots that hung over a slick, pinewood bar. The club was dimly lit with places to disappear into the shadows for those who wanted to. Those who were like me.

I'd been here before. I knew that in the academic sense. Only this time felt different. I rested my elbows on the counter and pretended to wait for a bartender while I searched the faces gathered there for one that I recognized. No luck.

I turned my back to the bar and scanned the crowd. *Come out, come out, wherever you are*, I thought darkly.

The small town of Dearborn, which neighbored Hollow Pines, only had a few hot spots to serve all of the college's campus. This was by far the most popular.

Five faces had been seared into my memory. When I recognized none of them at the bar, I slinked into the mass of clubgoers. My mind flashed through the lineup of them. Nameless. Heartless. They could only hide for so long.

I reached my hand into the light jacket I was wearing. A wash of comfort blanketed me as my finger traced the blunt side of the knife stashed inside the pocket.

Strobe lights flashed across the dance floor. I studied the face of every boy that I saw. Laughing. Smiling. Drinking from frothy cups. In the cutting lights, they all looked like they had fangs. I stroked the hidden blade, biding my time. *Soon*, I told it. *Soon*.

And in a soft voice, I began to sing:

"Hide and seek, hide and seek,
In the dark, they all will shriek,
Seek and hide, seek and hide,
Count the nights until they've died."

THREE

Cassidy

When I was a kid, I had a name for that place between sleeping and wakefulness. I called it Sleep Space. As in *outer* space. That little pocket of time when I was so relaxed in bed that I was practically weightless, a black hole between two different universes, left dreaming in no-man's-land.

Sunlight trickled through the blinds in my room, warming my face. I buried my head deeper into the pillow and clung to Sleep Space as though I could stop the pull of gravity.

The door of my bedroom creaked open. Through it, the scent of bacon wafted, causing my stomach to growl. When was the last time I'd eaten? I wondered as I finally lost my hold on Sleep Space. My last meal had to have been dinner. Did I remember to eat dinner? I couldn't recall. I took a deep breath in and my mouth watered.

"Cassidy?" My little sister's tentative voice came from the doorway.

When I propped myself up on my elbows, I had to remind myself she wasn't so little anymore. Honor was already one semester into her freshman year at Hollow Pines, tall for her age with cheeks splashed with freckles and hair two shades lighter than my own that fell to the crooks of her elbows. She'd been named after my grandmother, who passed away a few months before Honor was born, and ever since, the name had been a constant source of anxiety for her.

"Morning," I said.

"Mom told me to tell you that she made breakfast," she said, taking a step onto my carpet. "I told her you probably wouldn't come down, but she made me tell you anyway."

"Okay . . . well, what'd she make?" I moved a pillow behind my back and propped myself upright.

Honor looked at me like I was pulling a prank on her. "Mom's making chocolate chip pancakes and Dad's cooking bacon. Why?"

I licked my lips. My stomach growled loudly enough for both of us to hear. A smile tugged at Honor's lips.

"You had me at chocolate. I'm coming down." I wrestled my legs free from the covers.

"Uh, Cass?"

"Yeah?" My bare feet hovered a few inches off the pink floral rug laid across the hardwood floor.

"Did you go to a party last night?"

"Yeah . . ." I caught a glimpse of my reflection in the vanity across from my bed. "Oh." I was wearing the same dark skinny jeans from last night and a fitted black shirt. Mascara and lipstick were smeared on the side of my face so that I resembled the Joker. I covered my mouth with my right hand and stifled a giggle. "I guess I need to clean up first, huh?"

Honor's face brightened. "I'll stall Mom?"

"Don't let any of the chocolate chips get eaten without me."

She grinned and scampered off. I heard the sound of her footsteps fading down the stairs. My chest squeezed as I remembered that this was the first conversation in weeks that involved me responding with more than one word.

Wiping the last threads of sleep from my eyes, I made my way into the bathroom and twisted the nozzle on the showerhead. Steam filled the room, fogging up the mirror, and I quickly stripped off my clothes, which reeked of smoke and alcohol, and jumped under the downpour.

I'd never fallen asleep in my clothes from the night before. Why hadn't I changed when I'd gotten home? I closed my eyes and let the water cascade over my head. Actually, I had no recollection of getting home, period. I ran my fingers through my soaked mane, racking my brain for the last thing that I could remember. My fingers reached the ends of the front strands of hair on the right side too quickly. I felt around the chopped-off edge like I was touching the end of a missing limb and suddenly the sound of a scissor snip replayed in my mind. Liam barging into the bathroom, the tiny, yellow pill, and then . . . Sunshine.

Yes, the last thing I remembered was a warmth spreading through my hands, feet, and limbs as I danced gleefully around the party with Liam.

Here in the shower, I noticed that I was smiling at the memory. Well, I noticed that and that the water was beginning to get cold.

I didn't feel hungover. I had no headaches or stomachaches or grogginess. As I stepped out of the shower, I realized that I felt better than I had in weeks.

I ran a towel over my skin, but when I got to my left hand, I observed a dark smudge on the back. I held it up to the light to study, but I couldn't make out what it was other than an inky smear. That was odd. I put the back of my hand underneath the sink faucet and rubbed at the blotch with my thumb until it disappeared.

As the steam evaporated, I stared at my reflection. Bright eyes stared back at me. For the first time in a long time, I had the urge to comb my hair, put on eyeliner, and wear real clothes. I couldn't remember the end of the party or how I'd gotten home last night, but . . . so what? After I took the Sunshine, maybe I'd had too much to drink. Maybe I'd actually partied like I used to and had one of those miraculous mornings without a hangover. Clearly, I was fine. In fact, I was better than fine. I was happier than I'd been since before I'd met Adam, since before Knox died, since before that night in Dearborn.

Dearborn.

I abandoned my reflection in search of a pair of yoga pants and a soft fleece jacket. Real clothes and makeup would have to wait until after I got my appetite under control. I never wanted to think about Dearborn again. Except somehow it'd been all I could think about for weeks. I'd thought about it so much that it had chewed the gaping hole through my chest.

Dressed, I tugged a comb through my damp hair. Only last night and even this morning, it was like the gaping hole had vanished. It was like I'd never gotten drunk at that stupid bar or stumbled away from my friends or gone off with that stupid group of college guys.

It was like I was still me.

Like they'd never hurt me.

I froze, waiting for the memory to gnaw a fresh crater where my heart should be, but none opened up. I could breathe. In and out, in and out. I felt genuinely *good*. Maybe my friends had been right after all. A night out was exactly what I'd needed. Kids my age. Fun. *High school.*

There was no reason to worry. Everything was fine. People had little blackouts all the time after a party. I nearly giggled at the memory of Billy Ray, who once took off his shirt at a party, drew a smiley face on his ample stomach, using his belly button as the mouth, and went around using it like a ventriloquist dummy. When we brought it up at school, he had absolutely no recollection of his routine.

See? I was better than fine.

I returned my comb to the drawer, enjoying the scent of eucalyptus shampoo and the comfort of lotion on my skin, and then, without sparing another thought for Dearborn, headed downstairs to the kitchen.

Mom was using a spatula to wrestle a pancake from the griddle. She dropped the perfectly browned circle of batter onto a plate. Dad peered into the microwave while a plate of bacon spun around and around. He didn't know how to use the stove.

Honor was the first to look up. "Don't worry. I didn't let Mom use any blueberries in yours," she said. She sat on one of the wooden chairs at the kitchen table, knees tucked into her chest and pajama bottoms covering her toes.

"Thank goodness," I said with exaggerated relief. The tile was cool on my feet as I wandered over to the refrigerator and pulled out a carton of orange juice.

"Somebody's up and at 'em this morning." Dad stood up from the microwave. I couldn't count the number of times my mom had told him not to watch the food while it spun inside or else he'd get cancer from the radiation, but when it came to food, my dad was a little kid, always sneaking treats and never able to wait patiently for the next meal, which explained the endearing cushion of fat that protruded past the waistband of his weekend sweats.

"I guess so," I said, trying to sound casual, as though I'd never stopped attending our Saturday morning breakfasts in favor of sulking in my room.

Mom turned her back from the griddle. She had a dollop of batter stuck in her bangs. "You look . . . healthy," she said.

Healthy. That was nice, I supposed. But what had I been looking like normally, the Crypt Keeper? A few months ago, I probably would have immediately assumed she meant "fat." After pouring a glass of orange juice, I returned the carton to its spot in the fridge.

"Oh, Cassidy, can you grab the strawberries in there? We need something semi-nutritious."

"Since when?" The microwave beeped and my dad grabbed the plate of bacon, yelping when it was too hot to handle. *"Youch!"* He pressed his fingers to his mouth.

"Careful." I laughed—not that I was keeping score, but that was at least the second time in twenty-four hours. I slid the strawberries over to my mom.

"That's strange. One of my knives is missing," Mom said, studying the wooden block that held her kitchen set. "Are you using it, Darren?"

Dad shook his head. I plopped down on a chair next to Honor and pulled my phone from my pocket. Five unread text messages.

The first three were from Paisley.

Where are you? I can't find you anywhere and this party is past its expiration date. The message was sent at midnight. I scanned to her second text.

Hello? You're my ride home. Did you ditch me for Liam???

I chewed on my nail. Had I really abandoned Paisley? That did sound a little like me. Shit.

Ava's giving me a ride home. Next time you want to take a drive down easy street, you could at least let me know . . . Text me so I know you got home ok tho, promise?

A mixture of emotions swept through me. I'd always thought Paisley's jokes—that I was easy—were harmless until recently when I realized they could hurt my credibility. It felt too late and too convenient to try to tell people now that, sure, I liked to get drunk and kiss boys, but . . . that was it. Besides, maybe Paisley was a little bit right about me. I wasn't sure anymore.

The next text was from Ava.

Ignore Paize. She's drunk. Both glad to see you having fun. Ta-ta!

I smiled at that. See? I was right. I *had* had a good time. I still was having a good time.

Just then Honor reached for my phone and tried to snatch it away. "What's so important, anyway?" she whined. Years of being a big sister had trained me to be quicker than she was. I latched onto her wrist before she could swipe my cell away.

"Give it back!" I pried her fingers free from the screen. She had such delicate little bird bones that it was a relief, at least so far, that she didn't want to be a cheerleader like me. The poor girl would break.

She released her grip with a huff and sat back in her chair.

I closed my eyes for a moment and sighed. "Okay, okay, I'm sorry. One more thing and I'll put it away. Deal?"

She nodded.

The last message was from an unsaved number. I clicked on the message and knew immediately whom it was from:

That was fun. Where'd you run off to last night? Txt me if you want more. This # is my cell.

It had to be Liam. And I could only hope by "more" he was referring to Sunshine. After all, if *he* didn't know where I ran off to either, then that must mean I didn't "take a drive down easy street," as Paisley had so poetically put it, which meant I probably just got tired and decided it was time to head home. That was a relief. Sunshine was looking better and better. A smile tugged at the corners of my lips.

I pressed my thumbs into the keypad and typed out, *Later today?* And hit "send."

"I know that look." Mom set a heaping stack of pancakes topped with strawberries on the table between Honor and me.

"What look?" I said, setting the phone facedown.

"The *there's a boy I like and I can't stop texting him* look." She gave me a look that I was familiar with, too. The *I'm your mother and I know things* look. I scrunched up my nose and stuck my tongue out.

Dad joined us at the table and helped himself to the first pancake. "A *boy*?" he said with mock surprise. My dad wasn't one of those barbaric guys that acted as though his daughters should be locked in castles until they were thirty or else he'd pull out his shotgun. In fact, my parents shared an obviously pleased glance at the mention of a boy and me in the same sentence.

I flitted my eyes to the ceiling like I was annoyed when actually it felt nice to have my parents faux-worried about a boy as opposed to real worried about my constant bad mood. Dad slid the pancakes over to me and I forked the biggest one onto my plate and doused it with warm syrup. "It's not really like—" I stuffed the first bite into my mouth. The taste of the warm, sugar-laden flapjack exploded on my tongue and I nearly moaned. Usually I allowed myself only one cheat day a week and lately I'd been surviving on power bars and Gatorade more often than not. The effect of the flour and sweet and glorious carbohydrates was sinfully delicious and nearly short-circuited my brain.

I started to tell my parents that Liam wasn't a boy that I liked and, what was more, there weren't any boys on my radar period, but I stopped short. Maybe it was the digesting pancakes sending a wave of endorphins into my brain or maybe it was just the way our whole family was gathered around the breakfast table like nothing had changed in the last few months. Whatever it was, I made a decision. I may not have liked a boy exactly, but I did like something, so instead, I asked in the midst of shoveling in my next bite, "Do you guys mind if I meet up with him later?"

— — —

LIAM TOLD ME to meet him at the corner of Grimwood and Havelock Drive. At dusk, I pulled up to a ramshackle park with a public basketball court. If this was a date, I'd insist he at least take me to dinner and a movie, but since it wasn't, the park would do. A pair of headlights shined onto the court. Liam waved at me from the free-throw line. "Can you leave your lights on?" he asked when I started to get out of the car. I glanced at his Mustang. "The lighting sucks out here," he explained. When I looked around, I saw that he was right. There was only a single lamppost for the whole park and it was several yards away from the basketball court.

I nodded and left the car running and my headlights blazing. Outside, the sun had slipped below the tree line leaving behind it only a sliver of molten orange to dye the sky's hem a soft, cotton-candy pink. Everywhere else evening muddied the edges of things.

The concrete court was painted mostly green, but a rusty red color peeked through in places where sneakers had rubbed holes into it. Liam bounced a basketball in front of his toes twice and then shot it at the hoop. The ball bounced off the tilted rim. I caught it midair and ran my hand over its bumpy, leather skin. It smelled like gym class.

"How'd you get my number anyway?" I asked, twirling the orange basketball between two fingers.

He wiped his forehead off on the sleeve of his T-shirt. "Sports directory." He grinned and tapped his pointer finger to his temple. "Smart, huh?"

"Oh, right." I'd forgotten about the directory, which gave the names and contact information of all Hollow Pines athletes. It helped to coordinate pep rallies, signs of support, and general attendance at events. Why hadn't I thought of that?

"Don't worry. I'm not, like, a stalker or anything."

I rolled my eyes and bounced him the ball. "I didn't think you were. You're Liam Buckley."

"What's that supposed to mean?" He dribbled the ball to the hoop and this time shot a layup. It swooshed through the ragged net. He caught it on the other side and tossed it to me.

I hadn't played basketball since I was a kid, but my dad always told me that I'd stolen all the athletic genes in the family. Maybe that was true, since it looked like Honor was destined to be more of a drama geek. I dribbled the ball out to the three-point line. "Only that I hardly think you need to be stalking girls. They seem to flock quite willingly."

He stood underneath the net, waiting. "Yeah, well, you're Cassidy Hyde," he said with a shrug.

I scoffed. "So?"

"So, everyone knows who you are, too."

"I guess." I positioned the ball between my palms, bent my knees, and used my right hand to guide the ball as I hurled it toward the hoop. It bounced off the backboard and I squeezed my fist tight instinctively. "Darn," I muttered under my breath while Liam chased after the stray ball.

"Looks like someone's competitive." He returned with his easy lope. "So, are you glad I didn't let you chop off all your hair?"

I stared down at the ground. "I wasn't planning to chop it *all* off," I said, even though I wasn't sure what I'd been intending to do. The darkness that I'd felt in that moment was impossible to touch from where I currently stood. Still, I knew it was hovering nearby waiting to consume me and that was exactly why I was here. With Liam.

Liam's eyebrows shot up. A half smile played at his lips. He bounced the basketball through his legs, switching up his stride, left and right. "Okay . . . ," he said. "But you have to admit, it helped."

I took a deep breath. The park was deserted except for the two of us. "Yes, but . . . I have questions." As though to prove that the old Cassidy was clawing to return to life, I had come armed with all my best type A questions for Liam.

He stopped bouncing the ball. "I'm an open book. Come on." He set the ball down and walked off the court to a swing set nearby.

I chose the swing next to his and let my feet lift from the ground, grateful now that I had his full attention. "Right . . . well, first, did, um, did anything happen between us?"

Based on his text message, I was pretty sure the answer was no, and I was abundantly glad that he couldn't see the color spike in my cheeks when I asked. Nothing said "easy" like a girl who couldn't remember whether she'd been easy or not.

His chuckle was soft and low in the dark. "Like did we hook up? No. Nothing like that. Just danced. But now you're making me wish that maybe I'd made a move."

"No!" I snapped back too fast. The silence that followed was awkward. I listened to the creak of the swings' chains. "I mean, sorry, but I'm glad we didn't. I didn't think so, but I . . . was just testing. You know, for any side effects of . . . well . . ."

"Of Sunshine?" He completed the thought for me.

"Exactly." I looked over. Liam's back formed a *C* curve as he hunched in the swing's seat, too small for his lanky frame.

"I . . . wasn't sure how I got home last night. Has that happened to you when you've used it?"

He shook his head. "No. Nothing like that. And I've already taken it, like, a dozen times. Healthy as an ox." He thumped his chest.

I furrowed my brow. I guessed that was a relief. "So, are there any side effects I *should* know about? I ran a search on it, but I couldn't find anything."

He pushed off the ground and tucked his knees to float through the arc. "It's new. Designer. Totally the shit. My older brother got it at his college. Just that warm, gooey feeling, like everything is happy and perfect and fun. You know what I'm talking about." He reached over and nudged me.

I knew exactly what he was talking about. "Is it . . . addictive?"

"Christ, Hyde. You think I'd give you heroin or something? Haven't you ever taken a party drug before?"

I let the soles of my shoes drag along the dirt below. "No. Is that strange?"

"Oh, sorry, I just figured you had or whatever. I mean, I guess I've always heard you were a bit of a wild child."

Wild child. Easy. What had I done to earn these descriptions? "You shouldn't believe everything you hear," I said flatly.

He shrugged. I wondered what it would take to get a rise out of Liam Buckley. He seemed so annoyingly self-assured and relaxed.

"Look, I'm an athlete, too, but as long as you don't go overboard, you should be fine."

I pressed my lips together. Right. Everything in moderation. At least until the old Cassidy was back and here to stay. I'd been miserable for long enough. What I needed was a jump start. That was all.

"So, what'll it be? I'm not just selling to anyone, you know. Only people I know will be cool and not a bunch of shitheads. Shitheads are how people get caught."

"How much?" I asked, standing up to dig out the cash I'd picked up at the ATM.

"That depends on how many you want."

"I don't know. Two or three, I guess."

"All right." He smiled easily. "For you, forty bucks."

My palms were sweaty. I decided not to ask whether "for me"

meant the pills were more expensive or less. I handed him the money and he handed me back a small ziplock bag with three yellow pills inside. My heart beat like a jumping bean.

Sunshine.

A few minutes passed before I was back inside my car, fishing out a pill and placing the tiny droplet on the tip of my tongue. Now all I had to do was wait.

FOUR

Marcy

One hour, thirty-three minutes, and fifteen seconds.

It had been that long since I'd first seen the boys walk into the club and it'd been just over an hour since I'd left to wait outside for them. Five faces: The short one who I knew as the watcher, the one who'd hidden behind his video camera that night like the distance made him any less guilty. The surfer with the longish hair and laid-back attitude, the boy who'd told me to relax, *chill out.* The sexy jock with his backward baseball cap and silver tongue, who'd pulled me in like a mosquito to a bug-zapper. The thin-lipped skull face with a cigarette hanging from his mouth, a mouth I knew was armed with cowardly taunts and cheers and encouragement to go too far. And, of course, the mean one. Vampire-toothed, crocodile-skin boots, eyes that could eat your heart out raw. Circus

Master, I called him. I had nicknames for each and I checked them off mentally before returning the phone to my pocket. I traced the entry stamp on the back of my hand, a splotchy inkblot in the shape of a pair of cowboy boots.

"You know you can go back inside." The bouncer sat on a stool opposite the glass doors. "If you're waiting on somebody or somethin'. You're welcome to go take a look."

I nodded without looking over. "'Kay." But I made no motion to leave.

Instead, I propped one foot up on the brick wall behind me and folded my arms across my chest. It was getting late.

The door swung open. I held my breath. Two girls spilled out into the night, giggling and swaying arm in arm. I relaxed against the wall again. No sooner had I, though, than a shot of laughter burst into the dark sky like a gunshot. The laugh sounded to me like a living echo of a memory.

I wrenched my shoulders from the wall and glanced sidelong at the fivesome and immediately I stiffened. There was an extra person. Six total. And that sixth person was a girl.

She wasn't supposed to be there. I watched as Circus Master looped his arm around her shoulder and leaned in close to talk to her. I felt my mouth curve into a snarl.

The girl was young. Maybe younger than I was. She had an uncared-for look, like a stray cat, wide-eyed and with a narrow build. Clearly, she was just as lost, too.

As the boys turned left out of the club, I hiked the black hood I was wearing over my ears and followed. Over the fabric, I clutched the outline of the knife hiding underneath. Squeezed the hilt twice for comfort. It was there and it could wait, too, I reminded myself.

Only I wasn't sure how long.

At the corner, I expected the girl to veer off. *Go,* I willed her mentally. *Leave.* But she didn't.

I trailed a block behind. Watched the moments as they happened like snapshots. The two boys in the back—the one with the cigarettes, Lucky Strike, and the sexy piece of bait for the group, Jock Strap—jostled each other. The cigarette fell out of Lucky Strike's mouth and he left it fuming on the sidewalk. When I passed the spot, the sweet vapor from the wafting tip made me woozy. I crushed it with the sole of my boot.

Up ahead, California, who, like Short One, wore a shirt that read *Beta Psi,* crept up and pinched the girl's ass. She squealed and whipped around and I saw the fleeting look on her face change from anger to annoyance to a fake smile, like she'd been in on the joke all along.

The joke was theirs, though.

Short One jogged in front of where Circus Master still had his arm looped possessively around the girl's shoulder. Short One pulled out a handheld camcorder. "Smile for the camera." At least that was what I thought he said. He walked backward and panned the group. I edged sideways, out of the frame's background.

From this angle, the girl's face was hidden from me, but I could see as she raised a tentative hand to wave. Her shoulders pinched up to hide her neck. The boy got close. Zoomed into her face and let out another huge clap of laughter.

We passed one of the blue towers with dead siren tops scattered near campus. Big buttons begging to be pressed in the event of an emergency. But emergencies rarely happened in convenient areas. I should know.

I'd lost track of where we were walking. I quickly collected my bearings. We'd turned off the main road onto a dark side street. They entered a parking lot, nearly empty but for an old Chrysler with a FOR SALE sign tacked in the window. I hung back in the shadows of an old apartment building.

Observing. Studying. Biding my time.

Leave, girl. I needed her to go. No witnesses. No mess. Right now, she was in the way. I felt some of my anger peel off and gravitate over to her. She must have seen where she was by now. But she was still playing the role of good little girl. Pleasing. Compliant. She mustn't be rude.

Jock Strap found a littered bottle, picked it up over his head, and smashed it on the ground. Short One hid behind his blinking red light. Then, with no other toys to play with, nothing else breakable, they turned to the girl. My hands curled into fists at my sides.

It began as a shove. The girl stumbled forward like a marionette doll into the arms of Circus Master. I could feel his sneer, breath hot on my face, even from a safe distance away. Another echo of a memory. I forced myself to watch.

Another shove. This time back to Jock Strap. Around she went. Push. A kiss on the cheek. Shove. Another pat to her ass. Rage clawed at my stomach.

Circus Master gave an order. Gestured with his hands. And then the girl was lowering herself to her knees amid the broken bottle and the shimmering moonlit asphalt. The sound of her whimpering cries reached me. Rage boiled my blood until it thickened and hardened in my veins.

I forced the rage down into the pit of my belly where it'd be forced to stew with the other acids there until the next evening.

There would be no revenge tonight, I had to concede. The huntress inside me seethed, pulling at the reins to be let loose.

But the problem of the girl remained.

I observed her another moment before turning my back on her. It was official: Tonight had been a total waste.

As I disappeared around the corner, I could still hear cruel laughter. I could picture the humiliation spilling out in hot tears all over her face as clearly as if it was a portrait painted on a canvas in front of me.

It took me thirty seconds to reach the blue tower, to slam my hand on the button, for the sirens to swirl and to flash blue and white light on the pavement. They were thirty seconds the girl would never have back.

My breath shortened as I ran back to the apartment building adjacent to the parking lot. The boys had lifted their heads, listening. I pressed myself to the side of the old brick and cupped my hands around my mouth. "Hey," I said in as loud and as deep of a voice as I could muster. "You. Over there. I've called the police." The boys searched in my direction. I stepped partway out of the shadows, using the hood to mask my hair and face.

The sirens cut through the air. The police really would be there. Soon.

The red light on the camcorder blinked off. "Come on," I heard Short One say.

As he left, Circus Master took one glance back at the girl still on her knees. He ruffled her hair before spinning to follow his friends.

She fell on all fours, palms biting into the asphalt. Sobs dampened the air. My shoes crunched toward her. "Here." I grabbed her under the elbow and beneath her armpit and used my weight to pull her upright.

The girl squinted at me. Tears streaked her cheeks. She shook violently, lower lip trembling. Dark, sweaty bangs stuck to her forehead.

I let go of her arm. She nearly toppled over, but caught herself and still managed to stand there blinking at me like I was an alien who'd descended down from a UFO.

"My name's Lena." She offered it up like a gift. Her legs quaked and I steadied her.

"Marcy," I said gruffly, wearily, wishing there weren't any more girls like Lena but recognizing myself in her all the same. I held on to her until I was sure she could stand on her own. "Make sure you don't need my help again," I said, and there was nothing altruistic about my tone. It was a warning.

"But, w-w-wait, don't I—?" she said. "That's not your—" Her fingers slid down the sleeve of my sweatshirt as I pulled out of reach.

I didn't wait. I couldn't. I tugged the drawstrings of my hood tighter, turned, and walked swiftly away.

FIVE

Cassidy

Honor jabbed me in the ribs and I blinked awake.

"Watch it. You're about to start drooling," she said. Her feet were crossed at the ankles, nude flats tucked underneath the pew. Next to Honor, my mom followed along with the sermon in the Bible she shared with my dad.

"Is it almost over?" I whispered.

She nodded and turned her face back to the front. I wiped the corners of my mouth, just in case my sister had been right about the drool. This was hardly the first time I'd fallen asleep during one of Pastor Long's sermons, but today, I'd managed to sleep through my alarm, plus I was still groggy from missing my coffee. I'd only barely managed to throw on a wrap dress and pin my hair into a passable bun before loading into my dad's Tahoe. It wasn't like me to sleep through my alarm. Come to think of it, I wasn't sure I could recall setting it at all.

I yawned and shifted my weight on the pew's thin cushion. My family had been coming to Hollow Pines Presbyterian ever since we moved here. I'd always loved the purple and green stained glass and the way the windows refracted the light into geometric patterns that shifted on the red carpet of the church's stage. Everyone that was anyone went to church in Hollow Pines. It didn't matter if you drank yourself silly the night before or if you'd spent the entire six days prior getting to third base in the back of your boyfriend's pickup. On Sunday morning, your rear end was in the sanctuary.

I scanned the congregation for familiar faces. Even though I was sleepy, the effects of the Sunshine still hadn't worn off. Either that or I was truly getting over the last few months of my life. I knew because it hadn't annoyed me when Dad put his blinker on a hundred yards too early or when Mom sang the hymns too loud. And I was dying to discuss hair choices for Friday night's basketball game with Paisley. Hair choices! I couldn't remember the last time I'd cared about something as inconsequential as hair choices.

I caught sight of Paisley, her head dutifully bowed, which meant she must have been sneaking texts on her phone since no one else was praying. In the church's right wing, Ava sat with her mom. Every so often, she'd trace the sign of the cross over her shoulders and breastbone. Her family was Catholic, but since there were no Catholic churches in Hollow Pines, the Presbyterian church had to do.

In unison, the congregation rose and began to sing a song about peace and forgiveness. Honor balanced her hymnal on the pew back in front of us. She slid it over so that I could read from it, too. A black stamp on my left hand caught my eye. Quietly, I lowered my hands off the rail and knitted my fingers together, hoping that Honor hadn't already seen.

I'd seen, though.

My throat tied itself in knots. The stamp was a picture of two spurred boots and I recognized it instantly. A cold sweat cropped up among the tiny hairs on the back of my neck. I'd had that stamp on my hand before—once—the night I went to Dearborn. When I went to Ten Gallon Cowboy.

I closed my eyes and took a deep breath. The images flooded in, rushing through me like a tidal wave. The music. The sticky floors. The boys laughing. Without even trying I could feel again how the night had morphed into something ugly, first slowly and then all at once.

I forced my eyelids back open and pulled myself free from the memory. I would never go back. That was the promise I'd made to myself. Never, ever, ever and as far as I knew, I hadn't. Or at least that was what I would have thought if I didn't have the evidence stamped across my hand. My heart beat fast.

Pastor Long raised his hands and held his palms out to us. "The grace of the Lord Jesus Christ, the love of God, and the communion of the Holy Spirit be with you all," he said. "Go in peace to love and serve the Lord."

"Amen," I chanted. Then the organ blared and everyone was reaching behind them to pick up their belongings. I grabbed my purse and tapped Honor on the shoulder. "I'm running to the restroom before the line gets too long, okay? Tell Mom and Dad that I'll meet y'all in the atrium."

I darted out of the pew and up the aisle toward the double doors, panic slimy in my mouth and throat. "Peace be with you," an elderly usher in a khaki suit called to me as I hustled away.

"And peace be with you," I responded breathlessly.

The women's restroom was located at the end of the corridor. I hurried inside. Tiny green tiles covered the floor and walls. I squeezed out a dollop of pink soap, stuck my hand underneath the faucet, and began scrubbing it with my fingernails. I relaxed as the ink dissolved from my skin and I was left with reddening scratches instead. In a few short seconds, I would have never suspected it was there in the first place.

Ladies of the church began trickling in. Still shaken, I slipped into a stall at the end and closed the door. *Breathe*, I ordered my lungs. *Calm down and breathe.*

The stamp meant nothing. The night after Ten Gallon Cowboy, I'd woken to full body aches that stretched from the top notch of my spine down to the backs of my knees. Today, on the other hand, I felt fine. I had to keep reminding myself of that. I felt fine. For the first time in a long time.

I reached for my cell and texted Liam. **I thought you said there were no side effects?**

I waited as flashing dots appeared on-screen. Followed by his message. **There aren't.**

I dug my teeth into my lip, unsure how much I wanted to tell him. **Who else has tried it?**

The answer was immediate. **Confidentiality. Part of the job requirement.**

I rolled my eyes. It wasn't like Liam was a doctor or a lawyer. Still, it was nice to know my secret was safe. **But there are others?**

Of course :)

I tapped my foot on the ground anxiously. **And no one has had . . .** My thumbs hovered . . . **memory loss?**

Nada. U ok?

Fine. I typed a quick reply and switched my screen to dark. Without pulling up my dress, I sat down on the toilet. It was just me. Lots had happened to me in the last few weeks. And besides, nothing bad had happened. Maybe it was even a good thing. Maybe I'd confronted my fear and just, I didn't know, blocked it out or something. Like with PTSD. Was that my issue? What sorts of trauma could lead to a brain switch like post-traumatic stress disorder? I'd heard stories of soldiers getting it from war, of children having cases of PTSD when parents were killed, but what about what happened to me?

I still couldn't say the word. I couldn't even think it.

Was I . . . *traumatized*?

I turned the word over in my mind and thought of the near-catatonic shell of myself that I'd peered at in the mirror, the one who'd been ready to shave off an entire head of perfectly luscious hair. Then I paired that version against who I was before Dearborn: popular, in control, straight As, flirtatious, professional-level best friend. When I put it like that then, yeah, I supposed the word *traumatized* did seem to fit. Was I stressed, too?

Well, it certainly wasn't like me to forget to set an alarm. If I had the trauma and the stress and it was post the "Incident," was it possible that I'd been full-on disordered without even realizing it?

I wiped my hands down my shins. This felt like a positive step. A sign that the old me was just around the corner. Identify a problem. Solve it. That was what the old Cassidy would do and medical problems required medicine. At least until I recovered. And, since my problem wasn't exactly one I could talk to a doctor about without a dozen questions and a call to my parents—I could already hear Paisley's singsong voice chiding me about my strolls down easy street—then I would have to self-treat. My breath was coming more steadily now.

Just as much as I felt the old, better version of myself hovering tantalizingly close, I also felt the sad, nasty version haunting me like a ghost. If I wasn't careful, it would suck me under. I needed to preserve cheerleader, straight A Cassidy stat.

There was one thing that had made me feel the best I'd felt in weeks. If I was the problem, then perhaps it could be the solution. I opened my purse and fished for the small clear bag that contained another couple drops of Sunshine. Maybe if I took a half now and saved half for later that would get me back to the feeling I had the night of the party. And yesterday and—

I pinched a tablet between two fingers, positioned it between my two front teeth, and bit the pill in half. A chalky texture coated my tongue. I quickly swallowed the half-portion down, wishing I could get to a water fountain to wash the taste away.

Sealing the bag, I returned it to my purse. The reaction was slower this time. At first nothing happened. I listened to the flush of toilets and waited. Then, gradually, a warmth built underneath the beds of my fingernails. It spread to my knuckles and up to my elbows until, at last, the glow seeped into my chest and filled the cavity there with a pleasant heat, soft and wonderful, like a mug of hot cocoa on the coldest day of the year.

I slid open the lock and stepped out of the stall. Catching sight of my reflection in the mirror, I noticed that my skin had an attractive rosy tint to it. A faint smile pulled at the corners of my lips. No one would know that I'd thrown my hair up and my outfit together in five minutes flat. No way. I looked fantastic.

A silver-haired woman trundled past me in her floppy Sunday hat and scooted her way into the stall I'd occupied. I waved as she passed.

That was it. I'd been overreacting. About all of it. It was so like me. Type A. Closet perfectionist. Every ounce of worry, which had felt so pressing only moments before, floated off to an unreachable distance.

"There you are." Paisley strode over to the sink and washed her hands. "I thought we were going to go see a movie last night. Do you not return texts anymore?"

She wore a floral dress with a Peter Pan collar, perfectly tailored to fit her minute stature.

Movie . . . movie . . . It sounded vaguely familiar. Paisley fussed with a few stray blond strands, flattening them into her sleek shoulder-length bob.

I couldn't recall what movie we'd wanted to see or receiving any texts from Paisley, but this time, when confronted with the gap in my memory, the panic wasn't there. It felt almost funny, as though Paisley and I were in on a joke. "Sorry," I said cheerily. "Must have given my secretary the night off."

Paisley huffed as we wandered together back into the atrium. Organ music still trickled in from the sanctuary. Pastor Long stood at the main doors, shaking hands with families as they hurried out to catch their eleven o'clock brunch reservations.

I could tell Paisley wasn't actually mad. That was the thing about the two of us—we could never stay mad at each other. Especially because our popularity multiplied when we came in a pair. We both knew it. Blond and brunette. Pick your flavor. Or your poison.

"Okay," she continued. "So then what had you so occupied that you needed to subject me to another night of watching the Billys play Xbox in William's basement?" She idly strolled over to a nearby snack table and took a store-packaged cherry Danish from the tray.

"Liam," I replied without thinking. It was the first thing that popped into my head. That was what I remembered from last night. Liam. I was certain of it.

Paisley stopped before she could take a bite. "Liam?" She lowered the pastry. "So much for that long-winded speech you gave about swearing off boys. How long did that last? One month? Two, tops. That has to be some kind of record for you, Cass."

I remembered the speech in question. It was only days after Paisley, Ava, Ashley, Erica, and I had visited Dearborn for our big girls' night out. We were at our usual table in the cafeteria and Ava had asked who I thought would invite me to prom this year. When I'd insisted I wasn't going and that, even more shockingly, I was giving up boys altogether—like they were carbs or something—my friends had been ready to declare my depression clinical.

Maybe they'd been right.

"It's not like that," I said, trying not to stare at the jam-filled Danish.

When Paisley took a bite, some of the frosting flaked off and I fought the urge to lunge after it. I'd already gorged myself on pancakes this weekend, so church pastries weren't on the agenda. Not when I'd decided that I wasn't ready to return to chubby mathlete obscurity quite yet after all. Not when I'd just reminded myself of all I had to lose. Not when Sunshine had reminded me, that was. Girls did not claw their way to the top for nothing. That was important for me to remember.

Paisley followed my eyes, smirked, and took another monster bite. "It's Liam Buckley," she mumbled, mouth full. "If it's not *like* that, you're doing it wrong. Trust me."

I chewed on my lip, debating how much to tell her. Would Liam let anyone in on our little secret? Were other people using Sunshine, too, and I never knew? Part of me wanted to tell her. For better or worse—let's face it, many times it was for worse—Paisley was my best friend. But did that mean she had to know every little thing about me?

She didn't know about Dearborn or the boys or the aches that followed in my body and in my heart.

Paisley had been my best friend for years, but when I thought about the barbs in her tongue, the ones that could poke me and call me a slut with a laugh and an *oh you know it's true* smile, I wanted to recoil as though from a hot stove.

The more I thought about it, the more I saw that Sunshine worked like a really great tube of concealer. It matched my skin tone perfectly and nobody, not even Paisley, needed to know that I had a pimple.

"We just met up at the park and played a little basketball." I shrugged. "No biggie."

Paisley polished off the rest of the Danish and licked her fingers. She'd never had the same tendency toward chubby stomach rolls that I had. "Okay, so you're taking it slow. That's good, I guess. Different for you, though."

I rolled my eyes. "We're not taking it anywhere."

Her eyes widened. "Is he gay?"

"I don't know, Paize, and I didn't ask because I don't care." By now the Sunshine was flowing through my veins like liquid gold. I gave an easy smile. One that had the old Cassidy written all over it. "Stop being so uptight." I pinched her cheek like an overzealous great-aunt. Then, in my altered state, a thought seized me. "Hey, do you want to go for a run this afternoon? It's really beautiful out." Sun poured through the glass doors. Outside, churchgoers were shucking off their cardigans and enjoying the weather.

"Did an alien abduct you? Or . . . oh, I know, are you doing one of those Gwyneth Paltrow juice fasts because I've been debating trying the master cleanse, but wasn't sure . . ."

I kept my gaze trained outside, staring at the fresh air and the rustling leaves and the flowers, all brushed with a spring glow. "Truth?" I cut her off.

Paisley gave a light, frustrated stomp of her foot. "Truth. Yeah, of course. Always."

"It was, just, I don't know, getting kind of exhausting being sad all the time."

- - -

SWEAT DRENCHED THE neckline of my T-shirt and turned my legs slimy. I kicked my tennis shoes off on the front porch and shoved them next to the family welcome mat. My muscles burned and my calves were already tight. I'd run the mile to Hollow Pines High to meet Paisley where we'd then done two full sets of stadium steps. Even though I knew I'd be sore in the morning, I relished the surge of endorphins, the feeling of fistfuls of blood pumping through my heart and the way my body felt totally awake after a good workout. An Eminem song blared through my headphones, reminding me of the times that Paisley and I used to ride around in her car, windows down with nowhere to go, blasting rap songs and nailing every line word for word at the top of our lungs. The memory made me smile. I tugged the buds from my ears and wrapped the wire around my phone as I pushed open the door to my house.

"Mom, I'm home!" I yelled. My socks left cloudy imprints on the hardwood floor as I pounded up the stairs to my room. The door to my bedroom was closed. When I opened it, I let out a soft shriek once I found that it was occupied.

"Honor? God, you scared me." I blinked several times in quick succession, surprised to see her in my room when she wasn't supposed to be and even more surprised when I took in what she was doing.

"Cassidy!" She whirled to turn her back away from the full-length mirror. She didn't realize I could still see the phone clutched in her palm through the reflection.

My little sister was wearing a red thong and a black push-up bra. Both of them were mine. "What are you *doing*?" I lunged for her phone.

She jumped clear of me and held the phone out in her opposite hand to stay clear of my reach. "Nothing. God, don't overreact. I'm going to wash them and put them right back where I found them, okay?"

Underneath her constellation of freckles, her face flushed pink.

"You think *that's* what I'm worried about? Whether you return my . . . my *underwear*?" Her knobby knees bowed slightly inward as she tried to shift into a more modest position. I gawked at her pointy elbows and sharp collarbone, both of which would have made her appear more at home on a playground than posing in lingerie. "The question is what are you *doing* in them because I'll tell you what it looks like you're doing."

She rolled her eyes and in that moment it looked to me like my little sister had morphed into some kind of otherworldly being. "Please, Cassidy. Like you aren't going to parties and sneaking out with boys. I found you yesterday morning wearing your clothes from the night before. Remember?"

My mouth fell open. "I—I—*what*? That's totally different." And for a second it was like I had double vision. I saw Honor sneaking out to Dearborn. Honor flirting with college boys. Honor ditching her friends for a cute smile and a free drink. Honor being passed around, sneered at, called horrible names, names so poisonous they would burn a hole through her chest. And Honor not getting to choose her first anything because it was taken from her in one stupid moment.

She stood there twirling a few strands of hair around her finger.

"Give me your phone," I said slowly, stretching out my hand.

She lifted her chin defiantly just as she had when she was five years old and wanted to wear a tutu for a week straight. "No."

"Give it to me."

"No!"

"Honor Mary Hyde, give me that phone!" I charged and grabbed her behind the elbow. We tumbled onto my bed.

She flattened her face into the mattress. "Get off me," she screamed. She tucked the phone underneath her stomach. I straddled her, one knee on either side of her little-girl hips.

"Who did you send them to, Honor? This isn't funny."

"No one! Gross, Cass, you're all sweaty."

I wedged my arm between her and the bed. Cheerleading and two extra years had made me twice as strong as her. I felt for her fingers and pried them off the pastel blue case one by one until she lost her grip on the phone.

"Got it!" I yelled triumphantly. I kept her pinned down while I scrolled through the contents of her phone and found the pictures. Three photographs were saved side by side. One with Honor turned to the side, her back arched, her hair cascading until it reached the small of her back. One straight on, but I could tell she was using the sides of her arms to create the small line of cleavage. And one shot over her shoulder to get a view of her butt. "Oh, disgusting, Honor." My nose wrinkled and I hit "delete" on each of the photos. "Here's your dumb phone back." I tossed it on the mattress next to her head and crawled off of her. "Next time I catch you doing something like that I'm telling Mom."

She rolled over. Her chest was rising and falling like it was her that had just run stadiums. "Oh, I guess it's okay when you do this stuff because you're *Cassidy* Hyde."

"I don't do any of that." I wiped sweat from my forehead. But of course I remembered the boy behind the video recorder in Dearborn, red light blinking in my face, and wondered if she was a little bit right.

"That's not what I heard." She scooted off the foot of the bed. From the floor she grabbed a pair of flannel pajama bottoms and a sweatshirt. She pulled the sweatshirt over her head and immediately looked less like a cyborg had taken over her body. "You must be pleased now that you have Mom and Dad convinced that you're back to being Miss Perfect." She tugged on the pants.

"But it's not easy being Miss Perfect's baby sister, okay? You could at least invite me to one of those parties or something. We *are* related, you know, and we *do* go to the same high school."

My throat tightened. I wasn't sure I wanted my sister near a party ever. Especially not now.

She waited for a few seconds for me to respond. When I didn't, her shoulders sagged and she moved for the door.

"You'll thank me later," I called after her. But she was already down the hallway and I wasn't sure if she heard.

I shook my head and slid off the side of the bed. I'd left my purse on my nightstand after church. Honor was right about one thing. The relief I felt seeing my parents' faces now that they believed I was back to being the old Cassidy left me feeling a hundred pounds lighter. Better than any Gwyneth Paltrow juice fast. And besides, they didn't just believe it was true, it *was* true.

I felt strong again, functional, vibrant. The leftover effects of my run still hummed through me like a tuning fork. My sister was just naive. What did she know about the world? Nothing.

I unzipped the top of my purse, fished out the ziplock bag, popped the other half of the tablet into my mouth, then swallowed.

SIX

Marcy

If everyone's life was a story, then any given night was a scene waiting to be played out. Sure, those boys had momentarily stolen the show, but I was returning to take back the narrative. *Surprise*. I sure hoped they liked twist endings.

I'd left my car on a side street and now stood at the end of a wide lane. Lamps lit the redbrick street of fraternity row and I hugged the iron fences that hemmed in large colonial homes where I passed a boy with his arm draped casually over his girlfriend's shoulder. Her oversized sorority T-shirt hung down to mid-thigh. The boy gave me a slight nod as I slipped by and I wondered how well I blended in with the college students. Did I look young to the couple the way I should have looked young—too young—to those boys that night?

I supposed it didn't matter anymore. Not when I could already taste the coppery, metallic tang of revenge on my tongue. I studied the letters on each of the houses, searching for the funny-looking *B* and a symbol that resembled either a deformed *W* or a misshapen trident.

I went by three houses before I spotted it. A two-story house with white columns framing a porch. A sheet hung out of one of the second-story windows. It was painted with neon-green letters to announce a Monday night throwback rave mixer, whatever that was. It sounded pointless and barbaric. So basically, exactly what I'd expect. On the untended lawn was a long table, strewn with red plastic cups.

This was it. Beta Psi.

The fraternity from California's and Short One's T-shirts. Heat crept up my neck and burned my ears as I took in the evidence of the days and nights of merriment they'd enjoyed in the weeks since they'd stolen from me what was only mine to give. The one with the long hair who'd told me to chill out—California—and Short One—the boy who'd hid behind the blinking red light of the camera, watching. Funny how the pair of them had given me the clues I needed to track the group. A couple shirts and Greek letters. Not funny ha-ha, mind you. At least not for them.

I hated them both. Hovering outside the iron gate, I watched and listened. It was a Sunday night and the volume of campus life had been turned down to a dull hum of activity that seemed to take place behind closed doors.

Shadows moved beyond the orange glow of the Beta Psi windows. The gate creaked as I opened it. I didn't flinch. Cautiously, I crossed the lawn to one of the windows on the lower floor. I wore all black down to my Converse. My hair was slicked into a low ponytail.

Before I reached the glass, I lowered myself into a crouch so that my head wouldn't clear the sill. The sound of a boy's voice floated through the panes too quiet to make out what he was saying, but when he was finished, a chorus of male voices joined him, chanting a mix of jumbled words in unison.

While they chanted, I latched my fingers to the windowsill and pulled my nose over the bottom ledge. Inside, a group of boys sat in folding chairs listening intently to the boy at the podium. I dove back under the window to hide from view.

I knew about the weekly meetings of fraternities and sororities. I'd heard about them. The memory felt fresh, but I couldn't remember how or why, when I tried to place it.

Squatting outside of the Beta Psi house, I felt like a sitting duck, so I left my post there and rounded the building to wait on the side. Pizza boxes and beer cans piled waist-high around me. I leaned against the cool brick, loitering at the corner so that I could see the moment anyone from inside the house left. I pictured the Beta Psi T-shirts again and prayed to the gods I didn't believe existed that I'd be right. That they would be here.

I felt at home in the shadows. My fingers found the knife blade in my hoodie. I turned the hilt over and over again in my hand, wondering which ones would scream when I found them and which ones would go wide-eyed but wordlessly. The images formed in my mind like a delicious fantasy to be savored.

Meanwhile, the night ticked on and I lost track of how much time had passed. Five minutes? Ten? Fifteen? I was as still and immovable as the house. As I waited, I began to hum softly and then the song came back to me. Each line in bloody succession.

"*Hide and seek, hide and seek,*" I crooned as though in lullaby. "*In the dark, they all will shriek. . . .*" The words left a smile.

The song formed and re-formed itself in my head, weaving me into a trance. *"Seek and hide, seek and hide, count the nights until they've died...."* Until the door to Beta Psi opened. The first few boys trickled out, laughing and calling into the dark after one another. The hairs on the back of my neck bristled. My grip tightened around the thin knife hilt.

"Hide and seek, hide and seek," I hummed the words softly, observing.

And then there he was. Short One. He was walking out with California, a backpack slung over one shoulder. I held my breath, waiting. Were the others inside? Would Circus Master, with his devilish, lopsided sneer, be making an appearance or were there only these two?

As Short One and California turned left out of the gate, I realized I had to make a decision. At a spot still within the house's shadow, I hopped the fence into another fraternity's yard. Trees dappled the moonlight, shifting and stirring to create eerie shapes on the ground. I kept my eye trained on the two boys like a sniper rifle.

They chatted easily between each other as they strolled down the sidewalk and I felt the heat creeping up again, rising in me like fire up a stake. The more I saw how unperturbed they were, the more I wanted to watch them burn. California jumped up and touched a lamp at the top of a post. On the next one, Short One tried to copy and missed.

Two out of five, I told myself. Two out of five wasn't bad. I waited for them to pass the fraternity whose lawn I now found myself occupying and then I exited the identical iron gate and fell in step behind the pair. Two out of five was good, I tried telling myself again. My heart rate sped up.

I would follow them until they turned off somewhere unpopulated. Somewhere like where they'd taken me. My vision swam with red. I studied the back of Short One's neck and imagined the silky feel of his blood coating my fingers.

Easy, I warned internally. I had to be careful. Couldn't mess up. If I messed up, I might not get another chance. I might miss the other three. And that would never do.

To calm myself, I sang the song in my head. *Seek and hide, seek and hide, count the nights . . .*

We turned left again at the end of the road and I recognized the twinkling lights of the dormitory buildings sparkling in front of us. The window of opportunity was shrinking. Now was the time. I was sliding the knife out of my pocket and tightening my fist around the hilt when a squeal came from the direction of one of the sorority houses and a streak of tan legs and blond hair shot across the street and wrapped its way around California.

My scalp tingled. I seethed through my teeth and quickened my stride.

Go. Away, I willed the girl. *Stupid girl. Stupid, stupid, stupid girl.* Instead of going away, she linked her hands with California's and fell in step with him, smiling and tucking her hair behind one ear. She talked easily to Short One as well, a melody of words I couldn't quite make out.

Meanwhile, the boys had now halved the distance between themselves and the dorms. My empty hand clenched, nails bearing down into my palm.

"Think," I commanded myself quietly. *Think, think, think.* The need for revenge and for that revenge to come tonight buzzed in me like an addiction and sent my skin crawling.

I felt my instincts sharpen as we got closer to campus. I noticed the campus security golf cart parked on the side of the street, yellow light blinking. I took in the lights cascading from dorm rooms that overlooked the quad where the boys were now crossing, with me in close pursuit.

I felt them closing on the dorms. The sensation of being uncloaked shocked my system. My throat squeezed in protest as I watched my window of opportunity shrink from small to nonexistent. And when the girl's fingers untangled themselves from California's and she forked off in a separate direction, I experienced the moment missed like it was a cold, dead spirit moving through my body.

The girl looked casually over her shoulder. Her perfectly waxed brow furrowed and she cocked her head at me. "Can I help you?" she asked.

And then there were mere seconds between me and the moment the boys might look back, out of curiosity, and notice me. I flipped my hood up, sank my chin to my chest, and was already moving away, back into the shadows, back into the darkness, back home.

SEVEN

Cassidy

I lifted the whistle hanging on a hook outside of Coach Carlson's door and looped the string over my head so that it hung around my neck. The metal whistle bounced off my practice uniform—a black sports bra and stretchy yoga pants that hugged my waist. I caught my reflection in the glass of Coach's office window and noticed myself appraising what I saw there, the same way the old Cassidy would have. I'd lost some of my muscle tone since autumn and my ribs showed too prominently when I breathed. Both of these things would have to be remedied with extra conditioning. I was doing better, though. Feeling stronger, more me.

I'd taken a quiz in English and I was pretty sure I'd get an A+. My GPA could still be saved this semester. I'd even passed Ava a note in class on which I'd drawn some stupid cartoon of Ms. Minter that made her laugh. Perfect friend Cassidy to the rescue.

My hair was pulled neatly up into a high ponytail and I'd selected a peachy shade of lipstick that I'd actually remembered to apply throughout the day. As I pulled my captain's clipboard out of its slot on the locker room door, I felt in control for the first time in weeks.

In the gym, the basketball team was running suicide drills. They had made the play-offs and in less than a week's time, they'd begin their first tournament round for the state title. Still, maybe I'd make the girls do twice as many suicides at the end of practice today. Show the basketball players who the real athletes on campus were. This was my first semester as cheer captain and during an important time, too, what with the chase for the title and Hollow Pines's best chance at a varsity championship in twenty-odd years. My parents had been so proud when I'd been elected on the heels of being named Homecoming queen. At one point, it had seemed impossible for my life to get any shinier. Even then, though, the threads had started to unravel, only I couldn't have predicted, in just a few short months, how little I'd have left.

I took a deep breath and remembered who I was. I was Cassidy Hyde. And surely it wasn't too late to catch on to the ends of those threads and sew my life back together stitch by stitch . . . was it?

I lifted my chin and walked briskly over toward where the other fifteen girls were stretching. When Liam reached the baseline, his eyebrows lifted at the sight of me. A bead of sweat trickled off a tuft of his sandy blond hair. I gave him a broad smile and a flirtatious wave. Okay, so it wouldn't hurt to let the other girls think I had the eye of Hollow Pines High's starting forward, especially not when he looked like that.

As a former chubby mathlete I knew success in high school was a matter of both real and projected image. I had been a master sculptor, chiseling the rock underneath with long runs, restrictive diets, careful wardrobe selection, and a winning personality that was one part girl next door and one part flirtatious minx until what showed through on the outside was the type of girl that could hold a town like Hollow Pines in the palm of her hand. Not too shabby, I reminded myself. Now, all I needed was a few touch-ups to the Cassidy Hyde brand before the whole sculpture crumbled.

As I approached the girls, I placed the whistle between my lips and gave it two short blows. "Gather up," I said, putting my hands on my hips.

A few girls—Molly, Liz, and Kylie Beth—who were nearest to me stopped their stretching and looked up without moving. Paisley had been using Ava's shoulder for balance while she held on to her shoelaces with one hand to stretch her hamstrings. She let her fingers slide from Ava's shoulders and the two shared a look that I couldn't read. Nobody was budging.

"Hello, lazybones." I clapped. "Where's your hustle? Let's get practice started. I don't want to be here all night."

Erica moved to Paisley's other side and cast nervous sideways glances. I suddenly had the feeling that I was standing on the wrong side of an electrical fence. A queasy uneasiness spread in my gut, like that time I ate movie theater nachos.

"Okay." I folded my arms across my chest while attempting to hide the ricocheting of my heart against my ribs. "Can someone please tell me what's going on?"

Ava, who had added rhinestones to calf-high tube socks and to a bow in her hair, cleared her throat but looked down at her sneakers.

"Paize?" I said.

Paisley's blue eyes flitted to the ceiling for a split second, then she took a small step forward. "Fine, whatever, I volunteer as tribute." Her fingernails were painted a frosty pink and she curled them around her narrow waist. "Look, I don't want you to make a big deal of this or anything, but some of us have been talking."

An icy wave tingled the roots of my hair and crawled down the length of my back. "Yeah?" I said, fighting to keep my voice steady. "Talking about what?"

Paisley was four inches shorter than me, but with the way she carried herself, like she was Napoleon, it always caught me off guard when I noticed how tiny she really was. "Well, to be honest, we think maybe you shouldn't be captain anymore."

I felt myself go still as glass, worried that if I made any sudden movements, I might shatter. Paisley was the only one on the whole squad looking at me. Was that how much the lot of them had already dismissed me or were they just too cowardly to say this to my face?

"And you . . . don't want me to make a big deal of this . . ." My voice trailed. *Not a big deal*, I screamed inside. *Not a big deal?* "How long has this been going on?" I asked, keeping my internal monologue where it belonged. "The talking behind my back." Well, most of it, anyway.

Ava lifted her chin and stared at me with her deep brown eyes. She, at least, looked genuinely stricken. "Not long," she said quickly. "I—well, the last week maybe, but—"

"We think you've been distracted," Paisley interrupted so that I didn't get to hear what lay on the other end of that "but." "Let's face it, cheerleading doesn't seem like your number one priority anymore."

I held up my hand to stop her. "And whose idea was this?"

Behind me, I had the distinct sensation that the basketball players were beginning to stop and stare at the confrontation going on near this side of the gymnasium. Balls bounced and then seemed to fall idle and the squeaking of sneakers slowed. I began to sweat.

"Does it matter?" she said.

Something else was beginning to brew in the pit of my stomach. Fury. "That depends," I responded coolly. "Was it yours?"

Paisley rolled her eyes. "This is why I told you from the start not to make a big deal about it." I felt the other girls—more than a dozen of them, girls that I'd called my friends—crowding in on us like a pack of wolves.

"I'm not. I'm asking a simple question. Am I not allowed to ask questions?"

Beside Paisley, Ava tightened the bows around her braids.

Paisley's eyes narrowed. "You know, you're not the only one who's had hard stuff happen to them this year."

The words stung. My eyes pricked as if my cheek had been slapped. Paisley Wheelwright had no idea what I'd been through. Best friend or no, she didn't have a clue about Dearborn. I closed my eyes and for a split second, the words of the boy with the wolf-like grin came barreling through time and space to haunt me. *A new toy to play with, lads . . . How rough do you think I can be before this one breaks?*

The suffocating group of girls combined with the haunting shadow of the wolf grin returned me to the headspace of the chubby girl I used to be. The shame came rushing back and it felt new and fresh and worse because I'd been so used to holding this town in my palm that I'd nearly forgotten how bad it could be at the bottom of the dog pile, especially in a place like Hollow Pines.

No. My eyes snapped open. I'd worked too hard. I'd broken too many nails clawing my way to the top and it wasn't too late to stop the fall. Maybe I'd needed Sunshine to remind me, but I was still Cassidy Hyde and Paisley Wheelwright and everyone else that tried to stop me could suck it. I clenched my grip.

"Why do I get the feeling that the most tragic thing that's happened to *you* this year was *me* being named Homecoming queen . . . instead of you?" My question came out sickly sweet, laced with something unmistakably steely.

Ava and Erica both sucked in sharp breaths. Paisley's mouth formed a tiny *o* of surprise. *That's right, Paize, I'm still here and kicking.*

"We've just been worried about you," Ava said in a tone so sincere that I felt some of the gunmetal that had instantaneously built up around my insides soften. "But, I mean . . ." She fidgeted. "This weekend you seemed so much more like your old self, maybe . . . I don't know . . . maybe you just needed a little more time."

Paisley's mouth morphed into a barely visible scowl. "We talked about this. . . ."

I pulled my shoulders back. I almost laughed in Paisley's face. She saw a chance to be at the top of the proverbial pyramid without me at last and she grabbed for it. The funny thing was, she was only a week too late. A few days ago, I probably would have slithered away and skulked into social obscurity. Anything to avoid the confrontation. But I wasn't ready to go now. Not yet. Not this way.

I drew myself up to my full measure. I positioned the clipboard on my hip and tried to look authoritative. "Okay, I'll admit, things were a little tough there for a while and I apologize if I seemed . . . distracted, but I can assure you *this* is my first priority. The Oilerettes. Hollow Pines High. Making our squad the best it can be. Making sure that *we*"—I scanned the faces of the girls, making eye contact with each and every one—"are flawless. You can count on me." I smiled and there wasn't anything phony about it. I felt the warmth of leftover Sunshine pulsing through me. I could do this. I could win. "Give me this week. Until after the first play-off game against Lamar." We were gearing up for a long weekend of tournament games in quick succession that would decide whether Hollow Pines would be playing for states then regionals. It was a lot of responsibility and a big stage. "You'll see exactly what I mean."

When I finished talking, Erica actually jumped up and down and clapped, then let her hands drop when she caught Paisley's glare.

Paisley tucked her cropped hair behind her ears. As her best friend, this was a dead giveaway. She was nervous. "But we already talked about this, y'all," she said, turning to implore the squad. "We took a vote. This is a democracy. Votes are sacred. Doesn't that mean something to you?"

Ava waved her off. "Come on, Paize. The point was we wanted Cassidy to be better. And . . . well . . ." She gave a hesitant shrug of her shoulders. "I, for one, am thrilled to have Cassidy 1.0 back." Evidence that the real original Cassidy was so invisible that she still remained forgotten. Ava extended her arms and came to wrap me in a tight hug.

The warmth inside me flared. "Thanks," I said softly into her ear.

"Sorry," she murmured back.

Everyone shifted their weight and muttered signs of approval.

Molly, Emma Kate, Alice, Becky, they were all coming around to my side. *Back* around to my side. I rapped my knuckles on the clipboard. "Well?" I said to Paisley.

I watched as she rearranged her face before my eyes. I watched as the lines of her frown curved upward into a smile. I watched as she expertly pulled the fangs out from where she'd attempted to lodge them in my neck and reinvented herself as Paisley Wheelwright, certified best friend. "Totally," she said, in the same pitch she'd use if she were performing a cheer. "Just wanted to make sure you're cool."

I cocked my chin ever so slightly and responded drily, "Totally."

For the remainder of our hour-and-a-half practice, I worked the girls harder than they'd ever been worked before. We lunged up and down the court until all of our legs were consumed in a blaze of lactic acid. We ran laps, repeated jumps—straddle, pike, and herkies—performed push-ups and sit-ups in sets of one hundred. I let them feel a fraction of what it'd taken to build Cassidy Hyde, Homecoming queen.

Sweat streamed from our pores and, through my exhaustion, I felt like I was being baptized into a new person. I luxuriated in the feeling of weakness draining from my body.

And of course, I kept a careful eye on Paisley, making sure to call her out publicly for every lapse in form. As Coach Carlson was shutting off the lights to the gym and the basketball players were trickling into the locker room, I blew my whistle three times.

"Great work, everyone," I said. They wandered over to their gym bags, pulling out bottles of water and wiping their necks with fresh towels. "Time spent today means we're flawless on Friday." I caught Liam disappearing into the locker room.

"I swear I must have burned, like, a thousand calories," Ava said, unscrewing the top of a Gatorade.

"I'm stopping for a Big Mac," said Erica.

Paisley plopped down onto a bottom-row bleacher. "That totally defeats the purpose, dimwit."

Erica ignored her and so did I.

My muscles pulsed with endorphins and, besides, I had somewhere I needed to be. "I expect everyone to be on time and ready to run routines tomorrow. Got it? Picture them in your sleep," I finished. "I'll see you guys then."

With those parting words and feeling quite proud of myself, I spun on my heel and disappeared to replace the clipboard and whistle and to snag my belongings from where I'd stashed them inside the girls' locker room. Two minutes later, with a sheen of sweat still sticking to my forehead, I was waiting outside of the back entrance to the boys' locker room.

My spot overlooked the vibrant green football field, which, now that it was no longer football season, was being occupied by members of the track team busy running their one-mile cooldown. So much had happened in Hollow Pines this year. I knew the town that I'd worked so hard to master had been changed for good.

But staring out at the field beneath the glow of stadium lights, with the breeze cooling my flushed skin, I caught a glimpse of the Hollow Pines I used to know. Simple and safe. And I wished I could freeze time to keep it.

The door of the locker room swung open and a few members of the basketball team began to trickle out toward the student parking lot. I spotted the back of Liam loping away, his gym bag slung over his shoulder.

"Hey!" I moved from the wall and jogged after him. "Wait up!" He turned. His smile was easy. He'd parted his wet hair to the side and I could smell the damp scent of fruity shampoo from several feet away. He waved a few of his teammates on and told them he'd catch up with them later. "Everything okay?" he asked and, by the way he glanced at the door to the girls' locker room, I knew he was referring to the squad's would-be coup.

"Crisis averted." I fell in beside him and we walked down the paved sidewalk.

"Good to hear." We continued along side by side. Liam didn't volunteer anything further. If this were a guy I was interested in, that alone would have driven me crazy, but since he wasn't, I found myself envying how carefree and unflustered he always appeared. Maybe things were always easy when you were that gorgeous.

Then again, people used to think that about me.

"I need more," I volunteered at last.

He fished the keys out of one of the many pockets on his gym bag. "How much more?" He clicked a couple buttons when we arrived at his car and threw the bag into the backseat. Night was falling, turning the air hazy between us, and I found myself growing antsy, although I didn't know for what.

"I don't know," I said, shifting my weight. "A lot, I guess." I hoped I didn't sound overeager, like some kind of junkie. But Sunshine wasn't a normal drug. I viewed it as simply a boost. That was it. The fact that I had gaps in my memory? Worrisome, sure. But were they so bad that I'd give up my newfound happiness? No way. I had enough bad memories that I could certainly spare a few. "How much can you give me?"

He gestured me around to the other side of the car and told me to sit in the passenger seat. He dropped into the driver's side next to me and reached over to pop open the glove compartment. He pulled out a zipped leather sheath that looked like it'd contain a car manual. Once open, I saw that instead it held a number of plastic bags, no bigger than the size of a credit card. He sifted through the bags. I knitted my fingers together anxiously and stared out the bug-splattered windshield. "I can give you a couple pills," he said. "I'll need to call my brother for more next week. You're not my only customer, you know."

I pivoted in my seat and leaned just a fraction of a degree forward. I was still wearing only my sports bra and yoga pants. "But I'm your prettiest, right?" I joked.

He pressed his lips together and appraised me. "You've got that right. Okay, fine. I can do a week's worth, but that's it. Deal?"

I nodded. My fingers were jittery as I pulled my own gym bag onto my lap and dug around for my wallet. I did some quick math in my head, counted out eighty dollars, and held it out for him. "Discount for buying in bulk," I said.

A dimple cut into his cheek. "Whatever you say, captain." He passed me two of the miniature plastic bags and I quickly stowed them in my bag. Members of the Oilerettes were beginning to make their way into the parking lot.

"I should leave," I said. "Thanks for this." I popped open the door and climbed out.

"Pleasure doing business with you, Cassidy Hyde." He gave me a salute and, as soon as I closed the door, he was peeling out of his parking spot and away from the lot.

I stood there in the dust left behind from his tires spinning in gravel. I waved the cloud away, coughing.

"Cassidy!" someone called from a car nearby. "Cassidy, over here!"

My eyes strained against the darkening backdrop. I searched, following the voice, until at last I saw a hand waving through an open car window. I couldn't make out the face inside.

My shoes crunched the gravel of the parking lot. I walked slowly over to the other car, an old VW Bug, painted an uneven blue, as though that hadn't been the original color. A girl got out and stood kicking her toe into the ground. I didn't recognize her. She had thick, dark bangs, wide eyes, and wore a jean jacket that was too big for her.

"Hi," I said, plastering on a smile. "How's it going?"

Paisley and I had different philosophies on Hollow Pines's lower social caste. She preferred the "let them eat cake" approach and hardly deigned to talk to the girls that tended to try to get our attention in hopes of scoring a spot on the Oilerettes—or at least at our lunch table—while I leaned toward a gentler touch. After all, wasn't I living proof that any of these girls could be a shopping spree and a Weight Watchers membership away from the ladder's top rung?

I studied her for a moment. Dark clothes. Dark hair. Thin. Skin that had clearly never been touched by the sun—less Gwyneth Paltrow, more *Walking Dead*. I pegged her either for drama or band, with an outside shot of a glee club member. Either way, she wasn't exactly going to be up for any class superlatives.

The girl's bangs fell over her eyes and stuck to her lashes. "I . . . was hoping I could find you here. Sorry. I just wanted to thank you—"

My forehead wrinkled, not following. "Thank me for what?"

Had I donated to her bake sale or charity drive in the last few weeks without remembering? It was possible.

"The other night." She twisted a silver ring on her middle finger. "I know you . . . didn't exactly catch me at my finest and, um, I'm sorry for that. It's embarrassing. But I wanted you to know that I'm grateful."

I looked around to see if there was anyone else to whom she could possibly be talking. "I think you must be confusing me with someone else," I said, when I was clearly the only person within earshot.

She hesitated. She shook her head. "I'm sorry. Is it, like, weird that I'm here or something?" For a girl I didn't even know, she sure did apologize a lot. Then, she clapped her hand to her forehead. "Stupid me. *Marcy*. You like being called Marcy now, I guess, right? It was late. I wasn't sure if that was a joke . . . or something."

"*Marcy?*" So this wasn't the typical Oilerette cling-on. This girl was straight-up delusional. "Look, you've got the wrong girl. I don't know a Marcy. My name's Cassidy." I held out my hand, if only because my Southern manners were so deeply ingrained that I couldn't help myself. "Cassidy Hyde."

The girl unlaced her fingers and hesitantly took my hand. Her skin was ice-cold. "I know," she said, looking between my eyes and our palms pressed together. "I'm Lena . . . we met two nights ago . . . I—I know you remember."

Without meaning to, I snatched my hand away. She startled as if I'd burned her. "I don't know what you're talking about," I said more abruptly now.

"Is it because I'm a sophomore here?" she asked, beginning to take a step forward. She froze when she noticed me tense. "Because it's not like I'm wanting to sit at your lunch table or anything. I'm not trying to embarrass you. I just wanted to thank you. Properly. Sometimes I think I make people uncomfortable and—"

"Look," I said, moving my gym bag to the other shoulder. The parking lot was emptying out now. Exhausted, all the other Oilerettes had made it into their cars without the usual gossip and joking around. My own stomach rumbled, reminding me it was dinnertime. "I don't know you and, trust me, that has nothing to do with your age. It was nice meeting you, Lena, but I—I need to go."

"Wait." Her dark eyes held me in place. "Please, take my number." Before I could stop her she took a notebook from her bag, tore a corner off the top, and was scribbling on it. She shoved it in my hand. I pursed my lips and tried to decide what to do with it. The sound I made was noncommittal. A brush-off.

I backpedaled and then with a final glance at the girl with the dark bangs, deep-set eyes, and too much jewelry, I turned and headed for my car. I was several paces away and had just clicked the button on my keys so that the headlights flickered twice, when Lena called from behind me, "I think we should both stay away from Dearborn." Icy tendrils branched from my ankles up through my spine at the mention of Dearborn. "Be safe, Marcy."

Blood thudded against my ears. I didn't acknowledge her, didn't stop. I quickened my steps the rest of the gray distance between me and my car and, once inside, ripped the scrap of paper in two and let its remains flutter into my cup holder. And then I fled. Without looking back.

EIGHT

Marcy

The sound of a thudding bass floated down the street and shook the windows of the Beta Psi house. Construction paper blacked out the windows, but the painted white sheet still draped from the second story, announcing tonight's throwback rave.

A lucky break.

College students stumbled in and out of the house, talking in loud voices as though they hadn't adjusted to the drop in volume outdoors. I traveled up the walkway, slipping in among them, and made my way into the home of the Beta Psi brotherhood.

Immediately, I was plunged into frenzied flashes of on-off darkness. Strobe lights blinked and the world around me shrank disconcertingly to the distance I could see between blinding flickers of light. I hadn't known what to expect. What was a throwback rave, anyway? Now I saw girls dressed in neon spandex, ponytails crimped and swept to the side. Boys wore aviator sunglasses and tank tops with atrocious patterns, all homages to a much tackier decade. Glow necklaces were worn around heads, necks, and wrists, giving the illusion of moving targets. And from somewhere a black light shone over the crowd, turning white T-shirts electric blue and Crest-strip smiles eerily radioactive in the dark.

I hovered near the entrance, letting my eyes adjust. Gradually, I began to thread my way through the thrashing bodies, cups of beer, and swirling smoke. The music pounded my chest, egging me on as I searched the faces.

I wouldn't be greedy tonight. One boy. A tasty appetizer. That would be my prize. I worked the room, passing a banister, a tarp-covered pool table, and a keg.

"Do you know a Beta Psi brother about this height?" I yelled in the ear of a guy filling up his cup from the keg hose and held up my hand to suggest a person only an inch taller than me.

His grin was sloppy. He raised his cup. "Cheers," he yelled back.

I waved him off and moved on.

I tried again. "A Beta Psi brother. This height?"

The boy appraised me, shrugged, and pointed to his ear like he couldn't hear before wandering away. Frustration built up inside me.

I disappeared into the throng of people who were all oblivious to my hunt. Faces appeared and disappeared in stop-motion. Disorienting. A nightmarish haze. I was tracing the entire perimeter of the downstairs floor when my heart fell out of rhythm with the music. There he was. Short One. The one who'd watched from behind his video camera.

It was my turn to watch him now. He stood smiling over a red cup, talking with two boys that I didn't recognize. Their faces blurred into the background. Neither of them were part of my evening. They were collateral.

Short One wore a bright yellow T-shirt and white shorts that glowed underneath the black light. Target practice. Hatred bubbled up from my gut like a pot of water reaching its boiling point. *I found you.*

I removed the knife from the pocket of my black hoodie and stashed it in the side of my boot. I then unzipped the hoodie and draped it over my arm. Underneath, I was wearing a skintight black tank top. I cupped my breasts and pushed them higher up in my bra. Better.

It took me ten steps to cut the distance between us. I counted them. I also made them count. I walked with a swing in my hips that begged to be lingered over. He did.

"May I?" I asked, cocking my head and holding my hand out for his cup.

His brows pulled together, but he offered me his plastic cup. I brought it to my lips and took a swig. The sickly sweet scent of beer poured over my taste buds.

"Do I know you?" he asked in my ear.

"I don't know. Do you?" I said coquettishly, and took another sip.

"You look familiar." He squinted his eyes, trying to place me between the flashes of strobe light.

"Maybe it'd help jog your memory if my clothes were off?" I said this as though it were an invitation, not a jab. As though it weren't the figurative tip of a blade poised at his jugular.

The corners of his mouth tugged upward. He motioned for his

two friends to leave. They pounded fists together like they were the ones in on the joke and I was the one left on the outside.

"Did you say 'clothes off'?" he asked when they were gone. His eyes were bright and shiny. He was thick around the neck and stocky from there down. He didn't have the wolflike grin of Circus Master, but that didn't stop me from hating him.

Watching me and doing nothing. Recording me for entertainment value. Did he really think those were crimes I could allow to go unpunished? *Think again, Short One.*

"Not here," I said. I had to brush my lips against his earlobe so that I didn't have to scream. I imagined that he had a clear view down the front of my shirt. That was okay, I figured, when all he could do was take it to his grave.

"Where?" he asked. He snaked his fingers between mine. They were clammy. Up close, he smelled like a sour mix of cologne and alcohol.

I leaned in close again like I was going to tell him. Instead, I used my tongue to trace his ear and felt him shudder. Without another word, I pulled at his hand, leading him through the crowd. I was so close. When we reached the door, a thrill raced through me.

As we stepped into open air, I felt another rush; it was Christmas morning and any moment now, I was going to get to unwrap my present.

Short One blinked. Compared to the party, the world outside felt muted. He dumped the contents of his cup in a bush and tossed it on the lawn. "Back to your place?" he asked. He was so presumptuous. Good, let him be. I wondered if he'd placed my face yet or whether he was too drunk to decipher where he knew me from. Or even worse, whether I'd been too unmemorable for him to care.

"My car," I said. "It's not far."

He stared up at the dark windows. "We can use one of the frat brother's rooms, you know. We don't have to leave."

I wrinkled my nose and tried to sound nonchalant. Nonchalance was sexy. "This will be better," I said. "Trust me." I allowed myself an air of mystery. *Trust me.* As though I had some grand plan fully designed around his pleasure. He must think that was how the world worked. A whole universe orbiting around him and his friends for the taking. That was okay, though. I'd be a good teacher. I had a lesson planned just for him. I tugged at his belt loop and he didn't argue any further. He was so simple.

— — —

"WHAT'S YOUR MAJOR?" he asked.

Trees lined the end of the boulevard, enveloping it in a leafy canopy and blocking out the stars. I leaned into him, wrapped my arm around his waist, and played the part of a girl who wanted nothing more than to take off her clothes for a boy. I relished the feeling of control, the way that I could touch his arm and his skin would erupt in goose pimples or how I could bump into his hip and he'd make a satisfied noise and pull me closer. It was like pulling the strings on a marionette. Left foot, right foot, left foot, right foot and the closer we marched to his demise.

"Undecided," I said.

He hummed approvingly. "I don't know, either. I might blow this whole place entirely. I'm going to be a comedian. Like Conan or Jon Stewart or something. People think I'm freaking hilarious."

"Is that right?" I turned into an alleyway, pinched between two buildings. I'd read the signs when I found the place. One was a faculty-only library and one was a church fellowship house. Both were empty at this time of night. The walls blocked out the noise from the road.

"Hey, where did you park?" he asked, looking around at his new surroundings. I checked over my shoulder one last time to make sure that no one had followed.

"Just down there." I pointed. It wasn't a lie. My car waited at the end of the back street. "This is a shortcut. Why? Are you scared?"

He chuckled. "I think I'll be all right." Of course he thought he'd be all right. Guys weren't taught not to walk alone at night. Guys weren't taught not to leave their drinks unattended. Guys weren't taught to carry Mace or whistles or to consider carefully whether or not to fight back. That was his mistake.

He started after me toward my car. Puddles gathered into the alley's seam. A few stray trash bags lined the way, spilling their guts onto the blacktop.

"You're kind of freaky, you know that?" Short One said.

I smiled back at him. "You have no idea."

Noise roared in my ears. My pulse beat wildly. I could feel my heartbeat all the way up in my eye sockets. Chaos ruled every particle in my body. A few feet from my car, I stopped. I turned to stare up at him. "Here," I said softly.

He moved closer. "Here?" The corners of his eyes crinkled in confusion. In another life maybe he would have grown up to be a comedian. I nodded. I ran my fingertips up the back of his arm. His eyebrows raised. "Oh . . ." His voice was a rasp. "Here."

Short One bent down and kissed me. His tongue was rough and his lips were dry. I kissed back, hard, until our teeth knocked. His hands felt for the bottom edge of my shirt. I let his fingers play with the hem. Slowly, I bent my right knee. I let my hand slip into the top of my boot. I pressed the hilt into my palm and slid it across my jeans.

Cool air tickled my belly button. He kissed me harder. Gently, I held his bottom lip between my teeth, just like I'd seen in the movies. Slow, sexy, and just the right amount of dangerous. Only problem: This wasn't the movies.

I clamped down on his lip, biting through skin. My head swam with the taste of coppery blood.

He yelped and jerked away. "You bitch!" Anger flashed in his eyes. I saw my face reflected in miniature inside the dark fathoms of his pupils. I tightened my grip and aimed for the bull's-eye.

He wouldn't be watching anymore.

NINE

Cassidy

I knew it was too early from the moment that I woke up. My phone lay dark and silent on the nightstand beside me, the alarm clock still set. The first strands of dawn had begun to trickle ghostly tendrils through my bedroom shutters. Instinct told me to roll over, stuff my pillow over my face, and enjoy whatever bonus time I found myself with in bed.

But the overhead fan was giving me the chills and I noticed that I'd kicked my sheets to the foot of the mattress. No wonder I'd woken up. I shivered and sat up to grab the top edge of my duvet cover. Dark spots on the fitted white sheet underneath caught my eye. I leaned closer and rubbed my fingers into one of the stains. It smeared.

Outside my window, birds were beginning to chirp. As I adjusted to the light, I saw that the blotches were a deep, rusty red. I sucked in a breath. My cycle must have started during the night. I hadn't been prepared. "Dammit." I crawled off the mattress, clutching the oversized T-shirt I'd worn to bed to my legs.

But when I examined myself, I nearly screamed. Blood coated my hands. Smudged red fingerprints stained my shirt. I swallowed hard. It was so much. I patted my torso, my arms, my legs. I had to be injured somewhere. Nothing was hurting right away, though. Was I in shock? I rushed to the bathroom and locked the door tight. *Breathe*, I commanded. I stared into the mirror and saw that red flecked my cheeks and forehead. The whites of my eyes created empty saucers in my skull.

I stripped my T-shirt off and kicked it to the floor. Still no signs of a wound, though many parts of my body were coated in blood. I turned on the showerhead and jumped in without waiting for the water to warm. The cold was an electric jolt to my system. I scrubbed my arms. Russet-tinged water streamed onto the white porcelain and swirled around the drain. Steam billowed up toward the ceiling's air vent. I scrubbed until there was nothing left to scrub and my skin was pink with scratches, but otherwise, there wasn't a mark on me. When the water began to scald me, turning my flesh from pink to angry red, I turned the knob and the cascade died. Soaking wet, I dried myself in a towel and changed into a clean pair of sweatpants, a sweatshirt, and my old pair of sheepskin boots. I dropped the bloody shirt into the back corner of my closet and pulled the comforter over my sheets.

On the white paint of my bedroom door, I saw remnants of a red handprint. How did the blood get there if . . . if . . .

My heart thudded. I slipped out of my bedroom, careful not to make a sound, and padded down the hallway. A single droplet dotted the hardwood at the top of the stairs. My throat closed up. Gingerly, I lowered myself onto the next stair and then the next. Fear bloomed in my gut as I approached the landing, terrified of what I might find downstairs.

But as I entered the living room, then the dining room, then the kitchen, I found nothing out of place except that the back door was slightly ajar. On the bronze knob, there was another bloody imprint, barely visible. I wrapped my hand over it and twisted.

The morning in front of me felt dreamlike, the air cool, but swampy. Glancing once more over my shoulder toward the still-sleeping house, I ventured onto the dewy grass. My family's backyard wasn't fenced. Our home backed up to the greenbelt, a few miles' worth of untouched foliage with crisscrossing paths for runners and hikers.

My sheepskin boots swished through the wet blades. At the end of our property line, I let my fingers brush against the thick leaves of my mother's elephant ear plants. I'd helped her transfer them from the pots to the soil the first summer that we moved here. A few of them looked as though they'd been trampled. I frowned and bent closer to the ground. A patch of grass nearby was stained red.

Several feet after, I could see another streak of red and a curved path where the grass had been crushed, as though something heavy had been dragged across it.

The hour was still early. Fog hovered low to the earth. I followed the path of the red streak and the urge to run began to chew at my legs. The only problem was I couldn't decide which way.

Morbid curiosity drew me farther. I ducked under a low-hanging tree, crossing into the greenbelt's thicker foliage. I had to look more carefully for the signs of red now, for where the dirt and the leaves were smashed down together. I stumbled over roots and tangled vines until a small clearing opened up. There, I found a mound of freshly turned dirt. The smell of damp mud filled my nostrils. I stared at the embankment where the trampled path clearly ended.

I recognized the size and shape of the pile of dirt at once. It was a grave. Trembling, I squatted beside it and brushed the raised crest away until the ground was even. A bird took flight from a branch overhead and I nearly choked on a scream that didn't come out. *It's only a bird*, I told myself.

Then, *call the police*. That was my next thought. That was what I could do. Maybe what I should do. But I remembered the blood in my bed, on my hands, on my face, and hesitated. I stayed there, studying the earth until, after several long moments where my ribs pushed against the backs of my knees as I breathed, I dug my hand into the dirt and tossed away a clump.

Soon, I was on all fours, scrabbling in the ground like a dog. Only a few inches down, my mud-caked fingernails snagged fabric. I flicked away clusters of dirt until I'd uncovered a T-shirt and a torso. My mind struggled to recall the last thing I'd eaten. Whatever it was, it was slowly creeping the wrong way up my throat.

"It's okay," I whispered. "It's okay."

My movements became quick and sporadic as I hurried to excavate the rest. I pawed at the soil. My fingertips touched skin and hair and then it was finished. I sat back on my heels and covered my mouth with my hand.

There, lying in the cold ground, was a boy whose face I recognized. And he was now in a position that I'd found myself fantasizing about many times over the last few weeks.

He was dead.

I pressed the inside of my wrist to my lips and took shaky breaths, fighting to keep down the bile that was tickling the roof of my mouth. It was like I'd wished it to be true and now, inexplicably, it was. My tongue felt too big.

Dirt and blood coated the boy's hair. His right eye was closed. A knife wound pierced the left eye socket. The remnants of an eyeball filled the hole like the whites of an undercooked hard-boiled egg. Violent, red-soaked gashes tore open the T-shirt. Too many to count.

Sunlight had begun to trickle down through the leaves. Silver glinted beside the boy. I reached down next to his arm and pulled out a serrated knife. I turned it over in my palm. The hilt was black with a metallic border. I recognized the small logo at the end as the same brand as my mother's collection. Hadn't she been missing one this weekend?

I felt my lungs deflate, sucked of oxygen like a plastic bag. Soon my family would be waking up. Soon they'd be wondering where I was. I rose to my feet and paced back and forth past the head of the body. *Think, Cassidy.* What should I do? I tapped my fingers to my forehead. Minutes spiraled away from me. I had no idea how this boy—this corpse—had gotten here, but I knew there was blood on me and there was a body merely yards from my house. I was a smart girl. Anybody that did the math would think I had something to do with it.

From the road, I heard the loud grumble of the garbage truck trundling up the street. The world was stirring. Quick decisions were the only kind I had time for, so I made one.

I began to push dirt back over the cadaver, then stopped. I

patted down his shorts and felt underneath his muddy back for a wallet or a cell phone. Who was this boy? I knew his face. I knew what he'd done to me. But that was it. I wanted to know his name. Except he'd been stripped of his things.

Out on the road, there was the beep of a reversing truck. *Never mind*, I thought and resumed shoving dirt. I didn't leave a mound. Instead, I packed the mud as tightly as I could over where he lay. I foraged for leaves and sticks and branches and placed them over the spot where I'd reburied the boy to camouflage it.

When I was finished, I studied my handiwork. The disguise was good, good enough to nearly convince me this had all been a nightmare and I was coming to after some bizarre sleepwalking incident. Or at least it would have been, if it weren't for the knife cast in the soil nearby.

I picked it up and stowed it in the pocket of my sweatshirt before cutting briskly back into my yard. I shut the kitchen door and pulled it until the lock snapped into place. I slipped off my boots and held them in one hand so as not to track in dirt. Checking the wooden block where my mom stored her knives, I saw that one was indeed still missing.

A clammy fever swept over me, like cold hands had just wrapped around the back of my neck. I rinsed the knife under the faucet and stuffed it with the rest of the silverware in the dishwasher before returning to my bedroom to change for the second time this morning.

When I came back downstairs, Honor was eating an English muffin at the breakfast table. "What's up with you?" she asked.

I'd changed into clean pajamas. "Nothing, just sick," I said. The kitchen felt so normal now that it was filled with my sister and the sounds of our parents getting ready in their bedroom. My heart ached for normal. A wave of nausea swam through my belly and for a second, I really did feel sick.

"Since when?" She took a bite of her English muffin. A dollop of jelly stuck to her cheek. She smeared it with her finger and licked it off.

I went to the refrigerator and poured myself a glass of orange juice. The liquid sloshed inside and I hurried to hide my shaking hands. "Since this morning. Why the investigation?" I worked hard to keep the edge out of my voice and failed.

Honor shrugged. "I just thought you were turning over a new leaf or whatever."

I glanced out the window, beyond the trees, imagining the horror that was hidden outside. My knees threatened to buckle. I needed to sit down.

"I am," I said. "I'm just not feeling well, okay?" I snapped. "I'm *allowed* not to feel well. Even the president of the United States gets sick."

She rolled her eyes and brought her empty plate to the sink. I held my breath as she slid the dishwasher tray out and placed it onto one of the clawed racks. "If you say so." I ogled my sister, remembering how she used to draw me pictures anytime I had so much as a cough. Hello, new teenage attitude. "Have you told Mom yet?"

"Told Mom what?" My mom appeared from the dining room. She wore dark jeans and jeweled flats with a crisp white top. She sat her purse on the countertop and started digging through it. I nearly lost my composure when I saw her. What would she say if she knew?

I couldn't bear the disappointment.

"Cassidy says she's not going to school today." Honor tossed her long hair behind one shoulder. I forced myself to remember that Honor knew nothing. This new mood of hers was probably just about those stupid pictures I deleted from her phone. I supposed I should be happy that my sister didn't know what real problems were.

Mom stopped digging to look at me. A crease formed between her eyebrows and I recognized the return of the worried look, the one that held the smallest bit of mistrust and an even larger dose of frustration. "What's wrong?" Finding her car keys, she dropped them on the counter. "Are you sick? Because you know if you can just wait it out there's a three-day weekend coming up. Maybe you can catch up on your rest then."

I pulled the sleeves of my shirt down over my hands. They were shaking even harder now. I hugged myself. "I think I'm coming down with something. Really, I just don't think I should go today. Is that all right?"

All the while I kept replaying one sentence: *There's a dead body in the yard, there's a dead body in the yard, there's a dead body in the yard.*

"I hate you missing more school, Cassidy." The corners of her mouth turned down. I saw her shoulders sag with them. "I already agreed to volunteer for Junior League today. But..." She dug for her cell phone. "I suppose I can cancel. Just let me call Mary Beth and—"

Too far, I thought. If I overplayed the illness, I risked getting stuck with Mom guarding my bed and a never-ending supply of chili while she tried to get me to sweat whatever "it" was out of me.

"Stop, Mom. It's okay. I'm *seventeen*. I don't need you to cancel your plans for me." I sucked in a deep breath and channeled the old Cassidy, the one that she trusted. "Actually, I wouldn't even be missing school at all." I rested my elbows on the kitchen island casually. "But we have that big game with Lamar on Friday and I absolutely *can't* be sick then. The girls have been working really hard."

There was a spark of appreciation in her eyes. "Maybe a little too hard," she said with a knowing tilt of her head. But I could tell how secretly pleased she was. Oilerettes. Big game. Working hard. When it came to the daughter who cared, these signs were the trifecta. She immediately began to buzz around the kitchen, morphing into a mom who was concerned for all the normal reasons instead of a mom whose daughter was spiraling into a bottomless pit of depression. "You'll be missing practice then," she said as she pulled out a bottle of vitamins from a cabinet. It wasn't a question. With a pang, I remembered the almost-coup waiting for me at practice and wanted to argue.

Instead I gave her a weak smile and held up my hand while she poured two chewable vitamins into my palm. "The girls will be fine without me. Who knows, maybe I'll even give them the day off. I'll catch up on my work Monday when we have off school. Promise."

Mom leaned forward and kissed my forehead. "Fine, you girls all take the day off then. That'd be nice of you. Now go back to bed." She pointed a finger at me and lightly touched my nose. My insides throbbed.

I climbed the stairs, dreading being closed up in a room that now felt like a crime scene, even if it was just for a short time. At a glance, nothing in my room looked out of place. The ceiling fan whirred overhead. Light spilled in through the shutters and bounced off the glass of my vanity.

But when I pulled back the sheet, the smears of blood jumped out. Sharp red and unmistakable. My vision swam. In the daytime, the stains were more visible. It now looked as if I'd spent the night rolling around in a slaughterhouse.

There was a light knock on the door. I covered the gore with my duvet and spun to face the entry. A creak and then Honor's face poked through.

She had her backpack slung over one shoulder. Her long hair fell in angelic curtains around her face. "Sorry you're sick," she said. "Text me if you want me to bring you anything on the way home. Assuming you manage to dodge Mom's chili."

And just like that, my kid sister was back. "Thanks," I said. "I'll text you."

"Oh, and you better not let her catch you out of bed," Honor called as she pulled the door shut again.

I stared down at the comforter. I did *not* want to crawl into a mess of someone else's blood, but she was right. If Mom caught me out of bed, there would be the inevitable tucking in and taking of temperature, all with the distinct possibility of chili.

I held my breath and shimmied between the covers. "Oh god." I stifled a gag. This should so not be happening.

For fifteen minutes I stewed in someone else's spilled vital fluids until at last my mom came upstairs to tell me she was headed out for the day. I nodded and tried to strike a balance between pathetic and capable. She blew me an air kiss after which it took another five minutes before I heard the garage door screech open and her car start.

I kicked the soiled sheets down to my feet and leaped out of bed. The next four hours, I spent washing and drying the sheets, spraying the lawn down with a power hose, running the dishwasher, and wiping the house clean of any stray drops. At the end, I collapsed onto the couch and lost myself in back-to-back episodes of whatever sitcoms were playing on syndication, too lazy and spent to change the channel.

I jumped to a sitting position when I heard the doorbell ring. My mom never rang the doorbell. My first thought was: *cops?* Bleary-eyed, I looked up to realize it was evening and I must have been sleeping. I peeked out the back door and saw that Mom's car was back in the garage. She must have snuck in and let me sleep. I should have been figuring out what to do next, formulating some kind of plan. But what kinds of plans were available to someone who may or may not have killed someone in her backyard?

That was a stupid train of thought. I should have been trying at least.

Still dressed in my pajamas, I wandered to the door, on the other side of which, to my great relief, I found Paisley waiting. "Ugh, I can't tell if you're either really sick or just plain sad," she said, letting herself in.

Funny, neither could I. "Come right in, I guess."

She turned and looked back at me from the foyer with a look like, *please.* She was right. Up until the last few months, Paisley and I had practically lived at each other's houses. We'd traded clothes, slept over on school nights, and shared an unlimited supply of inside jokes. But ever since this fall, sometimes it'd seemed like someone had taken our photograph and torn it in half. Thinking about it, I felt a ballooning in my throat. Turned out, I actually missed Paisley.

I hovered close to the open front door, which I knew didn't exactly say make-yourself-at-home, but whatever. I was already at a disadvantage seeing as how she'd found me in my ratty pj's and would probably tell the whole squad how I was headed for breakdown city.

"I brought your assignments," she said. "Mrs. Van Lullen didn't want you falling any further behind this year after . . . well, you know. After everything."

"Great." I took the short stack of work sheets and folders from her and tucked them underneath my arm. "But don't worry. I've got it completely under control. I'll be back to school tomorrow."

She raised her eyebrows. Paisley Wheelwright was the Zen master of saying every condescending thing she wanted to without actually ever saying a word. Sure, it was convenient when you were in on the joke. But now? It was just a pain in the ass.

"Well, friend to friend," she said, "I'll just say that the girls thought it was a little strange you missed practice the day after your big rally cry."

"Really? Because Ava texted me to let me know she was worried about me and hoped I felt better," I lied. "You know, friend to friend," I added. I pulled back my shoulders and attempted to look as dignified as possible for someone wearing elastic-waisted pants with kittens on them.

A frown flitted across Paisley's face and then disappeared. "That was nice of her." Her voice rasped just a touch at the end.

I was Homecoming queen. I was a perfectionist. I was Cassidy Hyde. I smiled and it felt like I'd glued on somebody else's. "Well, thanks for this. I'll see you tomorrow, I guess."

Paisley nodded and moved past me toward the door like a stranger. "Yeah, take care of yourself, Cass."

"I always do."

As soon as I shut the door behind her, I twisted the lock into place and pressed my back into the wood, breathing heavily. All around me it felt as if reality was crumbling and I was standing at the bottom of the rubble heap waiting to get buried.

My hands trembled. I wanted to feel good. I wanted to get the old Cassidy back, the way I had this weekend. I didn't want to look at her through the wrong end of a telescope, barely recognizing the person I used to be *or* the person I'd become. I was too good for that.

But when I returned to my room and pulled the small plastic bag from the inside of my music box I felt a twinge of misgiving as I stared at the yellow pill balanced between my fingers. Something wasn't right about these, or was it that something wasn't right about me? I knew I needed to figure it out and I promised myself that I would start first thing tomorrow.

For now, exhaustion and depression picked apart my willpower until all that was left was crumbs. I spun the pill around and around in between those two fingers. Around and around. Until the crumbs were picked over, too.

Only half, I promised myself. That was all I needed. Just a half and then the calm would be there to carry me away.

Just a half and I'll be okay. . . .

TEN

Marcy

Whoever said murder was an ugly business hadn't tried it. The way the world bloomed red had been nothing short of poetic, but not even I had expected it to feel *that* good. With my fist closed around the knife as it sank through his skin, slipped between his ribs, and found his organs, I felt like a goddess. His blood had been warm—just how I'd imagined freshly churned cow's milk—spilling over my fingers.

Blood everywhere. So much blood. I replayed the moments, a reel of the night's greatest hits, and grinned like an idiot at the memory. Each recollection sat in my mind like a gift that could be unwrapped over and over. There was the second when he realized he'd made a mistake. The one when he knew with utter certainty that *I* wasn't the quarry. The heartbeat when he saw the knife. The shriek when he felt the first stab of pain. The space in time when at last the light went out in his one remaining eye.

I wanted to celebrate. I wanted to raise my glass to justice. And revenge.

I twisted my hands around the steering wheel impatiently as I drove along the dead street of Grimwood. At stoplights I revved the engine, craving the roar of it in my chest. I wanted more. I reached over toward the passenger's side and snapped open the glove compartment. Fishing around, I felt the phone and wallet I'd stripped from the body, the things that told me Mick Holcolm was dead. That was Short One's name, it turned out. I bypassed both of these things—for now—and pulled out the two scraps of paper with jagged handwriting scrawled across it that I'd found last night discarded in the cup holder. When pieced together, I'd recognized the name.

Lena.

I could easily picture the face that went with it, staring up at me from the pavement with big, frightened eyes.

Lena Leroux.

I read the numbers and punched them into the keypad. The phone rang in my ear. I was about to hang up when a breathy voice came on the line. "Hello?" I waited, listening to the thud of my beating heart against the phone. "Hello? . . . Is that you?"

— — —

THE GAS STATION at Third and Mulholland cast a flickering, fluorescent glow that made it look like the inside of a freezer display case. Oil stained the concrete in slick puddles. An overstuffed trash can spit up plastic soda bottles and cardboard. I found Lena standing underneath the white, cascading light, hand clutched around the top of a six-pack of beer.

I pulled the car halfway between two parking spots and rolled down the window. "Where'd you get that?" I asked. Lena wore a long-sleeved fishnet top that showed off thin, fuchsia spaghetti straps that poked out from underneath it. Faded gray jeans hugged her skeleton-skinny legs all the way down to a pair of black boots that stopped at the ankle.

Lena rested her elbows on the side of my car. Her chunky black bangs fell against her eyelashes. She jerked her head to gesture back at the gas station. "Inside. I paid the cashier twenty bucks to give it to me. You said you were in the mood to celebrate, didn't you?" I nodded. She reached up and parted the bangs to push them from her large, cartoonish eyes. "May I?"

I nodded again and Lena tucked her bony knees into the seat beside me where she cradled the beer in her lap.

Inside, the cashier who'd sold Lena the beer watched us over the top of a *National Enquirer.* "Were you sleeping?"

She shrugged. "Barely. I have insomnia. It blows."

"Me too," I said. The car felt ten degrees warmer with her in it. "But I don't mind it."

She hugged the cardboard carton to her chest and the cans rattled. "That's good, I guess. My dad says nothing good happens after midnight." She turned her face toward me expectantly. Everything about Lena was a paradox. Her wide eyes gave her a look of innocence and sweetness at odds with the dark fringe of hair that masked most of her face. She seemed equal parts helpless baby deer and streetwise feral kitten.

"Your dad's full of shit."

She laughed and I could tell she didn't mind. "Where are we going?"

I tapped my foot idly against the brakes. "I don't know. Should I know?" I'd wanted to burn off my energy with another human being, but now that she was here, there was still energy buzzing through in small shock waves, filling me up with the need for topsy-turvy anarchy but with nowhere to find it. "That's why I called you."

She hummed what sounded like classical music under her breath. "There's an old grain mill out there." She pointed past the gas station toward a field and the border of the forest known as the Hollows out back. "Not far. A few of the theater kids smoke out there sometimes. They invited me twice." I could tell by her tone that invitations for Lena were a rare occasion. "Cops never come that way." She tapped the six-pack.

The fact that she knew cops never came that way instilled in me a sliver of trust. "All right," I said, not much caring where we went as long as it was somewhere. "Lead the way then."

I felt jittery and a little silly as I followed Lena out of the car. Another girl who seemed equally at home in the dead hours of the night and the wee hours of the morning. We crossed behind the gas station into the field where the grass was unmowed and we had to high-step through it while the blades tickled our kneecaps.

The artificial glow cast by the gas station awning and the traffic lights faded until the only light we had to see by was the silver moon. We crossed through a thin layer of trees before I noticed the clearing.

The mill was a rectangular building with rows of windows that had long since lost their glass and now hovered like gaping eye sockets within the concrete's peeling red paint. Above us, a sign on stilts attached to the building's roof read, *Golden Heart Flour.* I couldn't guess how long since the mill had been open. Ten years? Twenty?

"It's a little . . . creepy, I guess, at this time of night." Lena's voice was a soft whisper in the night.

"Not if you don't have anything to be afraid of," I said, and pushed open the door. With a creak it opened up into a murky cavern.

The soles of our shoes scraped through sawdust. Lena pointed her cell phone screen outward and we stared up into a maze of wood beams overhead.

I ran my hand over a giant cogged wheel, then took a seat at the bottom of a metal staircase that spiraled up into levels unseen.

Lena giggled nervously. She handed me a can. The aluminum was barely colder than room temperature. "You drink beer?" she asked.

"Not really." I cracked the tab. The sound echoed in the abandoned mill and the amber liquid fizzed into a head of foam. I slurped it off the top.

She watched me. A funny little grin tugged at her lips and it reminded me again of a cat. "But since we're celebrating then," she said, opening her own. "What are we celebrating anyway?" She wrapped one hand around a metal cord that hung from the ceiling with a pulley attached to the bottom of it.

I took my time answering. "Us," I said.

She let go of the pulley cord and it swung in a lazy pendulum arc. "I didn't know there was an us." But there was. I'd been her, the stupid girl who went off with stupid boys because they were loud and handsome and older. The only difference was there'd been no one there to save me. "I didn't think you'd call," she said.

I let my head rest against the rusty railing. "Those guys were assholes." Like that was a response.

Lines of graffiti sullied the carcasses of empty grain carts. Lena's breathing was loud. The metal siding of the mill groaned eerily as if it were a part of the conversation. Holes in the roof let in light from the moon and stars.

Lena held her can of beer out to me. "To us," she said, meeting my gaze and holding it.

"To us," I repeated and we clinked cans and each took a long sip.

I noticed the three stars tattooed on her wrist. She seemed so young and insubstantial to have something as permanent as a tattoo. "Where'd you get that?" I pointed.

She turned her wrist over and looked down at the stars drawn in navy blue ink against her pale skin. "A girl I know." She touched the tip of her finger gently to the center of each one. "So that I'll always have three wishes. In case I ever need them," she explained. "You know how it goes. *When you wish upon a star . . .*" Her voice took on a melody and she whistled another bar of the song.

I watched as she idly traced the outside of the ink and felt interest grip me. Maybe it was that two-thirds of my can was now empty or maybe it was that I needed to feel the rush of last night in some lasting way. Whatever it was, the yearning for something crazy found its foothold.

"I want one," I said. "Take me."

"To get stars?"

"No, to get a tattoo. Will this girl you know, will she give me one even though I'm too young, too?"

Lena stood up straighter. "You're serious." Her eyes shone.

"Deadly." My mouth spread into a wicked smile.

"You're a little bit insane, Marcy. You know that?" She dropped her empty can on the floor and crushed it underfoot.

"Oh, trust me, I'm more than a little bit."

After another beer each, Lena and I headed the short distance back to where my car waited, a healthy buzz vibrating through us for encouragement. I drove and she directed me. She kept casting me sidelong glances like I might chicken out. She didn't know me. I didn't chicken out. When we arrived at the location, it was a freestanding shop with a slanted roof, neon signs, and a mural of a skull and roses painted on the side.

"They'll be open at this hour?" I asked, following her around to the front door.

"They're open at every hour."

A cowbell clanged on the door as we let ourselves inside. Dozens of framed drawings hung on the walls of the store where no one was waiting. I wandered over to study some of the artwork. An assortment of faeries were depicted in a cluster. As I stood examining them, I saw that none of them looked like a typical fairy from a storybook. Black tears ran down their pointed noses and miniature faces. Violent holes tore through the delicate netting of their wings. A shiver raced through me.

"Wren?" Lena called, moving deeper into the store past black leather chairs that reclined like at the dentist's office. "Wren, are you here?"

I leaned in to see a curved scythe clutched in the hand of one of the illustrated faeries. A thin trail of blood dribbled from the lethal point.

I heard footsteps and turned to see a short woman with breasts that spilled over the top of her shirt and sleeves of tattoos that ran from her knuckles up to her neck. A deep shade of plum painted her lips. Lena greeted her with a hug. The artwork adorning her body moved with her, giving it the appearance of animation.

"So you're in the market for your first tat?" the woman who must be Wren asked.

"Does anyone have this one?" I tapped the glass covering the faerie with the sickle-shaped sword.

Wren came closer and peered over my shoulder. "Keres? No. Not yet."

"Is she yours?"

Wren murmured an affirmation. "Do you want her? It's an interesting choice." She seemed to appraise me, looking for what damage I must have suffered to want the violent faerie marked on my body forever.

I stepped away from Keres but spared another appreciative glance for her. "Not yet. Maybe someday," I said. I loved the faerie, but I'd save her for once I'd earned it.

"Okay, then. What can I do for you today?" She crossed the room, pulled a cart of equipment over, and sat down on a stool next to one of the reclining chairs.

I passed Lena and took a seat on the cracked leather. "Just a line for now. Here on my wrist."

Wren raised her pierced eyebrow. "A line? That's it."

"It's more than that. It's a tally mark. One for now. More for later. That's what I want. Can you do it?"

Wren grunted, but took out a silver tool that looked like a gun with a needle on the end. "I'll try not to take it as an insult to my talent."

Lena edged closer and put her hand on the headrest behind me. "You can hold my hand if it hurts."

I didn't tell her that I wanted it to.

Wren wiped my skin with a swab of alcohol and dipped the needle into a pot of black ink. She flipped a switch and the gun buzzed like a mosquito. The needle plunged into the bulge of veins at the base of my wrist. I gritted my teeth to keep from flinching. The sharp point bit into my flesh. I felt Lena's sharp intake of breath beside me.

Wren expertly traced a line half an inch long on my wrist and then retraced it. Too quickly it was over. She swiped cotton over the spot and the excess ink smeared and then disappeared. "A line. Just like you asked for." Her tone was flat. Unimpressed. "Thirty bucks."

I pulled cash from my back pocket all the while staring at the razor-thin line branded on my skin. One down. Four more to go.

I paid Wren and thanked her. Outside the darkness was dissipating. The lamplight faded into hues of blue. An idea had been bothering me all night. For me, in the days, there was only darkness. It was an unreachable part of me, what happened during the daytime. I was nocturnal and, for the most part, I relished that fact. But it had its limitations.

"Lena, what if I said I needed your help?" I asked.

She froze on the spot. Crickets chirped along a nearby fence and above, the stars were beginning to blend away. "Anything. You name it," she said.

I realized there may have been more to my seeking out Lena to-night than celebration. I had a task and, as someone who needed assistance for mundane matters that required regular business hours, it just might be worth having an assistant of sorts.

The one standing in front of me was canine loyal, wide-eyed and eager. Perhaps saving her would serve its purpose after all.

"I need you to track down a room on Corbin College's campus for me."

ELEVEN

Cassidy

What do you do when the facts of your life no longer add up?
I woke up with a line on my wrist that wouldn't go away and no idea how it got there. The only thing I could be certain of was that I couldn't remember the last time I'd been certain of anything.

A coldness nestled into the pores of my bones, as though winter had come to live there.

I kept pulling up my sleeve and staring at the tattoo, trying to imagine myself going into a tattoo parlor, sitting down, stretching out my arm, waiting for a needle to draw ink into the skin. It was nearly impossible and yet there it was. In black and white.

Of course the bigger problem—the much, *much* bigger problem— was the dead body buried just beyond the lot line of my house. Now *that* was something I wouldn't mind being able to forget.

No such luck, of course.

My elbows were planted on a cold-surfaced desk in Mr. Yotsuda's classroom where I was supposed to be listening to him teach AP calculus. Instead, I'd been staring at the clock above the whiteboard watching seconds tick-tick-tick by.

Yesterday I'd made a promise to myself to start figuring out what the hell was going on with me. Tomorrow, I'd promised. And now tomorrow was today and I'd done exactly nothing to honor that commitment. Because that promise implied me actually *doing* something. Active. And for the past few weeks I'd been completely rebelling against that notion. I'd decided to give up. Let myself sink into the pit of depression and drown there.

I flattened my cheek into my palm. *Ugh, that certainly would be easier.*

Uh-uh. No way.

I had to snap out of that train of thought. That sort of thinking was exactly what had gotten me into this mess. At least I thought it was. Honestly, I didn't have a clue.

Besides, two days ago I quelled a coup on my cheerleading squad. Two days ago I'd been staging my big comeback. Two days ago I decided to grab life by the balls and take charge.

I sat up straighter, mustering my resolve. I had built Cassidy, Homecoming queen, out of two things: smarts and determination. I still had at least one of those. I chewed on my eraser. If I had a complicated math problem how did I approach it?

First, I figured out what variables were missing. Then, I followed the steps to solve for them. *Bingo.*

I glanced around and saw the students around me furiously scribbling notes from the whiteboard.

"Cassidy? Hello, Cassidy?" Coming out of a daze, I saw Mr. Yotsuda waving at me from the front of the room. I blinked, looked down, noticed that I'd already been shoving my belongings into my book bag. "Cassidy, are you paying attention?"

"Um . . . ," I faltered. I was out of my seat with my strap slung over one shoulder. I stared at the equation he'd scrawled across the board.

$$dy/dx = cos(x) \, / \, y2 \, , \text{ where } y\,(\pi/2) = 0$$

I read the line under my breath. The wheels in my brain turned over. "The answer is $y = (3 \sin(x) - 3)1/3$."

"Where are you going?" Mr. Yotsuda said as I turned my back to him. "Class isn't over."

"Sorry." I stepped hastily over a backpack in the aisle. "It is for me."

"But—but," he stammered. "That's correct."

My mouth quirked into a half smile. Of course it was correct.

Once out of the classroom, I hurried down the hallway, past the school nurse's office. I noticed it with a twinge of regret, wondering how things might have been different if I'd confided in a nurse or in anyone about Dearborn before there was a dead body to contend with, before the string holding me together was so perilously frayed that all I could do was cling to both ends and pray for dear life.

Nobody would have believed me. Everyone would have thought I deserved it. It would have ruined my reputation at this school. These were the things I'd been telling myself for weeks. But were they true? And could I have been any worse off than I was now?

I kept walking briskly. Nerves crept in with every step. When I reached the library, I was downright jumpy, worried that every move I made was a sign of guilt.

Baby steps, I reminded myself. Figure out what variables were missing, then follow the path to solve for them.

I tugged open the door and landed on the ugly orange carpet of the school library. I spotted Mrs. Petrie behind the front desk. Her hair was a mop of cotton ball frizz atop her head. I approached her and cleared my throat.

When she saw it was me, she visibly brightened. For all she knew I was still Miss School Spirit and, as far as I was concerned, there was no need to correct her.

I'd almost forgotten one very useful tidbit: Teachers adored me. In fact, though I hated to admit it, sometimes I suspected that even adults and, let's face it, *especially* adults like Mrs. Petrie, wanted to be me.

"Shouldn't you be in class, Cassidy?" She curved her mouth into a frown, but her eyes expressed no real disappointment in me. A girl like me must have a good reason.

"Totally." I leaned in close like I was telling her a bit of juicy gossip. "Confession," I said, and felt her drawing in even closer. Her strong, floral perfume stung my nose. "I procrastinated on this project for Ms. Langley and I need to knock out some of the research quick."

"I can help," she said too eagerly, picking up a pen.

I let out an exaggerated exhale. "Thank god. I knew you could. Okay, so I'm doing a project on the human brain and memory. Like . . ." I stared up at the ceiling, trying to think through the missing variables and the steps to solve them. "Like why we remember some things and not others and whether we can make ourselves remember things we've forgotten."

She deflated. "That sounds . . . like a complicated project. Are you sure that's for Ms. Langley?"

"God, I know, right? We, um, had to choose our own research topics. Stupid me chose the most complicated of the human organs—the brain." I thunked myself on the head like I was one of the Three Stooges or something.

Mrs. Petrie's mouth went pin straight. She turned to her old school desktop computer and began typing. "Brain could be housed in the science and anatomy section. But . . ." She punched another pattern of keystrokes. "I think what you're looking for is psychology, which is in . . . Ah-ha! Row F, halfway down. Would you like me to help you look?"

"No, no." I tapped the desk in front of me. "You're very busy. Thanks, Mrs. Petrie!"

I couldn't get away fast enough. The last thing I needed was ancient Mrs. Petrie Dish tagging along. But it felt good to act like myself again. Even if it was just that—an act.

I brushed past the rows labeled with the first few letters of the alphabet, slowing down as I approached *F*. I turned down the narrow rows until the words that were written on the spines began to catch my attention. *Brain & Behavior: An Introduction to Biological Psychology. Understanding Psychology. Thought Manipulation. Psychopaths.* I studied them all, trying to decide which one to choose.

As I scanned the shelves, I homed in on the fattest one. A leather-bound psychology reference book. I slid it from the top shelf. A puff of dust rained down on top of me, making me sneeze.

The library was fairly quiet. I lowered the tome to the ground and sat in front of it cross-legged, where I cracked open the spine and flipped to the index pages at the back.

I was dragging my pointer finger down column after column of tiny print words when I heard a small gasp, as if in alarm, and looked up to see the girl who'd introduced herself as Lena staring at me from the end of the aisle.

Her hair was pulled into two tight buns that perched on top of her head like mouse ears. She had her thumbs hiked under the straps of her backpack. It was like I was Medusa and the sight of me had turned her to stone and frozen her in that spot. It was like I was a ghost who'd jumped out and scared her when she least expected it.

We held each other's gaze for longer than social niceties would permit. My mouth had gone dry. Was Lena another missing variable? Was she a piece that I needed to solve for? The thought of Dearborn kept flashing in my mind.

I broke our staring contest first, returning to the page, to the plan. And away from the weird girl who'd called me Marcy of all things.

As I scanned through another page of columns, I felt rather than saw her slink away. My finger traced the font and I found the entry I was looking for. *Memory.*

The tattoo on my wrist poked through from under the sleeve of my shirt, causing the metronome of my heartbeat to pick up its pace.

I was about to turn to the page of the first entry for Memory, page 187, when a word, spelled out as one of the subcategories, stood out in my line of vision.

I stopped thumbing through the pages and stared at the index. I hadn't known it was a real area of study in psychology. But reading it now felt like a sort of suggestion. There it was. A step.

Hypnotism.

— — —

WHEN I LEFT Hollow Pines High, I'd had exactly two hours to get back and that was if I planned to only miss gym and Spanish, the two courses I thought I could most get away with skipping. Slipping off campus wasn't hard. The faculty was already beginning to mentally check out in advance of the three-day weekend.

I pulled into the parking lot of the redbrick strip mall and checked the clock. I was down to an hour and forty-five minutes. A wooden sign that was attached to the side of the building had white letters that read: *Dr. Crispin, Harmony Hypnotherapy & Transformation.* I parked nearest to the tinted entrance underneath the sign and got out.

Dr. Crispin's office was wedged between a row of sterile business fronts, next to an accountant and a mediator. There was no bell to announce my arrival and I found the squat reception desk completely devoid of human life. The legs of an anemically brown leather couch wrinkled the edges of a puke-colored oriental rug lying underneath it.

I thought about taking a seat there with the stack of magazines, but decided I didn't have time to waste pretending to be patient when what I needed was to be *a* patient. Like now. So instead, I walked over to the vacated desk and strummed the strange wind chime that was hanging like an upside-down xylophone.

I kept on strumming the instrument until at last I heard a cough from a back room and a short man with a concave chest and round tortoiseshell glasses emerged dabbing his mouth with a crumpled napkin.

"Do you have an appointment?" he asked, unnecessarily pushing the glasses against the bridge of his nose. His voice had a nasal quality as if he were suffering from terrible allergies.

"Not exactly," I said. "No."

He made a high-pitched noise that I couldn't recognize with any assurance as either a sign of annoyance or a hiccup. I leaned over the counter to watch him flip through an appointment book that appeared to have more blank slots than filled.

"Can you fit me in?" I asked.

He looked at me over the top of his glasses. "Today?"

"Right now," I answered.

Dr. Crispin—I presumed—furiously flipped through the appointment book. "But the website specifically says no walk-ins."

I sighed. "I took a gamble that the hypnotherapy business wasn't exactly booming in Hollow Pines. And what do you know?" I made a show of looking around the empty waiting room. "I was right." I placed my hands on my hips. "So assuming you don't happen to be booked for the next hour and it looks like you're not," I said, staring down my nose at the blank spaces in today's date, "I'll take right now. It's urgent."

Dr. Crispin blinked rapidly behind his lenses. "Fine, then, okay, if it's *urgent*, as you say. I suppose I can fit you in." He spread his palms over the page and picked up a ballpoint pen. "Name?"

"Um . . . Jessica . . . Faire," I lied quickly, remembering a character in a romance novel I'd once stolen from my mom's nightstand in middle school. This seemed a time to be better safe than sorry.

He printed the name in slow, methodical letters and snapped the book shut. "Well, then, Jessica, I suppose you can follow me," the little man said.

I trailed him through a narrow hallway painted an ungodly hue of mustard yellow and together we entered a box-shaped room. My palms were sweating now and I wiped them on my jeans. Inside, a silk plant scraped against the wall next to an armchair. Water burbled over a bed of rocks down a fake waterfall and into a bucket-sized pond of lily pads. He gestured to a long black sofa with a decorative pillow propped in the corner. Wordless music with a Far Eastern flair trickled through a set of speakers balanced on a dresser. I took a seat and stared at my shoes, feeling more uncertain about the reasons I'd come.

I didn't believe in hocus-pocus. I was a facts-and-figures girl. A former mathlete, for goodness' sake. Was I sure hypnotherapy was the way to go? The place looked as if it'd been decorated from the dregs of a Chinese restaurant's garage sale.

Of course I wasn't sure at all. But it was a step. A way forward. And it had seemed like a good idea back in the library. Back before I saw how cheesy it was.

"You'll need to be lying down." Dr. Crispin waved his hand through the smoke of a newly lit stick of incense. *Oh, brother,* I thought. I was confident my problems were beyond what aromatherapy could fix. I considered my options. I could still turn back. I could tell him there'd been some kind of mistake. Or that I'd call back for an appointment after all.

Except then where would I be? I'd come to a point where the facts in my life no longer added up, where I couldn't trust any of my usual instincts. So, instead of following the one I had right now, which was to run as far away as possible from this hokey hypnotherapy shop, I swung my feet up onto the couch and leaned back onto the pillow.

"Very good." Dr. Crispin's voice took on the tone of a massage therapist. I tried to relax. "Now, what can we do for you today?" *We?* I winced at the affected manner.

"I . . ." I took a deep breath and prepared to tell somebody something I hadn't had the guts to tell anyone, at least before now. "I'm having trouble remembering certain . . . things. There seem to be gaps. Chunks of time that have just vanished. And I want—I mean, I need—to know what's happening in those spaces that I can't remember. I want to know why this is happening to me." I wondered if this was a normal problem for a hypnotherapist or if I sounded certifiably insane.

"When was the last time you noticed one of these 'gaps' as you called it?"

I swallowed. "Two nights ago." I avoided glancing at my arm. The skin around the black line on my wrist was raised and angry. If I was being honest, last night would be the last gap in my memory. But instead I chose the missing space two nights ago because that was what I most needed to know.

"When approximately in your day do you think you lost this memory?" I could hear scratches on Dr. Crispin's notepad.

"At night," I answered.

The scratching stopped. "At night. When you should be sleeping. What makes you think your memory is misplaced at all?"

"I've . . . well . . . I've woken up in places, seen evidence that I've been places at night that seem impossible if I weren't awake."

"So you're sleepwalking."

I clenched my fists. At first sleepwalking had seemed like the most logical explanation. I'd even hoped for that to be all it was. A childhood habit brought out by some weird form of stress. I felt my mouth shift into a crooked grin. "Is there such a thing as sleep driving?" I asked.

Dr. Crispin let out a puff of air. "I would say not." He paused for effect. "Jessica, how much do you know about hypnosis?"

There was a second delay in my response as I was forced to remember that Jessica was the name I'd given him. "Only what I've seen on television."

"Allow me to enlighten you then. The conscious mind," he began, "is what you're used to thinking about. It's what you think of when you think of yourself. Who is Jessica Faire? That's the conscious mind. The unconscious mind is everything else. The unconscious mind processes two million pieces of sensory information every second. The reality of which you're aware is the product of what was sent to you by the unconscious mind. The conscious mind is more logical, rational, analytical, but it can only operate based off what the unconscious mind has chosen to give it."

"So, you're trying to tell me that my unconscious mind could choose not to send me all the information. It could be holding out on me?"

"Exactly. Have you ever gotten a bruise or a cut and not remembered how it got there?"

I thought about this. ". . . Yeah, I suppose so."

"That's because your unconscious mind decided not to share that piece of information with your conscious mind even though something clearly happened to cause it. Something capable of being remembered. Only you didn't remember it.

"Have you ever smelled something that you didn't even know was familiar and suddenly been flooded by a random memory seemingly long forgotten?"

"Yes." I nodded more fervently, thinking of my grandmother and the smell of cinnamon gum.

"The job of hypnosis is similar to that of the familiar smell. Hypnosis is intended to make the unconscious mind cough up additional bits of information that it's been hoarding for itself."

The pulse thudded in my wrist and at the base of my throat. I felt as though I was walking closer and closer to the edge of a cliff and very soon I'd be looking over to see what lay at the bottom. "Okay," I said. "I think I understand."

"Good." Dr. Crispin snapped the cover of his notepad closed and rested it on his knee. "You'll be able to remember everything that happened here today, and in your altered state, I will not ask you to do anything that you don't want to do. You understand?" I nodded again. "I'll need you to listen very carefully to my voice. Using only my voice, I will lull you into a heightened sense of relaxation, a technique known as induction by suggestion. My sentences will be in time with your breaths, my words repetitive. Boring, even. Keep your breathing steady. Gradually, I will move from suggestion and begin making commands. There we'll enter into the hypnotic state to explore the last time you can't remember. From two nights ago. Are you ready, Jessica?"

My mouth went dry at the same time that my palms needed to be wiped once again on my pant legs. "Ready."

"Okay, then. I want you to imagine a happy place. Perhaps a vacation from your childhood. Maybe at the beach or on a cruise or near a mountainside." I chewed my lip, fighting back skepticism, and conjured up an image of me, lying in a hammock at the Atlantis resort in the Bahamas a few years ago. "Let your feet relax . . . and your toes relax. Consider letting your hips relax . . . your waist." I nestled into the sofa, doing my best to release the tension that I'd been clinging to over the past few days. "What if you were flying? Imagine that the wind is whipping through your hair. No worries, no cares, no stress." I continued to listen. The rise and fall of my chest evened out. My limbs went heavy with relaxation. "Sinking down and shutting down, sinking down and shutting down." The sound of Dr. Crispin's voice became more distant, like he was speaking to me from the other side of a pane of glass. "Return to the time two nights ago. You are there now. You can envision what you're wearing." An image came to me. I was changing out of my yoga pants and sports bra from practice that night. I was changing not into pajamas but into jeans and a tank top and a black hoodie. "Follow your own steps. Stay in the moment. The deeper you go, the deeper you are able to go." I measured my breaths by his methodical intonation.

It was late. My house was dark. I was in the driveway, turning the key in the ignition. Driving. Driving toward Dearborn. In the direction of the university.

"Every word I utter is putting you faster and deeper into a state of deep, peaceful hypnosis. Where are you now?"

"I'm . . . at the end of a row of large houses. It's nighttime."

"Good. Continue walking down the street. Explore your surroundings."

In my memory, I saw myself stopping in front of a fraternity house. Going in. The music was loud. The lights flashed, blinding me, even in my mind.

"Sinking down, shutting down . . . ," Dr. Crispin murmured.

I was looking for someone. My pulse sped up. In the present, I felt my fingernails dig into the leather.

"The deeper you go, the deeper you are able to go . . ."

My fingers relaxed. In my trancelike state, I was able to find the face I was searching for. I seemed to know him, though he didn't know me. We were outside. I was thankful to be free of the merciless beating music and the attacking strobe. I sank into the shadows, coaxing the boy after me. Enticing him. Egging him on. Hatred hatched inside me, reached across the divide of time and space, and grew roots in my veins.

Deeper, deeper, sinking, shutting.

A blade was in my hand. A blade was in his face, his chest, his throat. And it was glorious, beautiful, exquisite.

It was red.

And I was in love with it.

Somewhere in the distance I heard a snap of fingers and a command to wake up and then I was hurdling through nothingness, falling upward back into myself, back up to where gravity could grasp on to my arms, legs, back, and shoulders. I was there. Gasping. Sucking thin air and not finding enough oxygen.

I sat up pin straight, my back rigid.

"What did you see, Jessica?" Dr. Crispin's voice hit me like ice water to the face.

I stared at him, wild-eyed. "I—I—" My tongue felt around for words other than the truth, which was difficult with the truth pinging against every molecule in my gray matter. "I remembered a fight with my sister," I said. "I don't know how I forgot. Or why. But, yeah, just a stupid fight. It was dumb."

Dr. Crispin adjusted his glasses. "Really?"

And I could have been imagining it, but I thought from the way that he was looking at me that Dr. Crispin didn't quite believe me. Had I said something while under hypnosis? Cried out? Screamed? Or could he see deeper than that. Did he know, like I now knew, that the eyes he was looking into were the eyes of a killer?

— — —

I STROLLED INTO the gymnasium exactly one minute before the official start of cheer practice wearing my biggest pair of sunglasses and feeling even worse than I looked. I took pains to keep my arms pinned to my sides, resisting the urge to scrape invisible coats of blood off with my fingernails.

I kept feeling it on me. Reams of red spilling over my hands.

"See, told you she'd show up." Ava jabbed Paisley in the ribs.

Paisley rolled her eyes and gave me an unenthusiastic wave hello.

"Haters gonna hate," whooped Erica from her straddle position on the floor.

My heart squeezed with longing for them.

"Wow, though"—Ava stretched to the side with one arm arcing over her head—"you really do look sick."

"She always looks sick," added Paisley.

"I'm not sick." I pushed the sunglasses into the bridge of my nose.

"Oh my god." Erica jumped up, her eyes wide. "Are you pregnant? You are, aren't you? That's exactly how my cousin looked when she found out she was pregnant."

The word *pregnant* flashed through my head like a migraine. I squinted in discomfort. After the night in Dearborn, I woke up feeling sore and impossibly stupid. I hadn't been able to look up from my wallet when the pharmacist slid the packet of morning-after pills across the counter. Every achy cramp that day and the next felt well-deserved as I hoped and prayed for the medicine to wash away every scrap of the night before. "I'm not pregnant," I said, which was true. "I'm fine." Which wasn't.

"All right, all right." Erica held up both palms like I had a gun trained on her. Then again, maybe she was right to be afraid of me. *Oh god.* "Then are you sure you're going to be okay?"

My abdomen was rigid. It had to be to hold all the panic inside. "Of course," I said curtly. "We have a game in two days."

I wanted to stamp out the shared glances from the squad. More than that I wanted to be a part of them again. I wanted to press rewind and erase the last six months of my life. The images that had been resurrected this afternoon thundered around in my skull. The migraine that had been triggered was busy exploding in short bursts like the Fourth of July.

A blade in his face, his chest, his throat. Glorious, beautiful, exquisite.

I wanted to push my thumbs into my temples. The other girls were all staring at me, waiting expectantly. "What are you all waiting for?" I pushed the words out slowly and deliberately. "Are you all warmed up? Because it doesn't look like it. Ten laps around the court. This isn't the freaking chess club, ladies." I clapped twice and the noise felt like something snapping inside me, but it got the squad moving.

Fifteen ponytails took off around the baseline. I excused myself into the locker room where I made a beeline for the farthest bathroom stall. I dropped my gym bag onto the tile beside me and collapsed onto my knees.

My breaths were coming in great, heaving puffs that blew my cheeks out and sucked them in tight.

Coughs of crimson. Deep maroon that oozed from holes that shouldn't exist. Torn shirt, torn skin, torn face. The smell of iron. Hot and pleasant like bathwater.

I thrust my head over the toilet and vomited the contents of my stomach into the bowl. Mouth still dripping, I retched again. Yellow mucus ran from my nostrils.

From outside the stall came the sound of footsteps. "Cass?" It was Ava.

I turned and lowered my backside onto the cool tile and leaned my back against the stall. "Yeah?" I tried to force my voice into a normal octave.

"Are you coming back out?" She sounded like she felt awkward asking. "We finished our laps a few minutes ago."

My hands were shaking. My stomach was still spasming. "Uh-huh," I said. "I'll be right there. Why don't you lead them in the first cheer?" I knew she'd take this as a compliment. Honestly, I meant it as one.

"Okay." I didn't hear feet shuffling away. "Are you sure you're all right in there?"

I closed my eyes and felt for the zipper on my gym bag. I pulled it open and started rummaging. My fingers found what they were looking for. I retrieved one of the plastic baggies I'd stashed. It contained only one pill. "Yep, don't worry," I said, emptying the drop of Sunshine out into my hand. "I'll be fine."

TWELVE

Marcy

I've always heard that if you want to bring the hurt, you've got to hit them where they live.

Unfortunately for the "them" in question, I happened to take things very literally.

I checked the time on my watch as I slipped through the door to Graves Hall on the tail of a legitimate student with a key card. Lena followed closely after.

I had the urge to sniff the air. Like a bloodhound. I was that close. My skin tingled with it. A step through the door and I had landed on Mick's former turf. The blood in my veins began coursing, pushing the valves of my heart to work overtime.

Short One. That was what I'd called him, the one who'd watched through the lens of his video camera.

He wouldn't be watching anymore. He wouldn't be doing

anything. A pleasant warmth rose in my gut at the unintention-ally conjured memory.

But the dozens of campus activity flyers plastered to the walls of the dormitory snapped me back. If Short One had watched, that meant someone else could, too. The recollection of the blinking red light taunted me.

A recording. A vestige of the night.

That would never do.

A girl, not much older than me, sat on a rolling chair with her feet propped up on a half-moon desk. She looked up from her copy of *Vogue* and gave us a distracted smile before returning to the glossy photographs in the magazine.

I moved without hesitating toward one of the hallways on the first floor, searching for a flight of stairs.

"What if someone recognizes us?" Lena's breath was hot on my neck.

"I thought I told you to be quiet," I replied through gritted teeth. I lifted my gaze to peer up the stairwell. "And there should be no 'us.' I asked for the dorm number; I didn't ask you to come along."

As far as I was concerned, an extra body was an extra liability and an extra witness, neither of which were items I'd included on my revenge registry.

My boots pounded the steps. Lena trotted after me. With her purple fishnet stockings under a black moto skirt, not drawing at-tention seemed too much to hope for. "You need me," she said. "Besides, it's only fair considering I did the bulk of the work."

I wanted to tell her that this wasn't some kind of game. And that I didn't need anyone, especially not a high school girl with a hero-worshipping complex. "You can be the lookout. But that's it."

I found the stairwell. *Room 255.* That was the number Lena had gotten when she'd called the school asking how to send a care package to her cool collegiate cousin, Mick Holcolm. At least she was proving useful for something. I wondered if she'd feel as cooperative if she knew that her pretend collegiate cousin Mick was dead.

"So are you going to tell me what we're doing yet?" The clang of our soles echoed. We turned onto the second landing. The faint scent of marijuana lingered in the cramped stairwell.

"Again with the 'we,'" I said coldly, and drew a hood over my ears to mask my dark hair. Near the exit a fire alarm blinked red to show that it was ready. Another taunt. This time the charged memory that resulted brought with it more—torn clothes, ugly tears, a girl too weak to stand. The reason I was here.

I scanned the numbers on the doors of Graves Hall's second-floor dorms. Every step was purposeful. Efficient. Competent.

A girl squeaked down the hall toward us in shower shoes and a towel. My muscles tensed before she veered off into one of the rooms without sparing us a second glance.

Music trickled through a few of the shut doors and I could imagine the students who lived inside. A studious music major listening to classical. A stoner with his Bob Marley.

"What if Mick's home?" Lena's head was on a swivel. For someone else, her nervousness might be contagious. For me it was just incomprehensible.

"He won't be."

"How do you know?"

I cut my glance sharply over to Lena. "Because I know, okay?"

"But what about a roommate? He could have one of those."

I stuffed my hands in my pockets and hunched my shoulders, wishing that I was alone. "That's what you're here for."

"I thought you said you didn't need me." Her tone held a hint of triumph.

My finger rubbed the dull side of the unfamiliar blade stowed in my pocket. Now that my knife was hidden and buried in the mud, I'd had to snatch a smaller version with a curved, irregular blade that looked like it was used to peel the skin off things. "I don't. But you're here and this way's easier."

I located Room 255 three doors from the end of the hallway closest to the boys' showers. It was an unremarkable door with no hint of the person that had lived inside. I knocked three times and waited. I knocked again and pressed my ear to the wood. When no sound came from the other side, I turned the handle and, to my surprise, it twisted easily underneath my grip. "That was simpler than I planned," I said. Funny how safe these boys felt, how untouchable. But they weren't safe now and I'd already proven that they weren't untouchable.

They'd created a monster.

Beside me, Lena's breath smelled like a Fruit Roll-Up. "Now what?"

I was already pushing open the door and poking my head inside. My fingers twitched, ready to get ahold of the last scrap of evidence. It was important that they didn't have the pleasure of owning my misery. Instead my misery would become theirs.

"Watch for anyone coming this way. Three knocks for me to get out." I stared hard at Lena to make sure she wasn't wavering. "Got it?"

She nodded. Sweat and cologne hit me squarely in the nose as I sealed myself inside Mick's dorm room. It was empty. I walked between two twin beds pushed against either side of the room. Sheets draped halfway off the mattress from the one on the left. Dirty boxers and T-shirts covered the foot of the other bed.

Two matching, standard-issue desks stood flush against the window. I studied the photographs taped to the wall beside one of them. I recognized the boy smiling out of them at once. It wasn't Mick. Instead, it was the one I'd been calling California because of his chin-length hair and flip-flops.

I stared at the photographs feeling like I was staring into an alternate dimension. There California was smiling in each frame with a rail-thin girl whose hair was strawberry blond and nose was dotted with freckles. I recognized her from the walk back from the fraternity house.

I could see her kissing his cheek, legs straddling his waist in a piggyback ride, arms wrapped around each other. White-hot rage scalded my throat like coffee, burning and bitter. California had a girlfriend. And I'd bet a thousand dollars that she didn't know what a pig he was.

No worries. I would show her.

Before moving over to Mick's desk, I quickly rifled through California's belongings until I found a worn paperback copy of *Catcher in the Rye* with a penciled inscription on the inside cover that read, *Property of Jessup Franklin*. I punched the name into the notes section of my phone and stuffed it back into my jeans pocket. Another one for my collection.

I moved across the room to Mick's desk, known only to me in life as Short One. An open math book lay on the wooden workspace. A paper airplane. A clean pair of socks. Everything left there like he was planning on coming back. A laptop was hooked into the wall by a cord. In the hutch above, I found what I was looking for. The lens of the handheld camcorder stared out at me like an unblinking eye. I reached for it on the shelf and turned the equipment over in my palms. They'd been smart enough not to take the video on their phones where access to the cloud and other Internet mysteries would be a constant threat. But still, what sick psychopaths wanted to videotape their conquests?

Posters of famous comedians plastered Mick's side of the room. *Late Show with David Letterman.* Johnny Carson on *The Tonight Show.* Conan O'Brien. Always a spectacle, I guessed.

With a spare glance toward the door, I pulled Mick's chair underneath me and sat down at his laptop. I opened the screen to find that the computer was password protected. So I logged in as a guest, removed the memory stick in the video recorder, and drummed my fingers impatiently while thumbnails of videos loaded on-screen.

Three rows of images popped up in neat lines. I chose the first. The picture consumed the frame and began to play. "Say hi, asshole," Mick's voice came from behind the camera. There was a shot of the back of a head that I recognized as Circus Master's. Without looking back, Circus Master saluted the air with his middle finger. I felt my mouth curl into a snarl. The camera shook. Mick's breathing was labored.

Off to the side I could hear someone else's voice carrying on a singsongy rap, "All the bitches love me, all the—all the bitches love me."

Mick gave a gleeful giggle and panned left where California was walking with a swagger. He formed his fingers into a peace sign and flashed a brilliant white smile. The screen went black and the reel automatically switched to the next thumbnail down the line.

The five boys were at the same club I'd first seen them in—Ten Gallon Cowboy. Their images were grainy in the dim, neon-cast lighting. The camera zoomed in on the face of a boy in a baseball cap. He pinched a shot glass between his fingers. "Get it out of my face." He wrapped his palm over the lens. "Coach finds out I'm drinking the night before a game, he'll suspend my scholarship."

There was rustling and then Mick must have managed to wrestle the camera free. The focus had changed to a group of girls standing at a high-top table. The shot homed in on one of the girls' butts. "There's your home run, Brody."

Brody. Baseball. I made another note in my phone. Got it.

I watched the playback from the next thumbnail with a sickening sense of dread as the girl whose ass had been video recorded laughed with the boys and then showed up in a room that looked much like the one I was currently in minus a few details. At some point, she was passed out, arm draped over the side of a bed, and the boys took turns taking pictures with her, lifting up her skirt and spanking the bare flesh. I couldn't watch the rest and quickly clicked on the next frame.

More of the same. More girls. More taunting. And all the while, they grew more brazen. The girls less drunk. In one clip, I heard the word *no* muttered just before I hit fast-forward.

And then her face filled the screen.

I hovered the mouse over the "stop" button, but the images were already moving before my eyes. Instead, I moved my hand into my lap and I let it play.

– – –

"HER." FROM A distance, the shot zoomed in on a girl who looked like me. Who I knew, deep down, *was* me. Except this me was red-cheeked and glowing. This me was happy.

"Small boobs," came one of the voices offscreen. On-screen, I laughed like something was really funny. Like things could still be really funny.

"Shut up, they're fine," said another voice.

"She's totally hot," replied the first.

I kept stealing glances in the direction of the camera. It was clear that I could see them watching me and that I was performing.

"Scale from one to ten?" said a third voice.

"Nine-point-five," responded the first, and there was the clink of a glass being slammed down on a table for punctuation.

"Well, what the hell are you waiting on then?" asked a fourth. "Christ, Brody, get her over here, buddy."

"Why does it always have to be me?" said the voice that was presumably Brody's.

The lens zoomed out. There I was with three other girls, but I still took up the center of the shot. Jock Strap came into view. It was clear why it always had to be him.

He turned his baseball cap backward and shoved his hands into his pockets. He had a handsome, square jaw. The face of an underwear model. The pleasure that came with his attention danced in my eyes. Eyes that said, he noticed *me*? His devastating good looks translated onto film. Honestly, it should be criminal for anyone to be that naturally attractive.

He put his hat on my head and I giggled. Then, he hiked his thumb over his shoulder in the direction of the camera. Offscreen, the boys whooped, a big welcoming whoop, a *come-with-us* whoop, a *we-are-great-guys* whoop. I squeezed the arm of the blond girl next to me as if to say, *Can you believe this?*

I glanced back at the girls as I followed Jock Strap over to the other table. Right away, Jock Strap excused himself to go to the restroom. My disappointment was immediately replaced when a tall boy with an expensive-looking shirt and crocodile-skin boots put his arm around me and hugged me to his side like we were long-lost pals, like I was the most special girl in the room. "Let us buy you a drink," the one I knew now as Circus Master said.

And buy they did. We all took a shot. My nose scrunched as the clear liquid went down. There were five of them total. I grew bolder. I told a joke. They all laughed.

The thinnest boy, the one with a cigarette tucked behind his ear—I couldn't help noticing he was the only boy who wasn't conventionally attractive, with acne scars in the hollows of his cheek; Lucky Strike—leaned toward me. "You're the hottest girl in the entire bar, you know that?" I blushed, but didn't look surprised. "That's why we chose you."

"Prettiest girl we've seen in real life," said the voice behind the camera. "Wouldn't you say so?"

"I wouldn't not say it," replied the long-haired boy, tucking a strand behind his ear and slowly taking a sip off the top of his beer. California. *Jessup.*

"Don't tell your friends." Circus Master slapped me good-naturedly on the back. "I'm sorry, did we offend you? We didn't mean to offend you. We know they're your friends, don't we, guys?" He surveyed the group.

"No, no," I rushed in to say. "You didn't offend me." There was a smile behind my glass as I raised it to my lips. "At all."

Circus Master flattened his palm to his chest. "That's a relief. Hey." He scratched his temple. "I just had a thought. Why don't we get out of here?"

I lowered my glass. The flash of disappointment that played

across my face would have been obvious to an astronaut orbiting the moon. "Oh. Okay."

California Jessup fished for his wallet in the back of his slouchy jeans and laid down a couple dollars on the table. "Chill. They're talking about all of us. You think we'd leave our best girl?" He raised an eyebrow to me. He was so tall I had to crane my neck back to see him.

"Let's blow this place." Circus Master gave a whistle and twirled his finger in the air as if to round us all up.

"Um, hold on," I practically squeaked. "Let me just tell my friends."

I hustled offscreen while the camera panned the group of faces. Smug. Eyes twinkling with laughter. Mean. Predatory.

When I reappeared, Circus Master welcomed me back in, reworking his face into that of a gracious host.

"I told them I'd call them tomorrow," I said with a hint of pride.

Circus Master grinned down at me. I looked around at the other boys. As we moved together through the crowd, there was a shot of Jock Strap's—*Brody's*—devastatingly handsome face, still gorgeous as ever, but wearing a look that was unmistakably distant, as though he were bored. Or indifferent.

Outside, Circus Master released his genial hold on me. The camera kept zooming in on me, sliding the focus down my body.

"God, it's so goddamn refreshing to meet a girl that gets it, that can hang with the guys. Isn't it?" Circus Master said in a loud voice.

"Hell, yeah." California Jessup high-fived me.

The camera caught only slivers of the background, but gradually as we walked, it shifted from rows of well-lit restaurants and bars to dark storefronts. Then parking lots.

"What did I tell you? Hottest girl in the bar," said the voice behind the camera. There was shuffling. The lens tipped and then righted itself, then resumed bouncing with the steps of its operator.

Lucky Strike sidled up to my side. His sunken eyes peered at me. "What's the hottest piece of her?"

My head whipped in his direction. My expression disappeared from the viewpoint of the camera lens.

"Look at that ass," said Brody, taking a pretend swing of a baseball bat through the air. He watched his follow-through like he could see a home run sailing overhead.

My neck swiveled now. I glanced over my shoulder. "Hey, where are we going, anyway?"

We were on a sidewalk. Unruly branches hung over the path. There were now more trees than lampposts and buildings. Untended lots speckled the area. We took a turn. There were rows of parked cars along the street with nobody in them. We were making our way farther from the main road. No signs of life up ahead.

"A party," said Jock Strap Brody.

The camera caught my mouth forming into a soft *o*.

"See, most girls aren't cool like you." Circus Master was walking backward now to face me. "They can be so uptight. You're not uptight, are you?"

I shook my head. Circus Master came to a stop, so the whole group did, too. I was looking around like I should understand where we were.

"Good, I didn't think you were," Circus Master continued, like I'd said it out loud.

"I wonder what she looks like underneath all that." Lucky Strike pointed to my outfit.

Was it something I'd said? Were they making fun of me or was I in on the joke? The questions played easily on my face. The heady buzz I'd been enjoying at the bar popped and fizzled out.

"I just remembered, my friends will be waiting for me to get back," I said, turning away from Circus Master, who blocked my path forward.

Jessup easily stepped between me and an escape. "Relax. You're fine."

Circus Master pushed his lip into a pout. "But you already told them you'd call them tomorrow. Remember?"

My body visibly stiffened. Jessup twirled me around to face Circus Master. He gave me a little shove in his direction and I stumbled forward. The cameraman backed up and the angle got wider. Circus Master stepped toward me. He gently put his hands on my waist. Then he slid one up to my shoulder and pulled the strap down on my tank top so that it dangled off. "Now, I thought you were cooler than other girls." I stood frozen. "Right?" I nodded. His voice lowered. "You don't want to be a bitch, do you?" I shook my head.

I actually lifted my arms as he slid my shirt over my head. I shivered in only my bra and skirt.

"Christ, I'm bored," said Brody. "Can we hurry this up?"

Circus Master's eyes flashed. Then he lifted his chin and he laughed. "I'm sorry. I wasn't being a gentleman. You first?"

"Wait." My voice wasn't a scream. It cracked and gave me away. I didn't sound cool. I sounded frightened.

I tried to back up. Lucky Strike caught me by the shoulders. "You're drunk," he said. I stared down at his fingers. Then his arms wrapped around my chest and he was pressing me into him.

I wrenched my chin to the right, trying to twist my torso. But

Circus Master latched on to my legs. I still wasn't really fighting. Not exactly. Somewhere in my mind, I thought: *If I fight, this all becomes real. I'll know this is bad.* So I bicycled my legs, but without much force.

"Relax, chill out," Jessup said, shaking his long hair from his eyes. "Don't make a big deal out of it. You want to be cool, right?"

From behind the camera there was a high-pitched squeal of laughter while on-screen I went limp. My skirt was off and my bare skin was glowing translucent in the nighttime air. Circus Master ushered Brody toward me. *Step right up to the center ring, the main attraction.*

I'd always worked hard to be the center of attention, but in that moment, I would have paid any amount of money in the world to switch places with another girl.

I didn't need to finish playing the recording. I knew the naive girl that had first come out of that club had died there in that lot and no longer existed. That she'd been reincarnated as me. I ripped the memory card out of the computer and shoved it into my pocket. I hid the camcorder inside my hoodie and zipped it away.

Fresh humiliation rose to the surface of my skin like festering boils. I yanked the laptop cord from the wall. No one could see me like that. I had to hide it. Get rid of my link to the boys, get rid of that night in my life in general.

And if I couldn't log in to delete the evidence from the inside, I'd just have to destroy the outside, too. I looked for a hammer. Something heavy that would shatter the traces of the girls broken by the video. Something to keep these boys from having the pleasure of rewatching our pain and to make way for theirs instead.

I was coming up empty-handed when I noticed the window

looking out over a modest quadrangle down below. I fiddled with the locks on the pane and shimmied open the glass. Leaning into the fresh air, I stared down at the brick walkway. "That'll do." I snatched up the laptop. The windowsill had a sharp ledge. I smashed the computer down over it. The hard casing dented. I brought it down again and again, impaling the sides. Power surged through my arms down to my fingertips and I felt like a heavy-metal drummer. Destructive. Catastrophic.

It wasn't a knife. And it wasn't flesh and blood, but the sound of electronics cracking open and breaking apart was still satisfying.

Lena's three staccato warning knocks on the door pulled me back into myself. My chest heaved. My neck was hot. *Shoot*. I imagined California walking in to find me destroying Mick's computer. Not here. Not now. I pressed my fist into my teeth, trying to think. Quickly, I leaned back over the open windowsill and stared down. There was a row of bushes underneath. I stared at the laptop still clutched between both hands. I wasn't exactly a technology buff, but I was pretty sure no history papers would be written on this thing anytime soon. I released my grip and watched as the computer plummeted down into the row of hedges, disappearing beneath the thick leaves with a barely audible *ker-thunk*.

I could hear Lena's voice outside trying to stall. The handle was twisting. I braced myself. Wrapped my hand tightly around the knife handle. But it wasn't California's head that popped through. It was a crop of strawberry blond hair and a freckled nose. California's—Jessup's—girlfriend's breath caught when she saw me standing beside the desks. I waited for an instant but then saw that she was alone. No Jessup in sight.

I relaxed slightly. If I felt sorry for people, I would have felt sorry for her. Stupid baby deer of a girlfriend. What would she do if she knew about the other girls hidden on the memory card? The ones that didn't get flowers on their birthday or take piggyback rides like she did. The ones that, as far as her boyfriend was concerned, didn't even have names.

"Who are you? What are you doing here?" she asked. "Mick hasn't been back."

"I wasn't looking for Mick," I said.

Her lips closed and her eyes narrowed. "Jessup?" By the way she said his name, I got the sense that maybe it wasn't so far-fetched that Jessup would have a lady visitor.

Good. Let her think it.

I moved toward the door and, as though it was despite herself, she shifted out of my way. Maybe this girl's interruption wasn't such a bad thing. Perhaps even if stupid baby deer girlfriend wasn't capable of seeing what a creep her boyfriend was she might still be capable of conveying a message. Or a warning. "Tell Jessup I'll be back for him later," I said with a casual look over my shoulder. "Another time."

Her skin reddened, blurring the freckles. "And why would I do that?"

I shrugged, halfway out the door. "Or don't. It doesn't matter. I like surprises just as much."

Her lower jaw dropped a centimeter. But she couldn't think of a comeback. I winked. And then I was gone.

THIRTEEN

Cassidy

I didn't trust myself.

Even when I woke up in sweatpants and a T-shirt and, as far as I could tell, nothing had changed, I didn't trust myself.

My limbs still felt pleasantly warm and lithe, the lingering effects of last night's dose of Sunshine, but the moment my alarm went off, doubt began creeping in. I stared up at the ceiling for as long as I could, trying to convince myself that all was well. I was in my bed. I felt healthy. Reasonably happy.

I once read an article in a teen magazine that said trust was the most important thing in any good relationship. I guessed they were right because I didn't trust myself and my relationship with me was quickly deteriorating.

I clambered out of bed and began dressing. Meanwhile, the

feeling of unease grew. I washed and blow-dried my hair. I put on pink lipstick and mascara. I shimmied into jeans that fit and a cream top with ruffles on the sleeves. When I looked in the mirror I saw a very convincing version of myself. Pretty. Put together. In control.

What was it, then, that gave me away?

I stared harder at my reflection. It felt like a ghost of someone else lingered right there with me, just out of sight.

I flicked off the light and called for Honor to hurry up or else we'd be late for first period. Then, I went downstairs and threw my bag in the backseat and climbed in to wait for her. When I twisted the key in the ignition the dashboard lit up.

My heart sputtered with the engine. When I got home last night, I'd checked the mileage. I'd memorized it.

Now staring at me from behind my steering wheel was a number that was fifty miles more. Nowhere in town would be that far. The closest city was about twenty-five miles away. And it was Dearborn.

Honor appeared, hustling out the front door. A flannel shirt hung halfway off her shoulder and she was trying to tug it up while balancing a stack of books. I turned my face into a mask of calm. Underneath, though, my heartbeat skipped wildly out of control. And my knuckles turned white as they wrapped themselves into a death grip around the leather wheel. I felt like someone was haunting me. But I was pretty sure that someone *was* me.

I repressed a shudder. Honor tumbled into the seat beside me with a huff.

"Sorry," she said, breathless.

I smiled at her and helped her push her book bag into the backseat. "That's okay."

I let her choose the radio station as we drove to school.

"You're an actress, Honor," I said, keeping my tone casual.

She sat up straighter and adjusted the chest strap on her seat belt.

"I guess. I only have a really small speaking part in the play this semester."

I shrugged. "You're only a freshman, silly. So, when you're acting, you're trying to convince the audience that you're someone other than who you actually are, right?" She nodded. "How do you *do* that?" I asked, for once genuinely interested.

She looked sidelong at me. "You never ask me about drama."

I lifted my eyebrows. "Indulge me."

"Well, there are different methods, I guess. The main ones we've learned about are Stanislavski's system—that's when an actor draws on his own emotional memory to portray a character's emotions on stage. The actor focuses internally. Like, if you wanted to depict a happy character, you'd call upon memories in which you were really happy and try to channel that outward," she explained. "And then there's Method acting. The two are really closely related, I guess. Only with Method acting, you don't just use your own memories. You kind of imagine memories, I think, using the circumstances of the scene. Mrs. White says that Method acting is more honest so it looks more believable on stage."

I jutted my lower lip out thoughtfully, only partially focusing on the road in front of me. "Interesting."

Honor perked up. "I'm a Method actor, you know," she said, not bothering to conceal the pride behind that statement.

My chest throbbed with love for my little sister. "I think I am, too," I replied. We pulled into my parking space.

She grinned back at me and unclicked her seat belt.

With the road I was going down I was in danger of losing her. I was in danger of losing all of this. She started to open the door. I stopped her. I reached across the center console and wrapped her in a tight hug. "Have a good day, okay?"

Honor was never skeptical of anything. In this moment, I loved that about her. She hugged me back, kissed me on the cheek, and then scrambled off to her first class.

Meanwhile, I prepared to spend the next seven hours Method acting.

Like when Ava and Erica sat down at our lunch table to talk about whether we should have matching hairstyles for tomorrow's game, I thought about what the character Cassidy Hyde would do, channeled it, and flipped through a dozen pictures on celebrity tabloid websites until we settled on a half-up, half-down look, light curls, lots of hair spray.

Or when the class president asked if I'd volunteer for prom committee, I pretended to be super flattered. In fact, I pretended so well, I nearly convinced myself. I even affected a slight strut in my step as my wedges clacked down the hall. *Prom committee, here I come.*

When I had the opportunity in class to drop the act, I got busy devising a concrete plan. I figured, at the end of the day, it was a bit like an exorcism. I needed to follow the steps to banish whoever I was at night. I *had* to stop myself.

This past week it was like a light switch had flipped on. What had I been doing the past few months? It was as though I hadn't realized how fragile the balance of everything was and how much I really had to lose.

So what if those boys had taken something from me? Was

I prepared to throw my whole life down the drain after it? I had best friends, an enviable position as the head of the most popular group in school, good grades, and a sister that looked up to me. That was *worth* something.

I should have been smarter than this. There was a mathematical theory in economics that said you shouldn't consider sunk costs when making future decisions. Well, wasn't that exactly what I'd been doing? That terrible night in Dearborn was my sunk cost, but I would be an idiot to let it dictate my entire future.

I sucked on the end of my pen, once again zoning out in Mr. Yotsuda's class. I'd haphazardly taken down the notes on the board, not bothering to solve any of the equations this time. Below, in my notebook, I'd written a numbered list, penned neatly on the bottom half of the page.

1. *Act normal, be normal*
2. *Stop all nighttime activity*
3. *Sunshine (?)*

I studied the question mark. I didn't want to believe that the drug could have anything to do with the gaps in my memory. After all, it had yanked me from the fog I'd been stumbling around inside for months. But, if I was thinking rationally—and I was determined to think rationally now—I couldn't take the risk. Sunshine would have to go.

I took my pen and drew a hard line through the third item on my list. No more Sunshine. I felt tendrils of trepidation curling around me.

But by the end of the school day, I was still acting my way into feeling strong and capable. In fact, I was ready to nominate myself for a Golden Globe. Even Oilerettes' practice went off without a hitch.

"So are you coming tonight?" Paisley asked as the team trickled out of the locker room and into the open evening air. "You have to."

"Coming where?" I asked.

"To my house," Paisley scoffed.

I felt two inches shorter and bone tired from a day spent trying to play a convincing Cassidy Hyde. I eyed the distance between me and my car longingly. "Why would I do that?" I asked, trying not to sound as exhausted as I felt.

"*Hello*, we talked about this last week. I sent out an e-mail. Having people over. Night before. Pregame before the *big* game? Any bell up in that head tower of yours to ring?"

"Oh. Um . . ." I shifted my weight on my feet. "I don't know. I kind of have a lot of homework."

She rolled her eyes. "Don't hold all your AP classes over my head. Those are *your* problem."

I felt the weight of my muscles dragging me down. Besides, nighttimes were tricky for me. I had to remember item number two on my list and, above all else, I absolutely could not trust myself, especially at night.

"Cass, it's really important." Paisley stamped her foot. "People will expect you to be there. We're a duo, remember?" She pouted. I couldn't help but be a bit touched. And if I knew my best friend, she wasn't going to let up.

"Okay," I said, cutting her off before she could freak out. "I'll think about it. *Think* is the operative word."

Her heart-shaped lips curled to the side in a triumphant smirk. "I'll see you tonight."

I shook my head, but didn't protest any further. I could deal with her later.

The drive home was short. I listened to commercials telling me how to get liposuction without any surgery. I ate dinner with my family. Mom asked me if we were prepared for tomorrow's game and if she needed to get me anything for it. Dad asked if I'd signed up for the SAT yet and even though he'd been asking me the same thing for a few weeks straight, this time I actually made a mental note to do it.

When I dragged my feet up the stairs carting a pile of textbooks and making a plan to finish a set of math problems in bed, I wanted nothing more than to curl up in my pajamas and fall fast asleep. But as I crawled onto my mattress, I remembered my promise to Paisley to think about coming tonight.

The whole team would be together. The old me would have gone in a heartbeat. My parents would have encouraged it, even on a school night.

It was then that I felt the pull of the Sunshine stashed in the music box on my nightstand. One teeny tiny pill and I could go and be the life of the party. I could be fun, beautiful, all the things that I wanted to be.

I took a deep breath and opened the lid. The yellow pills looked like candy drops, ready for the taking. I swallowed. My fingers pinched the plastic bag and retrieved it from the box. I unzipped the top, shook the remaining pills into my hand. So tempting. I stared at them, my mouth watering.

Then, I went to the bathroom, dropped them in the toilet, and flushed. *There.* I dusted my palms off.

I tried to ignore the deep groan of my psyche. I had to stay on track. No slipups. I needed something else to keep me grounded. So I scoured the medicine cabinet until I found a half-full bottle of nighttime cough syrup. I brought it to my nightstand. I dug my keys out of my gym bag, looked around for a place to hide them, and wound up throwing them under the bed. Finally, I took duct tape that I had left over from sticking up Homecoming posters and taped three long strips along the crack of my door from as high as I could reach all the way to the floor.

I tucked myself under the sheets and pulled my computer into my lap. I clicked through my e-mail until I found Paisley's message.

Put on your rally caps and get ready to rumble. Gathering at my house Thursday to pregame before the Big Game. 1130 San Alamo Way. Be there, bitches.

I smiled. Even though she drove me crazy, I still missed Paisley. I felt bad that I was skipping out, but someday maybe she'd understand it was for the best. Someday maybe I'd even tell her about Dearborn.

But for tonight, I typed out a quick message apologizing for not being able to make it, citing a history test that I forgot about as the reason. I pushed the laptop to the side, opened the cap on the cough syrup.

I sniffed the contents—grape—swirled the liquid around, held it up to my lips. *Try getting up after this.* "Bottoms up," I said, and took a long, hard swig.

FOURTEEN

Marcy

Every night I woke up in a room filled with things I'd never choose. Girly, frilly things that made me recoil like a vampire in sunlight.

I'd become aware of *her* right away. I saw her—*my*—face planted on the dresser in picture frames, cheeks squeezed against those of friends I'd never have. Would never want to have.

We seemed to move in parallel, her and I. I could never quite reach out and wrap my fingers around that life. Then again, I'd never really tried.

Tonight was different, though.

I woke up with a dull headache thudding at the base of my skull. My arms felt heavy and when I looked to my right, I noticed a half-empty bottle of cough syrup PM open on the nightstand. I didn't feel sick. I felt groggy. I resisted the urge to lie back and fade into unconsciousness and instead lowered my feet to the floor and cracked my neck.

That was when I saw the door. Three strips of silver duct tape covered the seam, sealing me inside.

The possibility that the cough syrup had been a coincidence— an attempt at curing an illness—now felt slimmer. I narrowed my eyes. Who—or what—did she think she was dealing with? A child?

I crossed the room to study *her* handiwork. I tested the edges with my fingernails. The tape was stuck tight. No matter. I went to the dresser to retrieve the keys to the car.

Only they weren't there.

I searched the nightstand, a gym bag nearby, blankets bunched on top of the mattress. Nowhere in sight.

I was beginning to get anxious. I felt cooped up. Trapped. I always got out of this place, her place, as soon as possible. Where were they?

I began to seethe. I went into the closet and began tearing clothes off the hangers, rummaging through the pockets. All of them were empty. In a fit, I emptied the contents of all the bedroom drawers. I didn't find the keys. I tore through every purse *she* owned without hearing the jangle of metal.

As a last resort I dropped to my knees and peered under the bed. There, I found the clump of keys hidden farther under the four-poster frame than I could reach. It was a spot they couldn't have fallen accidentally.

She had placed them there.

I shimmied on my stomach until my fist clenched around them. My hollow insides were transforming into a bubbling pit of anger.

How dare she? My teeth ground like a mortar and pestle. She'd tried to stop me. She'd attempted to affect what was mine. *Stupid, stupid girl.*

A computer sat dark-screened and opened, still warm. I swished my fingers over the mousepad. It came to life. In a window on-screen was an invitation to an e-mail address for Cassidy Hyde.

Hello, Cassidy.

A party. Now that could be interesting. I liked having a good time. I liked parties. And it was clear that Cassidy needed to lose her privileges. *This is why we can't have nice things, Cassidy.*

Swinging my feet over the side of the bed, I stripped off the flannel pajamas she'd put on in favor of black jeans and a tank top. I shoved my feet into a pair of boots and laced them up to my ankles.

By the time that I'd stretched and shaken out the tension in my wrists, the spiderweb threads of Cassidy had been shed and it was go time.

The drive to Paisley's house was short. Nearly walkable. I pulled up to a three-story pink house with white shutters. I'd never seen something so large and pink before and the sight of it made me want to tear off the siding and burn it in a fire.

Instead, I parked. My boots made scraping noises against the brick walkway that led up to the house where I rang the bell glowing softly beside the little blue door. Several seconds passed. Commotion behind the door. Then a girl with short blond hair appeared. This girl's face appeared more than any other in the photographs on Cassidy's dresser. She was sharper and a bit meaner looking in person and I hated her instantly. A laugh died on her face the second she saw me.

"What are you doing here?" she asked. She was even more petite than she seemed in pictures.

I walked straight past her into the foyer, where I stopped and stared at her home. Porcelain plates were affixed to the wall as decoration. I ran my fingers around a few of the smooth edges. "You seem surprised to see me."

She still hadn't closed the door. "I—we—you said you weren't coming."

My boots looked too thick and military against the clean marble. "Why?" I turned my attention from the china plates and waited expectantly while she seemed to decide what to do about that door.

At last she made a choice. The door clicked into place and she slid the lock. "Are you okay?" When she frowned she looked like a pouting doll. "You seem . . . off."

I raised my eyebrows. Good. This was a start. Time to teach Cassidy and her band of playthings a lesson once and for all. "Never felt so alive," I said.

"All righty then. Well, we're all in the upstairs game room." I decided the conversation wasn't worth it as I followed her through a kitchen large enough to feed a full restaurant's clientele and up two flights of steps. My boots pounded the stairs too loudly.

The game room was outfitted with two thick-cushioned leather sofas, a real live pinball machine, and Skee-Ball. How spoiled did a kid have to be to need their own pinball machine? French doors opened onto a balcony overlooking a shimmering blue-green pool underneath.

I noticed that my boots were tracking light footprints of dirt into the carpet. And just because I had the urge, I ground them in a bit deeper until I was sure to leave heftier smudges.

In the room, I found ten kids my age playing video games and nursing beers. The conversation fell to a hush when I entered and I had the not-so-sneaking suspicion that the room's occupants had been talking about Cassidy before I'd come in.

"Look who's here," the blond hostess said, by way of introduction. I stared at everyone. They all stared back at me like a bunch of lazy dairy cows in a field. Too stupid to keep from being tipped over.

"Hey, Cassidy," one boy piped up. He was attractive in a very obvious sort of way. Slender, slouched shoulders, an easy, imperfect grin.

"Well." I scanned the room, ignoring him. "This sucks. I thought this was supposed to be a party, but you're just sitting here playing, like, Mario Brothers or something."

I walked deeper into the room and punched some buttons on the pinball machine. Nothing happened.

"Excuse you." The pitch of Paisley's voice shot up. "Since when did you become Miss Social again? Last time I checked, you were still busy blowing off the world."

"Christ." I shook the pinball machine, trying to make a ball appear. "Now I see why."

"Nobody forced you to come." The girl's pitch went up an octave.

"Oh god, is that why the rest of you look so glum? Are you being held here against your will? Blink twice to call for help." I smirked as everyone stared at me dumbfounded.

In one of the corners, there was a guitar display surrounded by vinyl records. I wrapped my hand around the guitar and pulled it off of the wall brackets to examine it. An autograph was scrawled at the bottom.

"Um, can you not touch that, please?" the blond said, still hovering.

"You mean like this?" I strummed my fingers across the strings and it made an off-tune chord.

She flinched. "Yes, like that. Now can you please put it down. It's autographed by Dolly Parton."

I stuck out my lower lip. "But I feel so rock and roll."

She rolled her eyes. "Stop being stupid, Cassidy. What's gotten into you? You're making me nervous."

"God, have you always been so uptight?" I strummed a few more misguided notes. The room collectively sucked in air so hard you'd have thought it may cause a vortex.

The only boy that had spoken to me stood up off the arm of the couch. "Can I get you a drink, Cass? Beer? Water?"

"Cass . . ." I practically hissed at the name. "What are you, my waiter . . . or my boyfriend?" Amid a dead silent room, I laughed at my own joke.

My phone buzzed in my pocket. Reluctantly, I set the guitar down and checked the message that was waiting. *Where are you?* The text had been sent by Lena. Instead of responding, I pushed the button to darken the screen and stowed it back in my pocket. *Cassidy* wasn't finished yet.

Something like power was rushing through my veins, filling me up and hollowing me from the inside out. The boy hovered near the couch. "Are you okay?"

I ignored him. "Doesn't anyone do anything fun? Doesn't anyone do anything *interesting*?" I threw open the doors and stepped out onto the balcony. The night was clear. I peered down at the shimmering pool below.

I studied the balustrade. It was flat on top, mounted on wooden posts.

"What are you doing?" The hostess rushed to the balcony.

I clutched a gutter running from one of the roof eaves down the side of the house and climbed onto the rail. "What does it look like I'm doing?" Slowly, I straightened my knees and stood upright. My arms went straight out for balance.

Others had crowded the balcony's opening.

"It looks like you're being a raving lunatic," she huffed.

"Who are you to tell me what to do?"

"I'm your best friend, moron," she pleaded with me.

I peered down my nose at her. "No, I mean literally. Who are you?" I let the edge in my voice slice through her.

"P-Paisley. What the hell are you talking about, Cassidy? This isn't funny." She looked around to her other friends for help.

I stared down at the pool, trying to calculate how deep it was. "Somebody here needs to not be a total bore." I enjoyed the pounding of my heart in my chest. The way it knocked so hard it threatened to pull me over with the smallest puff of wind. "Who here dares me to jump?" I twisted my chin over my shoulder to several gasps.

"Cassidy . . . don't jump." Another girl's—not the pixie blond Paisley's—voice trembled.

My calves burned with the effort of balancing. Any second I could tip over. Adrenaline pumped by the fistful.

"Cassidy, you're not acting like yourself," said Paisley.

"No, that's exactly right." I grinned. "I'm not. That's the entire freaking point, isn't it? So who *am* I acting like?"

Paisley looked anxiously between the faces in the crowd. "Stop this, Cass. Is this some cry for help? Are you trying to prove you were sadder than me or punish me for trying to take over the Oilerettes? Forget it. You win. Just don't splatter your brains all over my parents' imported Italian granite, okay?" She chewed on her lip. "Look, you've got our attention. Now maybe you should go home. You're making a fool out of yourself."

"I'm making a fool out of myself? Really? Says the skinny, frigid witch. Come on. Who here dares me? Anyone?" Silence.

Another text. Feeling more confident with each passing second, I pulled my phone from my pocket to read Lena's number across the top. **Did something happen? I'm waiting. You said you'd be here.**

I clicked "ignore."

The crowd parted. The boy who'd spoken up not once but twice now threaded his way through the opening. He came so close, I half expected him to shove me over. He was tall but standing on the balustrade I was much taller. He gritted his teeth and spoke in a low tone so others couldn't hear.

"Look, Cass, maybe the Sunshine was a mistake for you. Call it a bad trip. Or whatever. I don't know. But you're wigging out right now." He leaned a couple inches forward and studied the drop into the pool. "Why don't you go home and sleep it off. It'll all seem better in the morning."

I bent down closer to him. "See, that's the thing, though. Maybe I don't want it to be better."

Paisley threw up her hands. "That's it. I'm calling the cops."

The boy whipped around. "Wait." He ran his hands through his hair and gripped the back of his neck. "Wait, wait. *Dammit.* Wait. I gave her something. It's just a stupid pill. I don't know why she's acting like this. But she'll have it in her system. Don't call the cops."

Paisley folded her arms over her chest and shook her head. "You little sneak. You little druggie sneak."

"This is my fault," he said. Then he turned to me, pleading. "Cass, please, you're going to hurt yourself." He reached up and wrapped his fingers around my wrist. I went rigid for a split second before I pounced down from the flat rail, like something feral.

His eyes went wide as I spun him around and pressed his back to the railing. He hung, back suspended partway into open air, my forearm pressed against his Adam's apple. "What's your name again?" I asked.

His pupils darted in between the corners of his eyes. "Are you serious?" I pressed my forearm harder into his throat. "Liam," he choked.

"Okay, then, *Liam*. If you touch me again, you'll come away without any fingers." He gargled as I pressed hard one more time and then released him. "Besides, this place is dead."

I shoved my way through the group, not caring if I stepped on toes or knocked an elbow into someone's rib. On the way out of Paisley's house, I closed the door so hard, I heard the crash of china as it shattered on marble behind me. I felt as though my heart was separating from my chest, as though my humanity was shattering into a trillion tiny pieces lying scattered on the ground, as though I was getting stronger with every step. Taking over.

Once in my car, I jammed my foot on the accelerator. The wheels spun and the scent of burnt rubber sprung from the asphalt. I peeled away from Paisley's house feeling like I'd burned more than my tires. I'd burned the bridges to Cassidy's life. And soon, nothing could raise it from the ash.

FIFTEEN

Cassidy

Cassidy, what are you doing? We're here." Honor unfastened her seat belt.

I blinked and my eyes felt scratchy and dry, like I'd been staring off into space. "Huh?"

She nodded and gave me a *you're crazy* look. "We're at school," she said in a tone like I couldn't understand English. "Aren't you coming?"

I looked around. Outside of my windshield a typical morning at Hollow Pines High was taking place. The bright light of day burned my pupils. I squinted and fished around the side compartment for a pair of sunglasses. "When—how—?" I stammered because I had no recollection of driving here. Like at all.

I stared out at the students filing into the school building and rifled through my memory for the last solid one I could find. As soon as I located it, my insides lurched. The duct tape. The hidden keys. The cough syrup.

It took a moment for that to all sink in. When it did, it wasn't pretty.

"*Crap*," I said, which felt like a totally inane thing to say given the circumstances. "*Crap*," I repeated, lowering my forehead to the steering wheel. The horn blared.

I tried to steady my breathing while something like hysteria began to stampede around in my chest. How did I get here? What was I doing? *Focus, Cassidy. Try to remember. You must have gotten up this morning. Gone through your morning routine . . .*

Honor yanked me back by my shoulders. "What are you doing?" she hissed. "You're embarrassing me. Scratch that, you're embarrassing you."

Honor squirmed in her seat and looked around to see if anyone was watching.

She leaned toward me. Her hazel eyes searched mine. "What are you freaking out about? You haven't said a word all morning."

Cue: another round of terror. It wasn't the obvious kind that had me reaching for a paper bag to breathe into. That kind of terror would be far, far better. Instead, this panic was like a thousand termites hatching eggs inside my throat, multiplying and gnawing at my fleshy guts.

"I—I haven't?" I held my hands in front of my face. Sure enough, they were trembling.

She gritted her teeth together. "You're being weird again." She said it with the air of a childish playground insult.

But this was real. I was losing control. I racked and racked my brain, but I didn't even have a flash of brushing my teeth this morning or putting on my deodorant.

I looked down to study what I was wearing. I was dressed in a pair of tight black denim jeans, a fitted black tank, a dark hoodie, and lace-up boots that I bought for a Halloween costume two years ago. "What *is* this outfit?" I asked, pinching the tank top's fabric off my stomach.

Honor's mouth twisted. "I don't know. I figured you were making, like, a statement or something." For her part, Honor was dressed in a delicate cream cardigan and a knee-length plaid skirt.

"Of *what*?" I exclaimed.

She gave an exaggerated shrug as though I was missing the point entirely. "Who cares. Everybody will probably be copying your outfit by tomorrow anyway. But the tragic teen thing? *That* is getting a little old."

I tilted my head back and laughed, not caring if I sounded like a catatonic lunatic. "Oh, it's getting old, is it? I'm sorry, Honor, that my little phase"—I curled my fingers into air quotes—"isn't quite working for you." Honor's face fell.

I let my foot off the brake. The car gave a little bump as it settled into park.

"I—I'm sorry," I said. My sister looked as though she was frightened I was about to tell her that the Easter bunny didn't exist.

The Easter bunny didn't exist. There were no magical Homecoming nights or balloon-arch fairy tales. No matter what I did, I was losing my grip on everything that was mine.

"I just need a second to think." I pressed two fingers to my temples and rubbed, hard.

"Cassidy, you're scaring me." Honor hugged her arms across her stomach.

I turned to her and put my hands on her shoulders. I took a deep breath. "I'm sorry, I'm not trying to scare you. Everything's fine. I just . . . felt a little faint is all."

Honor's forehead relaxed, ironing out the wrinkles. "Maybe you should call in sick."

Something about her worry had shifted me into the calm one. Take charge. I could do this. "And miss the first game of the play-offs? I think not."

She grinned. I felt a wave of guilt at the way she looked at me. Like I was a hero. The panic was now only lapping at me, surging and then receding in my veins. I felt helpless. Nothing I'd done was working. I was lost. Alone. All I could do was move forward and pray the ship didn't sink before I got wherever it was I was going.

But I was taking on water fast.

I pinched Honor's cheek and gave it a hard shake that left red indents where my thumb had been. She squealed in protest. Maybe, just maybe, we looked almost normal.

Outside the car, the sun microwaved my face. I lowered my head and trudged forward in my ridiculous black boots.

All this and I hadn't even taken Sunshine last night. That was the only thing that felt true. And as proof, a round of tremors quaked through my body.

Now more than ever, I craved the flood of warmth I got when I'd first taken Sunshine. When I glanced around at all the smiling, laughing faces, it seemed like everyone else must have a secret stash. How else could they all be so darn happy?

From a few steps behind, I could hear the crunch of Honor's

shoes following me. The first bell rang as I entered through the glass doors and was sucked into the soulless hallways of Hollow Pines High.

I may have been losing my mind, but I didn't think I was imagining the dozens of sets of eyes trained right at me. I moved; they moved. I hurried my steps.

I should be used to people watching me. I was somebody at this school, which meant that, for the rest of the student body, keeping up with my social life was practically a sporting event. But today was different.

I navigated the crowded corridors, trying to ignore the feeling that I was an animal at the zoo, trying to ignore the fact that I still couldn't remember how I'd gotten to school.

Just go with it, I told myself, meanwhile wondering whether the cough syrup had kept me in a deep sleep last night and what I'd done with the strips of tape. Had I peeled them off? Cut through them? I couldn't recall.

Paisley was leaning up against the locker next to mine, waiting for me. "So you're alive," she said.

"Morning," I answered without making eye contact. I spun the dial on my combination lock three times until I heard a click.

"Nice try." She pushed my locker door closed. I blinked at the wall of aluminum siding. "You caused two *thousand* dollars worth of damage to my mother's wedding china. You are not getting off that easy."

"What are you talking about?"

"Last night. Maybe staying home to study was the way to go." My face must have gone ghostly white because she grabbed me by the elbow, turned me so that my back was to the hallway traffic, and drew me close. "What is with you?" she asked. Her breath smelled like wintergreen. "I don't even recognize you anymore. The drugs. Your little stunt on the balcony."

"*Shit.*" I pressed my hand to my forehead.

Paisley raised an eyebrow. "Yeah, now that's more like it."

"I—" My mouth tried to form itself around words. "I—I—last night—I was at—your house, then? I was at your house?" I pointed between us.

Paisley scrunched her nose and she let her eyes cast side to side like she was looking for someone to complain to that I was crazy. "Look, I know you've always kept up the reputation of a party girl, but don't you think you're taking it a bit too far? I mean, there's the party train and then there's the train wreck. Word to the wise, you, my friend, are off the tracks."

"*Shit.*" She frowned. I didn't have time to figure out what the stunt was that I'd pulled on the balcony. Or question how it was that Paisley knew about Sunshine. I had to grab tight to whatever ends I had left before I ran out of rope. "I'm sorry, Paize. It was a stupid joke," I tried. She looked skeptical, but I pressed on anyway. "Tell your mom I take complete responsibility. I'll pay for the damage." How I was going to make good on *that* promise was a problem for future me.

Paisley's lips parted. Then, they closed again. They opened. And then they closed. It was clear she hadn't been expecting that response. Finally, she spoke. "Cassidy, we're worried about you." I rolled my eyes. Probably unconvincingly, but I rolled them anyway. "Okay, *I'm* worried about you. Tonight we have the play-offs and . . ." She hesitated. "Maybe you should step down. Give it up. Clearly it's too much stress on you."

I stiffened. "Give it up to who?" I asked. *"You?"* Her mouth was sealed. This time she didn't stop me when I opened my locker door. I grabbed the notebooks I needed and stuffed them in my bag. "That's what I thought," I said. "I told you for the last time, Paisley, I'm fine."

One of my cheeks dimpled in a half smirk as if to say to her, *Don't know what else to tell ya.*

And I didn't. I couldn't give up the Oilerettes because giving up the Oilerettes felt like giving up, period. And if I started giving things away, I wasn't sure what parts of myself I'd get to keep.

— — —

I AM FINE. I am fine. I'm fine. I'm fine, I'm fine. I'mfinefinefinefinefine.

"Uh, Cass?" I jolted at a tap on my shoulder.

"What?" I snapped, and then softened when I saw Ava peering at me. Outside the locker room doors, the crowd roared for game one of the play-offs against Lamar.

"Pines, Pines, Pines, Pines," the fans chanted. Their voices trickled into where the Oilerettes were gathered, ribbons in hair, laces tied, muscles limbered.

Ava pulled back her hand as if I'd literally tried to bite it. "Whoa, you look . . . totally wigged out."

The girls turned to me expectantly, cracking knuckles, stretching hamstrings. This was it. Last night—whatever had happened—had clearly been a setback in the girls' trust for me. But they'd given me until the Lamar game—the first night of the play-offs and the weekend-long tournament—to prove myself as captain and, true to their word, here I was, still captain. The stakes were high. It was time to put up or shut up . . . and get out.

The thunderous roar of feet stomping at bleachers split my aching skull. "I'm not *wigged* out." I pulled my spine straighter, drawing myself up taller. My tone was brittle. "I'm focused. Big difference. And can't say I'm loving *your* lackadaisical attitude." A sickly sheen of sweat coated my forehead. I could use a dose of Sunshine right now. I was practically kicking myself for throwing it down the toilet.

Ava wrinkled her nose. She had splashes of glitter on her cheeks. "Lacksa-what-ical?"

I'm fine, I repeated internally. Only I knew exactly what Ava meant. Three layers of concealer couldn't hide the purplish circles seeping out from the skin underneath my eyes. The space between my ears rang, I hadn't taken a bite out of anything all day, and now my stomach felt as hollowed out as the inside of a jack-o'-lantern.

I scanned the fifteen pairs of eyes that circled me and reminded myself not to feel claustrophobic. They were supposed to be looking to me for guidance. I was, after all, their captain.

"Erica," I snapped. "Spit out your gum before I chew you out. Ashley, core tight. Paisley, less bitch face, more smiles. Remember to put the 'cheer' in *cheer*leader."

"Okay, captain, whatever you say. But remind me again. Who's going to put the *leader* in there?" Paisley pinned a phony smile across her face.

Several girls snickered but stopped when I shot them a poisonous stare. I could tell the events of last night left them a little more nervous around me than usual. I seemed to have something of a ticking bomb effect.

Sweat pooled between my fingers. I shouldn't have stopped

taking Sunshine only a day before the big game. Everything felt wrong. Like I was half a beat off and couldn't tell whether I was too fast or too slow.

I mustered up my best can-do attitude. "It's a full house," I said. "Let's get ready to bring it." I put my hand in the center of the circle, hoping that the girls wouldn't notice the way it trembled, the way *I* trembled like a junkie in rehab. More hands stacked over the top of mine. "One, two, three, break!" In unison we all raised our hands to the ceiling and whooped.

I was the first one barreling out the door. I sashayed and waved my pom-poms. The smile I held felt as though a Barbie manufacturer had molded it into place. *Do what they expect*, I commanded.

I caught sight of Liam near the sidelines where he was stripping off his warm-up layers. I pulled my eyes away and hoped he didn't notice. The fabric of my already fragile world was tearing apart. No more Sunshine. No more gimmicks. Like it or not, I was going to have to do this on my own. We arrived in front of the home crowd bleachers. I bumped elbows with Oiler Dan, the school's big-headed mascot, as I found my place in formation.

"Watch it." The kid underneath the mascot head staggered, catching himself on the table with the Gatorade dispenser.

"Sorry," I whispered.

Get it together. I stretched my fingers at my side and rolled back my shoulders. *Nerves.* I made sure I was in alignment with the other girls. I was Cassidy Hyde. Cassidy-freaking-Hyde. And I could do this.

But as I stared up into the screaming sea of faces a wave of nausea nearly knocked me sideways. Cold perspiration popped up on my upper lip. I closed my eyes and blew out a long breath. *Shut it all out. Everything that happened in the last week, shut it out.* This was my chance.

"Ready?" I clapped my pom-poms—one orange, one black—twice. "Okay. Five, six, seven, eight." The other girls joined in with our first cheer of the night. "Beat 'em, bust 'em, that's our custom. Beat 'em, bust 'em, that's our custom. Let's go, Oilers, readjust them!"

I executed a high kick, spun on my toe, and finished with my hands straight out and forming a *T* with my body.

"Go, Oilers!" Ava bounced out of the ending pose. She raised her eyebrows and nodded at me as if to say, *good job.*

Behind us, the first quarter had begun. Each time our players got the ball, we encouraged the fans to cheer and when the other team charged for their basket, we led the fans in a cheer of "Defense!"

When I looked up, I saw the weird sophomore girl with the VW Beetle that I'd first met outside of practice a few nights ago, this time just staring at me. Her black bangs framed the pale moon complexion of her narrow face. A prickle worked its way up from my toes all the way to the top of my scalp. What was her name? Lena? She wasn't watching the game. She was watching me.

The sight of her distracted me. I leaped into a straddle jump. My knees knocked together hard as I landed and I had to force myself not to flinch.

Lena's eyes unsettled me. They felt so familiar, more so than they should. I recovered from the jump and tried to ignore her. But my legs were feeling shakier, whether from withdrawal or something else, something worse, I couldn't tell. But Lena's presence pushed on my consciousness like a finger kneading a bruise.

I counted out the beats. *Four, five, six.* This time, when I twirled in step with the other Oilerettes red swam in front of my vision and I saw myself clutching a knife and plunging it deeper and deeper into cold skin. I stumbled out of the spin and righted my balance using Ava's arm.

Her eyes bugged, but she held me upright. "Are you okay?" she asked through gritted teeth.

"Fine," I said. I missed the next two dance moves and then fell into formation. My teeth pressed into my tongue, giving me something on which to focus besides Lena and the images swimming before me. My stare couldn't help landing on Lena every few seconds. Why was she watching me like that? What had she been talking about the other night and why didn't I remember her when she clearly thought she knew me?

I didn't remember a lot of things.

It was nearly halftime. My throat was bone dry. We were in the middle of one of my favorite cheers—"Let me hear you stomp your feet!"

I ducked to set down my pom-poms in preparation for our first stunts. We'd been working on the lifts for weeks. My body was fever raging, forehead flushed with burn. The sellout crowd stomped their feet in response and it shook my heart. I huddled in with my stunt group. Ava held a poster with the word *Fight* painted on it. Ashley took the other side. I tried to focus. But all I could see was blood. All I could see was me in it. The hypnotist's memory hovered halfway between real and a dream, but how could it not be real when the evidence was buried in my backyard . . . wasn't it? Statistically speaking, any other option didn't make sense.

"Count, Cassidy," Ashley hissed. She had her fingers locked together, ready to grab Ava's—our flyer's—foot in the hold.

"What?" I blinked. "Right. Sorry." I clasped my hands together, too. I realized I'd lost track of whether the Oilers were winning or losing in the game behind us. "Five, six . . ." Ava gripped my shoulder. "Seven, eight."

The soles of Ava's sneaker found my hand. I bent my knees and rocketed her into the air. Her body went rigid. I watched her from my vantage point on the ground as she held up the sign. Days ago, I'd felt renewed strength coursing through me. Today, my arms felt flimsier than cooked spaghetti.

Holding Ava's foot in one hand, I turned out and thrust my fist into the air at an angle. I held the pose and recited the lines of the cheer. My enthusiasm was bleeding out. I couldn't focus.

Just a little bit longer. I watched Ava closely. It was time for the catch. I felt the pressure on my hand as she bent her knees. She jumped and touched her toes. A shooting pain split through the center of my skull and cracked open the camera-eye view in which trickles of red streamed down a boy's face like a sad, violent Harlequin doll.

"No!" I screamed, and jerked away reflexively.

But gravity worked fast. Ava was free-falling. Her dark hair trailed her like fluttering streamers. One foot nailed Ashley in the mouth. As she stumbled back, Ava's other foot hit the floor at an unnatural angle. There was a sickening crack and she crumpled on the gym floor. A collective gasp sounded from the crowd. A whistle blew and the sneakers behind us stopped screeching.

I turned to see the basketball clutched at Liam's side. The whole team stared. On the ground, Ava was writhing. Her thigh bone jutted out in a way that it shouldn't. A thick bulge showed a sharp split in the bone of her leg. My stomach churned.

I glanced wildly at Ashley. She was hunkered over. Blood poured into her cupped hand. Erica's arm was already wrapped around her back. Ashley's red mouth worked and then she spit a tooth into her palm.

The weight of the entire gymnasium's stares bore down on me. "I—I'm sorry." My voice was paper-thin. "I didn't mean to—"

Faceless adults began rushing onto the courtside. I took a step back. Then another. And another. I turned my back and I ran. My shoulder crashed through the double doors and I sprinted through the halls of Hollow Pines High until, half-blind with panic, I found the exit and fell gulping for oxygen into the fresh air.

I crouched in the fetal position outside where my knuckles pushed against the concrete. What was happening to me? What was wrong with me?

Oh god.

I squeezed my eyes shut and prayed that the earth would either swallow me whole or self-destruct.

"Cassidy?" Liam's voice came from behind me. It now seemed a lifetime ago that I would have swooned at the mere mention of my name on his lips.

I wiped my eyes with the back of my hand and stood up. "What?" The word scratched my throat.

"I figured someone needed to check on you, too."

"Don't you have a game to play?"

Sweat glistened off his arms. "We're taking a brief intermission." He flashed me the same lopsided grin that had managed to sneak through my walled-up defenses that night at the party when all I'd wanted was to be alone. Didn't he realize that he was intruding again? "While we wait for the ambulance to arrive."

I grimaced. I tried to imagine myself through his eyes. Did he wonder what had happened to Cassidy Hyde the Homecoming queen? Or did he think that he had it all figured out?

"It's not like she's going to die, you know," he said. "Ava's too big to be a flyer anyway."

"That's not true," I mumbled.

He glanced back over his shoulder at the closed door. In the distance, I thought I could hear sirens.

"Do you have any on you?" I peered up at him, forlorn. I hadn't taken it last night. I hadn't taken it and it hadn't helped. What more did I have to lose? The answer felt like a resounding *nothing*.

"Cassidy . . ." He ran his hand over his face.

"Do you?" Here was Liam, temptation staring me right in the face and I wasn't sure I cared enough anymore to resist. He didn't answer. I took that as a yes. "Please," I said.

"Last night—"

"I don't care about last night." I shook my head. "It's been a really shitty day. I'm asking you, as a friend." Which was a lie because as of this moment, I didn't have any friends.

He reached into the top of his sock and extracted a recognizable, clear plastic baggie with two pale yellow pills inside.

My heart performed a stutter step.

I licked my lips and eyed the tablets, tantalized. "I'll pay you later, I promise."

He shook his head. He was no longer making eye contact with me. It was like I was a beggar on the street. "Forget it," he said. "I think you'd be doing yourself a favor if you tried to forget this whole day. Pretend it never happened and move on. Life's long, Cass." He flicked the plastic bag to me and it floated down into my lap. "You've got to stop dwelling on the past." Tears brimmed on my lower eyelids.

Forget. That was what I'd been doing. My unconscious mind was chewing holes in my memory, leaving missing pages, the plots of which I could only guess at. In this tiny plastic bag was happiness, however temporary.

"Thanks," I said. "I will." He wanted me to forget because he thought that what I didn't know couldn't hurt me, but maybe it could hurt someone else. Maybe it already had.

My nerves were worn to fraying, sparking wires. I had nothing to spare. No willpower. I thought I was a better person than this, but maybe, right now, I just wasn't.

The ambulance screeched to a halt in the parking lot. Red and white lights flashed. Doors slammed and urgent, hurried voices riddled the night. Seconds later men in white scrubs were hustling up the walkway, carrying a stretcher between them.

I waited for Liam to leave before emptying one of the pills into my hand and popping it in my mouth. Then, I stood up, brushed past the medics on their way into the gymnasium, and waited to forget.

SIXTEEN

Marcy

Corbin College lost the baseball game 4–2. This wasn't Brody's lucky night.

My first thought for tonight had been California—Jessup. I knew where he lived. Now that I knew where he lived I could find a way. But then there was the baseball connection with Jock Strap. And the moment I had seen the team schedule, the opportunity had seemed too good to pass up. So I didn't.

I had listened to the groan of the crowd from the bottom floor of the stadium, waited while the fans departed, deflated with mustard stains on their cheeks and foam fingers pointed down at the ground. I was there as the lights clicked off one by one, shutting down the top floors, the middle, and then the corridor where I stood lurking in an empty alcove.

A janitor pulled a squeaky mop bucket past, humming along to a tune that was playing in his headphones. The locker room exit swung open and I was there to watch. Suddenly interested again, I straightened. A gradual trickle of baseball players began to flow out, having changed out of their dirt-streaked uniforms into street clothes, mostly of the T-shirt and jean variety.

My fingers twitched at my sides. I felt the closeness the way one might sense subtle movement by the quiver of water in a still glass.

I first saw him in profile, walking out with his head down, punching the buttons on his phone. He was alone, though a few more players straggled out behind him.

"Brody!" I called softly from the shadows. He paused, looked around. "Pssst, Torres! Over here." Brody backed up a few steps, narrowed his eyes, and stared into the darkness where I imagined he could see my two eyes gleaming. I stepped forward just enough so that he could see the outline of a girl.

One of the other players stopped. "Brody?"

Seeing me, he furrowed his brow, but he looked over his shoulder and waved his friend on. "Nah, man, I'm good."

He slid his cap from his head and ran his hand through wet hair before replacing it. Brody Torres stared into my face. He had a dark beauty mark at the top of his right cheek, tan skin, and full lips that gave him the look of a Latin pop star. "Have we met?" he asked.

"Not formally," I said, taking another step forward. The stadium was beginning to have an emptied-out feel, like a hollowed carcass. "I'm Marcy. You weren't going to leave without giving me an autograph, were you?"

"You know we just lost in the last inning, right?" He sounded bored again. I was just a girl, after all.

Internally, my brain ticked off the reasons I hated Brody Torres. Cocky. Arrogant. Way too good-looking. Moody. I could shut my eyes and remember the way he baited me in only to drop me dead at Circus Master's feet like a cat with a bird in its mouth. The memory of his disinterested laughter played.

I pushed my lower lip out into a pout and leaned against the side of the alcove. "Oh, come on, it's for my little brother. He's a big baseball fan." I appraised Brody. Rounded muscles filled out the shoulders of his shirt. "Now I guess I can see why."

He scratched his temple. "Fine, fine. What do you want me to autograph?"

I shrugged. "I don't know. How about a ball?"

"The team's already closed up for the night."

I lowered my chin along with the tenor of my voice. "So unclose it."

He looked over his shoulder, but there was no one there except the sound of the janitor around the corner singing to music only he could hear. "A ball." He rubbed his fist into his eye. "Okay, sure. Just—" He started to turn. I could tell he wanted to get this over with, to go home and watch *SportsCenter*.

"Can I come?" I cut him off.

"Girls aren't allowed in the locker room," he said.

I took another step forward. I doubted Brody was the only one that could act as bait. "What's the required amount of time to pout in baseball anyway?" I asked.

"I'm not—" Half a smile showed up in the shadows under the brim of his cap.

"Now that's a better look on you," I said.

"You think so, huh?" His voice was gravelly. I had his interest.

We listened to the wet *swish-swish* of the mop and the off-key notes of the janitor.

"I've always wanted a tour of a locker room," I said.

Brody's skin was dewy from a fresh shower. He made a throaty noise somewhere between a scoff and a snort. "Why's that?"

I dropped the decibel of my voice. "We're all allowed our little fantasies, aren't we?"

He wasn't moving to leave anymore. "You go here?"

"Transfer student."

"Oh, I'd have thought I would have recognized someone like you."

I lightly touched his arm. *Gentle, easy does it.* "I would have thought so, too."

"I suppose I could show you around real quick," he hedged. "If you really want." He spun his hat backward and the shadows cleared from his eyes.

This time my grin was genuine. "Sign me up."

He looked both ways down the corridors. "Don't tell anyone I did this, okay?" But he said this with a light chuckle. Like he was used to doing things he wasn't supposed to do. A hint of sweat and grass stains still lingered underneath his freshly showered scent.

"Not a soul," I promised.

He fished a key card out of his wallet. My heart pounded, mouth salivated. I followed him in. He flipped on a set of lights. A big, square room materialized lined with navy blue lockers. Damp towels were slung over benches. There was a hamper for dirty uniforms. Cleats tied by the laces hung off a few of the open metal doors.

"Not quite as exciting as you pictured, is it?" he said.

I walked thoughtfully around the perimeter, taking my time. I let myself relish the space like it was sacred. Because this is where it would happen, where I'd earn my second tally mark. *So close*, I thought.

"It's running low on shirtless men. That's for sure."

Brody's beauty mark disappeared into a dimple when he smiled. "Shirtless men were a key part of your fantasy?"

"Among other things." I stopped to study a poster tacked to the wall that had been signed by Derek Jeter.

"Hang on. Let me see if I can rustle up a jersey or at least a T-shirt." He crossed the room to a stack of folded clothes. "What size is he? A small?"

"Yeah, sure," I replied absentmindedly. I pressed my hand into the pocket of my zip-up hoodie next to the knife that waited there. But a bag of equipment strewn on the floor caught my eye.

"Hey, cool," I said, pulling out a bat from the mesh carrier. "Is this what you use?" I flipped the metal bat around in my hands and tested the weight. I tapped it against the floor.

He looked over his shoulder. "Not much of a softball player, huh?"

"What, am I gripping it wrong?"

He set down the pile of clothes and came around to wrap his arms on either side of me. Then, he helped me to adjust my grip. "Like this," he said.

"That feels good." And I knew it was left up to interpretation whether I meant the new grip or the feel of his chest pressed up against my spine. I twisted my hands and tightened my hold. "Mind if I take a couple swings?"

"Swing away."

He was standing in front of me. Instead of turning, I stepped into him and took a pretend swing, halting the bat halfway to his kneecaps. He flinched and held out his hands, instinctively backing up.

"Whoa." His eyes widened.

"Just kidding," I said, and winked. He relaxed. "I got you, didn't I? You thought I was going to hit you in the knees."

He gave a chuckle. Now he was the one that wasn't sure he was in on the joke. "Maybe that's it for batting practice."

I didn't lower the bat. I took a step closer. "But I was just warming up." Then another step closer.

Blood rushed to his cheeks, turning them red. "Are you crazy?" he said.

And another step. I still had yet to lower the bat. It rested on my shoulder. "How's my grip now?" I asked. He glanced down, and in that split second, I pulled my elbows back and took a hard swing at his head.

The bones above his ears offered more resistance than I'd have thought, and the brains beneath his skull dulled the satisfying firecracker snap I'd been looking forward to. I tried again.

Brody stumbled sideways, clutching his temple. He made a guttural noise but no words. He didn't even look at me. I swung and this time the bat crunched through his cheekbone and it sounded like a rotisserie chicken leg being snapped from the carcass.

I felt myself grinning like a madwoman, almost cackling as I went in for another swing.

Blood spotted his shirt, dripped down his skin, covered up the beauty mark. The whites of his eyes spun like Chinese marbles in the sockets.

My heart sang with revenge as I watched him come undone. *Seek and hide, seek and hide, count the nights until they've died. . . .*

On the fourth blow he fell to his knees. Pain rained down on him until he could feel no more and his body lay still. Red crept out from his figure like a halo. It was like I'd made a piece of artwork in reverse.

I stood over him and dropped the bat, now splattered with blood and brains. It made a hollow *ker-thunk* as it teeter-tottered to the ground. The broken, crumpled silhouette had twisted into a sickening fetal position.

As I watched him lying there, I swiped a dash of blood from my nose and touched it to my tongue. I smiled down at him, even though it kind of was a shame, because he'd had such a pretty face.

SEVENTEEN

Cassidy

The next day, I slept past noon and wallowed in my bed, dozing off and on for several more hours. Mom brought me chili and left it at the foot of my bed like I had a head cold. But I wasn't hungry, instead waking up to a stomach full of regret.

The effects of the Sunshine had waned over the course of the morning, now leaving me feeling like I'd fallen hard into a mucky pit of despair and making me wish that I didn't still have another one of the tiny yellow pills stored underneath the lid of my music box. A cruel temptation, it seemed, only left there to mock me and test my self-control before I'd even had time for coffee.

When I felt I was on the verge of developing bedsores, I hauled myself out from under the covers.

The sound of Ava's leg snapping in half replayed in my mind, the memory of it getting louder and louder, sounding more and more like a gunshot. I might as well be dead.

I glanced around the room, looking for items that might be out of place, signs that pointed to what I'd done last night and where I'd been. But it was almost creepy how normal everything appeared. Like out of a catalogue.

I wandered to the bathroom to relieve myself, where I found a pile of black clothes, wringing-wet and lying on top of the bathtub drain as if they'd been soaked. I lifted them out and when I did, they dripped red water onto the white porcelain. A ring of pink stained the area surrounding the drain.

My insides clenched. I rushed to the toilet and emptied a couple tablespoons of stomach acid into the bowl.

This time there were no images that came unburied like they had with Dr. Crispin. I half contemplated making a return visit to him, but I didn't have the nerve. Then I considered checking the backyard for . . . well, for something, but I felt my guts come unglued at the mere thought.

Eventually, I splashed water on my face at the sink. In the mirror was the same face that I'd been used to seeing for the last seventeen years, except I couldn't help but think that something was different. There was a new hardness to my features. My pupils were pinpoints in my dark brown eyes. My eyebrows were arched at a steeper angle. Lips thinner and tauter. This all seemed impossible. But there was a sort of double vision, like someone had traced me and the lines on the two layers of paper didn't quite match up.

The second game of the play-offs would be starting soon. I didn't even know whether we'd won or lost last night. We'd be short a flyer at least.

My phone started buzzing from on top of my nightstand. Three short staccato bursts. I steeled myself for a giant Paisley I-told-you-so, but when I lifted my cell, there was a text message from a number I didn't recognize. I slid my thumb across the screen.

Thought you should see this, it read.

My forehead wrinkled. I scrolled down to a picture and sucked in a hard breath when I saw that the photograph was of Honor posing before the mirror in my room dressed only in my lingerie. She used her inner arms to squish together her barely-there cleavage and she held a kissy-face for the camera.

A deafening roar started in my ears. My fingers pounded the letters on my cell. **Who sent this?**

The response was instant and painful. **Everyone.**

My heart throbbed like someone had smacked it with a hammer. *Since when?* I scrolled through a number of missed messages and checked one from Paisley, marked with a simple "FYI" and the photographs.

Who sent it first? I asked, returning to the nameless phone number.

That was my little sister in that photograph. *That* was all that mattered.

An ellipsis dotted the text box. **Teddy Marks.**

Sophomore. Basketball player. Teddy Marks. I rolled the name over in my mind. So that had been the boy my sister had a crush on, the one she was thinking about when she stood in front of my mirror and posed like she was thirty instead of fifteen. I would ask how she could be so dumb, but I knew it wasn't that hard. After all, I'd suffered my own brand of stupidity. Besides, it wasn't her fault that she'd wanted the wrong person to love her. Honor's taste in boys probably didn't fall far from the tree.

I went out into the hallway and knocked on her door furiously. No answer. I knocked again. When there was still no answer, I pushed it open. It was empty. There was a deep throb in my joints as I saw the pink satin blanket she'd slept with since she was a kid peeking out from underneath her pillow.

I felt like two people living in one body. I wanted to rage and scream and cry and hide underneath my desk all at once. It hadn't been my sister that night in Dearborn but here she was in our hometown of Hollow Pines and she, too, would be an object for their consumption. And somebody had to pay.

I put on the first clothes I could find and threw my hair into a messy knot on top of my head. The team should be arriving any minute to start warm-ups. I was shaky on the drive over. I kept losing my focus and nearly missing a stop sign or a red light.

My heart beat hard against my ribs. As I was getting out, I noticed a ticket stub in the center cup holder. I pulled it out and read the event details. It was for a baseball game. A baseball game that happened last night.

Of all the things that may or may not have happened in the wee hours of the night, this seemed like the most innocent. I tucked the ticket into the pocket of the driver's side door.

My chest was already an emotional wasteland and the reminder of yet another missing memory hardly registered. It was like the bruise the hypnotist explained to me, the source of which would never be remembered. It wasn't important enough. Not right now anyway because the only thing that mattered right now was Honor, and the world and everyone in it could strip away everything I had, but they couldn't take away the fact that she was my little sister.

As I walked toward the gym of Hollow Pines High, I felt the

universe slow down around me. My lungs tightened. I had to force my feet across the parking lot to the double doors where I'd just been the cause of a disaster of unnatural proportions. There was a flyer pinned to the doors that warned of a new county curfew from the Department of Health and Safety. I barely paid attention. The county had done the same thing last year and, as far as I'd been able to tell, it hadn't kept anyone safe. Maybe there wasn't even such a thing as safety. After all, nobody had protected me.

The moments ticked by and I could hear only my breath. Then I was inside the gym where the scoreboard was still blank, the bleachers had yet to fill. Liam glanced over at me, did a short double take. He was still dressed in his warm-up sweat suit as was most of the rest of the team.

Paisley's face was unreadable the moment that she saw me. She'd dashed sparkles on her cheeks and fastened a ribbon to her hair. She nudged Erica and Molly. They both turned. A look of disappointment and sadness flooded out the friendship we'd shared and a gulf opened up between us.

Paisley separated from the group. I wasn't even interested in her. My eyes searched for Teddy Marks, a do-nothing boy from the sophomore class that I knew only by his mop of black hair, olive skin, and giraffe-like stature.

"I can't believe you showed up." Paisley arrived like a bucket of ice water.

"Get over yourself," I said, trying to move past her.

"No way." She put her hand to my chest to stop me. "We need to talk."

"Don't worry. I'm resigning." She stared at me as if she didn't believe me.

"As captain?"

I rolled my eyes. It was the last lame thing I had in my repertoire from my numbered days as an Oilerette. "From the squad," I said.

"But—then what are you even doing here?"

Deep in the pit of my stomach I knew that this wasn't all her fault. I hadn't told her about the night in Dearborn. I'd been the one to clam up, shut down, scared that no one would believe Cassidy the good-time party girl. But maybe it shouldn't have been up to me. Maybe I should have at least given Paisley the chance.

But there were things in life I'd never know, I was coming to realize. What might have been if Paisley was more of a real friend and less of a partner in popularity was one of them.

She followed the path of my gaze to where it had landed on Teddy Marks, who was emerging from the locker room, pulling a sweatshirt over his head. My palms instantly went slick with sweat. I lost all feeling in my legs. I was worried that my throat would close up.

"Cass . . ." Paisley started. "He's not worth it."

But I was already walking toward him. The closer I got to him, the shorter I felt. When he saw me coming toward him, he glanced away. Just like that. A quick once-over and then he turned his attention from me.

"Hey." I stopped him as he was picking up a basketball from the rack. My voice squeaked. I didn't sound like a badass older sister at all. "What—what—" I stuttered. I didn't want to stutter. "What did you think you were doing?"

He smirked and my cheeks went flaming hot. "What are you talking about?"

I swallowed hard. When I blinked I saw the mean ringleader with the vampire-toothed smile leering at me and the boy with the long hair telling me to relax. *No.* I pulled myself back to Teddy Marks, who was just a stupid sophomore, I had to remind myself. "You know what I'm talking about." Whiny, that was how I sounded when I meant to sound tough. "The pictures of my sister."

He shrugged. "She never told me not to send them to anyone. Relax. It's not a big deal."

At this my throat closed up entirely. I tried more than once to speak. It took a monumental effort to unclog it. "Not a big deal? Not a big deal to who?"

He twirled the basketball on his finger. "Honor's fine. Don't get all crazy again, Cassidy." And then Teddy Marks took his mop of black hair and he jogged up to the net for a layup. He made it and never looked back.

I stood alone on the far side of the gym, away from my former squad, away from Liam, away from everyone. Blood roared. My head throbbed. Fingers tingled. Then, all of a sudden, black spots started to crop up on the edges of my vision until I wasn't sure if I could stand up straight.

Then they were gone. I could see, and a force beyond my understanding or control seemed to drive my legs to action. I left the gymnasium behind without another word. The hallways lay dormant. I walked quickly through them until I found the spot I was looking for—the janitor's closet. I opened the door. A cloud of dust swirled in the air around me. I swatted it away and closed myself inside.

Using my cell phone as a flashlight, I searched the shelves. Lysol. Paper towels. Sponges. Windex. Ammonia. I ran my finger across the labels. My eyes continued to scan the remainder of the shelves' contents while my finger stayed put. Bleach. Another promising contender. And lastly, rat poison.

I wavered between the bleach and the poison. Turning both over to read the labels, I studied the horrors of their digestion. Stomach pains, vomiting, skin rash, burning sensation, blurred vision. Then, I replaced the carton of bleach on the shelf and stowed the small can of d-CON rat poison in my jacket pocket.

When I looked down, I was surprised to see that my hands weren't shaking. I poked my head out of the janitor's closet and made sure no one was watching.

I waited outside the gymnasium until I heard the telltale signs of the game beginning. There were cheers from the crowd as the teams were announced. The Oilerettes did an opening number without me and without Ava and Ashley. At the concession stand, I purchased a bottle of water then excused myself to the restroom.

I kept expecting the anger to subside, but as I took out the container of d-CON, it remained there, bubbling just below the surface. I shook a few sprinkles of the rat poison into the bottom of the bottle—just enough to make him sick, not kill him, I reasoned. Then, I swished it around to mix.

When I was finished, I entered the gymnasium again at last, taking stock of where the team sat in a row on the benches. I hovered on the sidelines, waiting for my conscience to set in, but my conscience, it seemed, had taken a vacation day. Or maybe it was just as fed up as I was with "boys being boys." Especially when it involved my little sister, Honor, who still slept with her childhood blanket and watched kitten videos on YouTube.

My eyes narrowed into slits as I homed in on the back of Teddy

Marks's head. He was hunched over on the bench with a towel around his neck.

I had to cut close to the dancing Oilerettes to get to the bench. I walked down the slender aisle between the first row of fans on the bleachers and the bench. When I got close, I leaned in to speak softly into Teddy's ear. "Mess with my sister again, and I will claw your eyes out."

His chin jerked in my direction. He swatted me away. In one swift motion, I replaced the water bottle that had been sitting next to him on the bench with my own.

"Hey!" he barked.

"Relax." I backed away. "It's not a big deal."

— — —

I FOUND HONOR an hour later sitting on our back porch, picking blades of grass. Her hair was plaited down her back. Snot slithered down the tip of her nose. I closed the back door gently behind me. We weren't more than a couple stones' throws from a boy whom I'd apparently murdered in cold blood.

But Honor could never know that. I still couldn't believe it myself.

"You're going to yell at me," she said, without looking up.

I stood behind her, wishing I could wrap her in my arms and hold her there. I could have sworn I'd deleted the photographs when I'd caught her in my bedroom, but I should have thought to check the sent messages. Maybe then I could have gotten to Teddy before it was too late.

"I'm not," I said. "I promise."

I walked around to her other side. My shoes pressed into the space of lawn from which she was picking idly. Her cheeks were streaked with old and new tears; the skin around her eyes was raw and thin as an onion peel. I felt so much older than the two and a half years between us.

"You'll see, it's all going to be fine," I said. "I'm going to help you."

She sniffled, then looked up at me through watery hazel eyes. "How?" she asked with a hint of defiance. "You're nobody now."

EIGHTEEN

Marcy

Y ou came back for her?" Wren stopped sweeping the broom back and forth across the black-and-white floors of the tattoo parlor. Her healthy bosom heaped over the top of her sweetheart neckline, rippling underneath the storied mural inked onto her skin.

I let the door close behind me. My insides thrummed like I'd been trapped for days and was just now plotting my escape from cabin fever. "Came back for who?"

Wren's burgundy lips were in stark contrast to the whites of her teeth. "Her. Keres." She nodded at the illustrations pinned to the wall next to me. "Isn't that the one you had your eye on last time?"

My focus was immediately drawn to the lithe faerie with her

tattered wings, curved blade, and trail of dripping blood. "How did she get her name?" I asked.

Wren resumed sweeping. "Keres was the name for the daughters of Nyx. Legend has it, they were female death spirits and sisters of the Fates. That one's my favorite. The black Ker, which meant Violent Death."

I lingered over the beautiful portrait a moment longer. "I haven't earned her yet," I said. "So just the same for now."

"Another line then?" She shook her head. "What is it with you? It's hard not to take line drawing as an affront to my artistic abilities."

I stepped forward and took a seat on the same black leather chair that I'd occupied on the previous visit. "It's not intended that way. I'm saving her. For a special occasion."

Wren shrugged and leaned the broom in the corner. "Aren't you a little young to be out tonight?" she said, rolling her stool and equipment alongside.

"What do you mean?"

"I'm hardly a stickler about the rules, but you're missing curfew." My face must have read blank because she continued. "The county's on lockdown again. Don't you watch the news?"

"No," I answered honestly.

The mosquito buzz of the needle switched on and she dipped the sharp end into the pot of black ink. "A boy's gone missing again. And another one's been found dead. This time they're college boys, but I don't think that makes it any better." I clenched my fist just before the needle broke skin. "This place has seen more than its fair share of death, don't you think?"

"I don't know." I watched the ink bubble over my flesh. "Who gets to decide what's fair?"

She paused. Her green eyes lifted and met mine. The door to the parlor opened and we both instinctively turned to see who was there.

Lena was brushing dark strands of hair from her forehead. "I got your message." She held up her phone. "You shouldn't even be out." Her glance passed between Wren and me and I could tell she wasn't saying all that she wanted to say. She crossed the room to us and stared down at my arm, the line on which Wren had begun retracing. She took a step back and gawked. When she spoke, her voice was a croak. "You're getting a second one," she said.

Wren wiped away the excess ink. I watched. As the darkness of the line deepened, so did my giddiness.

The surprise on his face. The sound of smashing skull. The spray of blood fanning out as though from a sprinkler system.

The line encompassed every bright point in my mind's eye. "Yes," I said, unable to fight the smile that was dancing at the edges of my mouth.

"There are cops everywhere." There was a quake in her tone that told me she wasn't worried the cops would haul us in for breaking curfew. She knew—or at least she guessed—the meaning of the second line and now the first.

"I tried to tell her," Wren said. She pulled out a wad of gauze and taped it over the fresh tattoo on my wrist.

The thrill of the needle's pain dissipated as the meaning of what Lena and Wren had been telling me crashed like a giant gong being beaten within five inches of my eardrum. I'd been stupid. So stupid. If cops were on the scene, if cops could be led to me, the end of my plan was in mortal danger, which in turn meant the remaining boys—California, Lucky Strike, and Circus Master—were not. I might never finish. There might never be justice. My throat squeezed like I was having an allergic reaction.

"How much?" I said, standing up too quickly so that the blood rushed from my head. Even I could hear the strangled note in my question.

Wren rolled her equipment back against the wall and stripped off her plastic gloves. "You can get me next time." Next time. The thought was comforting even if Wren had no idea what she was saying.

Lena let out a quiet whimper. I cut a glance at her and she shut up.

"Definitely," I said, rolling down the sleeve of my hoodie. Because there would most certainly be a next time. The problem had just gotten trickier to solve. Luckily, I was good at solving problems.

Lena followed me outside where the air was leaning on the side of warm and the first hints of cottonseeds could be caught in the breeze.

"I thought you wanted me to meet you." Lena stopped me with my fingers on the handle of the car door.

"I did. I didn't know about the curfew, though. Sorry about that. I shouldn't have asked you to come." I wasn't the type to apologize, so I wasn't sure why I was bothering now. All I knew was that Lena had chosen to be blind, but when Brody's body turned up, she couldn't pretend any longer. Not once she'd made the connection. I began to climb into the car.

She took another step forward. "You're not going home."

I hovered, partway in, partway out. "Yeah. So?"

She shook her bangs away. "Then why call me? Or better yet, why leave now?" The thing was, Lena didn't seem angry or scared;

instead she seemed like a girl whose boyfriend was breaking up with her.

You know something now, Lena, I wanted to tell her. *You know something and I don't want to have to hurt you, but I will . . . if you get in the way.*

Lena had been useful. She'd been my eyes and ears during the day. She'd been part of my new ritual celebration at night.

When I looked at her, I saw the girl kneeling and crying on the asphalt and found a tiny cranny in my entire destructive being that wanted to save and protect her. But even more than that, I felt a sort of sisterhood with her and all the other girls on the videos. "I told you," I said. "I didn't know about the curfew."

"Wait," she said before I could close the door. "I know what you did. What you're doing now." White-hot fury passed over my face. *Don't threaten me. Don't back me into a corner like an animal.* Because despite the desire to protect her, despite the kinship, I couldn't quit.

"Oh?"

Lena glanced over her shoulder, toward the tattoo parlor behind us. She hugged her frail arms around her body. "You killed them. Both of them. The boys that hurt me . . ."

"It wasn't just you. There were others. Me for one." My lips curled over my teeth as I wrestled back the memory.

"I know you saved me. You're the only one who's ever done something like that for me. Everyone else would have thought I deserved it. But you stopped them. I'm not going to tell anyone. You can count on me."

I tried to read her face for any hints of insincerity, but couldn't find them.

"Get in," I said. "Before anyone sees us." She obeyed. We sat side by side, the radio turned to low. "Okay, then tell me what you know."

While I stared out the dust-streaked windshield, Lena filled me in on the news reports and the theory that a killer had come back to Hollow Pines County.

"I suppose that gives me a little less room to work with, then, now that people are paying attention."

"What are you going to do?"

I leaned back into the headrest and closed my eyes. "Work faster, I guess."

I listened to the sound of her swallow. "And how are you going to do that?"

I hummed as I thought. What I needed was to process in bulk. Like an assembly line. Or a fast-food restaurant. But processing in bulk meant they needed to be in bulk. Which meant—"You know anything about editing video?" I opened one eye to ask.

— — —

BOTH OF OUR faces were cloaked in the shadows of the school building, which completely hid the moon from view. I held Mick's camcorder tightly in my grip. "I don't know about this," I said. An uneasiness had settled in my belly at the thought of entering Cassidy's territory where I didn't feel at home as I normally did in the dark, abandoned places of the city.

Lena fiddled with a key ring and fitted it into the lock. "It's fine." She twisted it and wrenched the door open, propping it open for my entry with her elbow. "I'm here all the time."

I peered into the high school auditorium, lit only by the glow of a few sparsely placed battery-operated emergency lights.

Inside, velvet curtains hung on either side of an abandoned

stage. I kept my footsteps light. Rows of empty seat backs stretched upward on a steady incline. My teeth were set on edge. I peered up into the rafters where the sleeping spotlights hung, waiting. The school felt like *her*. Cassidy. It was as though I could feel her imprint now that I was inside, haunting me like a ghost.

Lena let the door fall shut behind her. Her eyes twinkled in the dark as if the stars had come inside with us.

My eyes began to adjust and I hopped up on the stage. I strode to the center and stared out at the imaginary audience, picturing what it'd be like to have a spotlight blinding me. "Look at you," I said with a note of pride and trying to ignore the invisible presence of something other. "Breaking and entering already."

The thought was attractive to me even in my discomfort, the idea that we were invading Cassidy's space, taking over another piece of her life, or at least we could try.

She crawled up on stage after me, crossing toward the back where the set pieces of a play loomed like forgotten dolls. The mural behind her depicted waves of grain and an old windmill. Lena gleefully kicked back into a wheelbarrow, crossed her legs, and propped herself up to look at me.

"It's, well, it's a little bit sexy," I admitted.

She laughed softly. "There has to be some perk to being a theater geek, I guess."

"What play's this for anyway?" I went over and lifted a sheet from a hanging clothesline. The laundry tag on it read *Pottery Barn*.

"*Oklahoma!*"

"*Oklahoma?*"

Lena quirked an eyebrow. "You're not saying it with the exclamation mark. I can tell."

Absently, I ran my finger over the fresh line tattooed into my wrist. The skin there still stung. "So you're an actress? Do you sing?" I asked, exploring the set pieces. A wood facade stood on its own. Out of it was cut a window with tattered curtains that looked like old tablecloths.

"Hardly." She crawled out of the wheelbarrow. "Lights and media specialist," she said. "Fancy name for someone whose face nobody wants to see on camera."

"I don't know about that." I grinned and flipped the viewer on the camcorder open and peered through the lens at her. Lena's figure had a yellowish night vision tint to it. I hit the red button at the top and a caption on-screen popped up to read, "record."

Lena ducked behind one of the hanging sheets and poked her head out. "What are you doing?" she squealed and disappeared under the prop. "Are you seriously recording this?"

"Say hello," I said, moving around to the front of the stage to get a better angle.

She stepped out. A compressed smile pinched her cheeks. "You're insane, you know that?" She cocked her head. "Hi there." She waved and then suppressed a round of giggles with her fist.

"Do something," I commanded. If we were going to be here, I wanted Cassidy to somehow feel it like I felt her. I wanted to exorcise her.

"Do what?"

"I don't know. Something, anything."

Lena hesitated, then cleared her throat. "To be or not to be . . ."

"Lame." I lowered the lens. "Tell me something that nobody else knows."

She shifted her weight. "Nobody?" Her hands twisted together.

She stared off into the auditorium wings where a tangle of ropes and pulleys waited.

"I . . ." She started to say something and then appeared to change course. "Hate sleeping with socks on my feet. I can't go to bed."

I rolled my eyes. I lowered the camera to my chest so I could look at her dead on. "Something real," I said. "Something for just us." I raised the camera up again, nodded, and waited.

Lena looked off to the side wings of the stage and then, slowly, back at the camera. "Okay, then . . . ," she said. "I tried to kill myself last year." I zoomed the shot tight on her pale face until practically all I could see were her eyes. I heard her sigh. "I took a handful of my dad's sleeping pills and swallowed them all. Ten seconds later I realized what I was doing and forced myself to throw them all back up." She looked straight into the camera. "Not too impressive, I know."

"Why'd you do it then?"

"Because my mom committed suicide when I was little. I guess I just figured the same thing was probably in me, too. Bound to happen sooner or later."

I walked left, and shot her profile. "But it's not, then?" I asked, trying to imagine the Lena in front of me cold and lifeless with bluing lips.

"I guess I just don't know yet. Like if you hadn't found me that night. If those boys had . . . I don't know. Maybe then . . . Maybe I'm just, like, waiting for my first big tragedy before I fall completely apart."

I let the camera scan from her eyes to her mouth. She licked her lips nervously. She turned to me. Outside the viewfinder, I could see her roll her eyes. "Okay, not funny anymore. I feel like a moron.

What is this, reality TV?" She walked toward me with her hand outstretched until it blacked out the screen.

"Hey!" I protested.

She wrestled the camera away from me. "Now let's see who's camera shy. *Do* something," she said, mimicking me.

I held up my two middle fingers and walked back from her and then held them up to where the audience would sit, to the rows and rows of empty chairs. Somehow when I did this I felt like I was showing up Cassidy. A rush of power pulsed through me. I was here. I was invading her space. It was happening at last. I was taking over.

"Oh, that's nice. Real nice." Lena kept the camcorder aimed at me.

"I wasn't made to be nice."

"Hey, you called me lame."

Then at once, Lena and I both froze. She lowered the camera. The whites of her eyes ringed her pupils. "What was that?"

"Shhhh . . . keep your voice down." I listened. There was a metallic click followed by the whir of the air-conditioning starting up overhead.

My muscles unwound. "Just the unit clicking on." I felt the flush behind my cheeks, radiating like a sunburn. My breathing was heavy. "Let's go, though. We need to make sure we get this finished. We don't have much time."

She didn't stop to ask why. Whatever I was, whatever we were, Lena had accepted it. She snapped the camcorder shut. "It's this way." I imagined her heart pounding beneath the thin sweater she wore and wondered if the possibility of getting caught made her wary or made her want to chase the rush, too.

I glanced once more at the stage, then followed Lena up the dark center aisle. We reached a short flight of stairs, scaled them, and found ourselves in a small glass room with a bird's-eye view of the auditorium.

"This"—Lena plopped into a rolling chair and spun around—"is my domain." She brushed her hands over the controls. There were two large monitors in the corner and a panel of switches and sliding knobs.

I took the seat beside her. "Great. Now tell me, what can you do with this?" I pulled out the memory card and placed it on the soundboard.

Lena took it and inserted the memory card into the side of the computer. She punched a few buttons and the screens lit up. She tilted her chin to stare into the blue glow. One monitor populated with the rows of thumbnails that I'd first seen in Mick's room. This time, I told myself, I wouldn't flinch.

Lena double clicked and the beginning of the video loaded on the first monitor with an editing bar along the bottom ribbon. I watched her face as the video began to play on low volume. Her forehead wrinkled. She chewed the side of her thumb and scooted her chair closer to the screens. "What *is* this?" She clicked to another clip and sucked in a sharp breath. "Am I on here?"

"You're in good company," I said.

She followed up with more taps of the mouse and then she froze the screen and zoomed in on her own tear-streaked face. "What do you want me to do with . . . all of these?" she whispered. "Marcy, I'm not sure I like this."

"I want you to make them come to me. All of them. Tell a story. Make them understand that if they don't come, they all have something to lose and the whole world will know who they are. Oh, and I'm going to need to ship you a few things. That I order. Okay?"

I'd pulled closer to Lena as I spoke. She smelled sickly sweet, like overripe raspberries and Bath & Body Works lotion. I could hear the spit slide down her throat when she swallowed. "Okay." Her breath tickled my face. "Okay, I can do that."

She returned my gaze for another moment and then turned back to the computer and began a maddening flurry of keystrokes. She was possessed. It was like seeing a girl get sucked into a screen and disappear before my eyes. That was how entranced she was by the work. I watched her slice and cut reels of footage and rearrange them. She placed earbuds into her ears and replayed the bits until she made a decision about them. Occasionally, she'd twitch at what she was watching on the monitor, but mostly her face stayed neutral, businesslike.

I began pacing the room behind her. Late night hours slid into early morning. I leaned on the back of her chair and watched over her shoulder until at last she pulled the headphones from her ears and tilted her chin up to me. "It's finished, I think," she said.

I nodded and she pressed "play." At the end, we had the story of three boys. Jessup Franklin, junior, "devoted" boyfriend, son of wealthy Silicon Valley parents, the one I'd called California. Alex McClung—the skeleton-faced, cigarette-toting Lucky Strike— senior, son of a respected professor at the university. Then there was the worst of them all. The face of nightmares. The smile with a forked tongue. Tate Guffrey, senior, former backup quarterback, son of a Dearborn congressman. Circus Master.

The faces flickered across the screen, each one prominently featured, zoomed in on, examined, and interspersed with taunts and jeers and girls. I was noticing that both Lena and I were missing from the reels when the final shot panned. It was Lena on her knees.

"You included yourself," I said in a soft voice. "Why?" When there were so many girls to choose from, I wasn't sure I understood. She hadn't included me, after all.

"This is the part I can contribute to. This is the part of my story I get to direct. They have to watch. You'll make them."

She tapped the "escape" button and the video player disappeared.

Below us, the auditorium was empty, but as I stood behind Lena, I applauded. With the video clips, she'd created a movie. It was all I wanted and more. Now, they would have to come.

"It'll work?" she asked, resting her hands in her lap and staring down at them. I could feel more than see the blush in her cheeks.

"It's horrific," I said. "Which is actually perfect."

She stared up at me and I looked down at her, our eyes finding each other. And without asking, I bent down and kissed her.

NINETEEN

Cassidy

The second line had appeared sometime during the night because there was now another black mark drawn into the skin at my wrist, side by side with the first.

I knew what it meant by the wet clothes I'd found soaking in the bathtub yesterday and by the sick pit burning through the base of my stomach and chewing an ulcer there.

They were tally marks.

And if they were tally marks, I knew what the final tally would be.

Five.

My mom reached over to squeeze my hand during the chorus of "Holy, Holy, Holy." Sometime after the song was over—I didn't know how long—Dad tapped me on the shoulder to tell me the service was over. I realized then that I was just sitting there, staring at the cross over the pulpit with my mouth hung slightly open and my vision blurring into watercolor.

"What? Oh, sorry," I said, startled when I looked up to find that the well-dressed, polo-wearing family beside us was trying to leave, but my knees were blocking the way. My parents shared a look over my head. I hadn't caught a word of the sermon.

Honor and I hadn't spoken since yesterday. Her shoulders were slumped and she stared at the ground, ignoring me with a mix of icy defiance and indifference. Not having the energy to make inroads with her, I trailed them up the aisle and out of the sanctuary as the organ played a recessional that sounded unusually melancholy to my ears today. I smoothed the wrinkles on my navy blue dress. Usually I would rush off to try to find Paisley or Ava so that we could quickly rehash what had happened that weekend and catch up on any gossip we'd missed out on before. But there was too much distance between Paisley and me, most of it put there by her, but I had to take credit for widening the gulf until there was no swimming back across it. And Ava would still be home nursing a leg that I'd helped break. She was probably BeDazzling her cast, I thought, and felt an unwelcome and bittersweet tug at my heartstrings.

Today, I just waited for the moment when my dad would start jingling the car keys and talking about traffic and I even vaguely hoped that there might be talk of waffles this Sunday given that there was no reason to care about my figure any longer.

Mom stopped the family in front of the table filled with store-bought Danishes and coffee dispensers. "Honor," she said. "Why don't you go find Meghan and thank her mom for helping with the Junior League bake sale the other day."

Honor, who clearly had no interest in looking me in the eye, didn't protest. Instead, she disappeared into the throng of churchgoers.

Mom smiled at me. She'd put her lipstick on crookedly this morning and the peaks were uneven. "Cassidy, honey, your dad and I thought that maybe it was time for you to talk to somebody. About your"—she lowered her voice—"well, about your depression. We've arranged for Pastor Long to meet with you."

My mind went blank. I still felt as though I was just waking up. And now I was supposed to go *chat* with Pastor *Long*? "But . . . but I don't want to." This was a stupid way to object. Childish even. But it felt ridiculous that they thought a church pastor could fix my problems.

"Cassidy." Mom rubbed her hand between my shoulder blades the way she used to when I was sick. "It'll be fine."

"When?" I asked, blinking my eyes rapidly as though I was still adjusting to the light. Everything about the church felt vague and unfamiliar. Like it was a scene happening to someone else.

"Now," Dad said. The wrinkles around his eyes formed little starbursts. "He's waiting for you in the elder offices. You shouldn't keep him waiting, sport."

"But—"

"Cassidy." Dad didn't sigh, but he did look very tired. Almost as tired as I did, I bet. Was that the effect I was having on people? "He only wants to talk. Maybe you'll even feel better."

At this very moment, I felt terrible. Worse than I had in my entire life. And I only knew that I didn't want to make them suffer, too. It seemed that I could only accomplish small things now. And this was one of them.

I felt my parents' collective gaze on my back as I trudged up the red carpet stairs to the elder offices. Lately my tongue had begun to feel as though it was made of wet cement.

I walked down the hallway lined with office doors. I wasn't in a hurry. Since we were in church, after all, I didn't think it was too much to hope for a miracle that would get me out of a heart-to-heart with the head reverend at Hollow Pines Presbyterian.

The desire to get out of the talk continued to grow with each step until a voice began to materialize. *Duck into one*, something inside me urged. I glanced at the office doors next to me, the lights inside turned off, vacant. *Duck into one and skip this charade.* My pace slowed and I came to a stop. I looked at the door closest on my left, indecision brewing in me at the same time as temptation drew my hand like a magnet.

"Cassidy!"

I jumped at the sound of my own name. My eyelashes fluttered and it took a second for the man in robes to come into focus. Pastor Long waved at me from the end of the hall.

"I'm in this one down here," he said.

My cheeks flushed. "Right, sorry."

I dusted my palms off on my dress, lowered my head, and hurried the rest of the distance to the church's lead pastor. He ushered me into a small room where I took a seat on a yellow couch and pinned my knees together. Pastor Long pulled up a chair opposite me, crossed his legs one over the other, and leaned back.

"Tell me why you're here, Cassidy." Pastor Long was a man old enough to be my grandfather. He had long earlobes and grooves etched into his forehead so deeply they might have been irrigation ditches.

I twisted the hem of my skirt between my fingers and shrugged. Pastor Long waited. "What I mean is, why did your parents arrange this meeting?" Another long pause. "Do you think ... in your own words ..." He twirled his hand as if to say, *go on.*

I chewed the inside of my lip until the skin lifted and I could feel the salty sting underneath. I pressed my tongue into the small gouge. "I don't know," I said finally. "I told them everything was fine. I'm just tired. I'm not ... sleeping very well."

Pastor Long nodded and folded his hands in his lap. He'd always been a kind man. One time he'd even given Paisley and me bite-sized Butterfingers that he kept in his robe pockets when he caught us sneaking out of Sunday school. I'd, of course, given mine to Paisley, but I had associated the reverend with chocolate and peanut butter ever since and, as far as I was concerned, there were worse things to be reminded of by a person.

"Let's try another tactic. How's cheerleading going? What do you kids call yourselves, the Oilerettes?" His patience didn't waver.

I sighed. "I'm not on the squad anymore."

I watched for any flicker of surprise. A raise of the eyebrows. But instead, Pastor Long leaned forward and rested his elbows on his knees. His robes and pant legs hiked up so that I could see maroon socks with a pattern of bears marching across. "Cassidy," he said. "You don't have to talk to me if you don't want. I'm not here to make you." I shifted in my seat. "But there's one person you can and probably should talk to." Pastor Long lifted his eyes to the ceiling. "God. He sees everything, Cassidy." An uncomfortable wad of spit worked its way up my throat at the mention of "everything." "But he also forgives everything. Do you understand?"

His eyes were gray and comforting. What would Pastor Long say if he knew who I really was? What I'd really done? A thousand truths piled up on my chest and it felt like I was being buried alive. Every choice now twisted around me like a straitjacket. The drinking. The kissing. The flirting. The boys. Dearborn. Sunshine. Teddy Marks. And all the frightening blank spots in my memory too dark for me to see.

I tried to open my mouth, wondering if I did, what might come out, but my tongue stuck to the roof and the words stuck in my saliva like it was a fly trap. *Don't tell him.* The voice that had winnowed its way to the surface moments earlier now bubbled up again. My teeth ground into each other. My jaw twitched.

Even if someone would believe me about that night in Dearborn, that it had all happened and that I'd wanted none of it, the truth wouldn't set me free. It didn't take a mathematician to know that, if I confided in anyone about the night in Dearborn, it wouldn't take long for the cops to solve for *y*—and that *y* would be me.

"I promise, your problems may seem big now, but I've been working with kids your age for a long time and I can tell you that the problems of high school—the gossip, the boys, the cheerleading—they are never as cataclysmic as they seem." The pastor's office was hot and stuffy. I needed him to open a window before I suffocated. "Another year and you'll graduate, then— *poof*—all these problems will disappear."

Disappear. Poof. Gone. I was having trouble breathing.

He winked at me and leaned back again, probably confident that he had told another teenage girl exactly what she'd needed to hear.

And for the first time ever, I kind of hated Pastor Long. Because it never occurred to adults that we might be capable of having real problems, too.

THERE WERE NO waffles after church. My parents and I hardly spoke a word and Honor and I spoke none. I wanted desperately to make things better for Honor, but what could I say to fix things? I'd be repeating the same advice as Pastor Long and I couldn't bring myself to do that.

I kept staring at the two lines tattooed into my wrist, becoming more and more fearful that I might go to sleep and wake up to another one. The black marks felt like explosives, counting off seconds, hours, minutes of the time I had left. With every new one, I understood that another part of who I was would be lost forever.

Pastor Long had spoken about forgiveness. Aside from that, I'd been attending years' worth of church services that all talked about forgiveness. I didn't know if it was for me, but how could I possibly be forgiven if I sat around and did nothing?

My stomach churned at the thought, but I could think of only one thing to keep another line from materializing. If I could offer a warning, then maybe this nightmare would stop. Nothing worse would have to happen. I wasn't stupid enough to think that I could return to my old life. The thought of going back to the Oilerettes was laughable now. But I did still want a life, one outside of Hollow Pines.

Which was what had led me here, back to Dearborn. I'd left the moment our family had returned home from church.

Sunlight flooded the picturesque campus where I stared up at the brick buildings with concrete steps lined by scrolling iron handrails. On the greens, students lounged on blankets where they read and enjoyed the day off from classes. For a moment, I allowed my head to tilt back and I closed my eyes and imagined myself as a college freshman. A new state. New friends. New me. The setting looked straight out of a college recruitment brochure. It said: Nothing bad could ever happen here. . . .

Only I knew better.

When I opened my eyes, I quickly promised myself that wherever I ended up, it wouldn't be here in Dearborn. Ever since I'd crossed the city line into Dearborn, my insides had begun to slosh around in my belly like a bowlful of slugs. I hid my hands in my pockets so that I didn't have to watch how they trembled. I swore I'd never come back to this town, but here I was. As the saying went, *Never say never*, I supposed.

As I wandered the campus, I felt self-conscious and too young. How could I have ever thought I had any business being here at all? I checked the time on my phone. Eleven o'clock. The morning sun was a half step away from directly overhead. I followed a series of signs to the dining hall. Surely, at one point, at least one of the boys had to eat.

The dining hall had a triangular front made entirely of glass that reflected the sky. I took a seat on a bench at the top of a short flight of stairs, curled my heels up underneath me, and prepared to wait.

Reflexively, I turned over my wrist again and ran my fingers over the two lines tattooed. I knew it wasn't a coincidence. If that night hadn't been seared into my memory, I might not know how many would complete the set, but without having to stop to add up the faces, I could tell anyone with absolute certainty that the number was three more. The tattoos would end once a complete tally mark had been inked into my skin for eternity—four hash marks, plus one crossed over. It would end once my entire life had been ruined and then whose skin would it be, really? Would there be any Cassidy Hyde left over?

The numbers on my phone's digital clock read a quarter till noon. My tailbone was beginning to ache and I leaned back on my palms, watching the students that came and left through the doors of Broomwood Dining Hall.

Even though that night had been branded into me as physically as the lines of ink, I still nursed a needling worry that even if I found the boys, I wouldn't recognize them in the light of day. It turned out, I shouldn't have been. I heard before I saw. A clap of laughter sounded like a thunderbolt in my chest. I pulled the weight off my palms and twisted on the bench to see behind me. At three minutes after twelve, I laid eyes on him. The meanest of them all. He was nameless to me. The sight of his face felt like touching a spot of skin that had been burned. It stung and flared. The pain pulsed in time with my pounding heart. I lost my ability to breathe.

There he was. I sat frozen a safe distance away, watching his profile as he chained a bicycle to the rack. He chatted with another boy that I didn't recognize while everyone else faded into a blurry background. All I could see was him.

I remembered the feel of his hands around my wrists. The weight of his torso. The hotness of his breath. Slowly, I rose to my feet. But my knees went weak. My arms shot out to steady myself like a tightrope walker and I felt just as off balance as I forced my feet down the three shallow steps and nearer to him. His presence pressed me away like a repellent. My head was going fuzzy. One, two, three steps, I counted them out.

Screw him. The voice emerged nearly stopping me cold. *Leave him.* It was the same voice I'd felt in the elder offices. *Turn around. Run.*

My pace faltered. Something about the sound of the small but significant voice made me recognize it as someone's other than my own. I gritted my teeth, willing my mind not to listen.

My walk was stiff and robotic while at the same time tremors raced from my scalp clear through to my toes. I was close. Soon, I'd be close enough to reach out my hand and touch him. The conversation between the two boys faltered as they each noticed me.

"What do you want?" I shut my eyes against the sound of his voice. Knife wounds through my chest. Keep going.

"Are you all right? Are you sick?" The other boy's voice was an echo in my ears. I waved him off.

"I—I need to talk to you." It took every ounce of strength for me to open my eyes and look at the boy I recognized in my soul as my tormentor. *Circus Master*, the name came to me like a memory. Like the hiss of a snake. "You remember me," I said.

One corner of his mouth lifted and his chin snapped back. "Oh. That kind of talk." He snapped his bike lock into place and slung a backpack over one shoulder. He narrowed his eyes to a cocky squint. "Well, face doesn't ring a bell." He waved good-bye to the other boy and moved to pass me. "Excuse me."

"Wait—" I turned and trotted several steps after him. "I . . . I have to warn you. You must recog—"

He shook his head. "Look," he said, talking over his shoulder as he rounded the steps to the dining hall. "I'm sorry if we, like, talked at a party and I forgot to call or whatever. But you got the wrong idea. Trust me, I'm not really looking for anything right now."

My legs stopped working. My mouth turned into an *o*. He didn't recognize me. This boy had no idea who I was. To him, I was nothing. *It* was nothing. Another night. Another party. Another girl. The force of gravity seemed to double. Was it possible that the same night and the same set of events had been two completely different things for us? Was he not even the villain in his version of the story? Or did he just not care?

The distance between me and the back of his head increased and I couldn't get myself to close it. I felt as powerless as I had that night. And the snake voice wrapped around me. *Let him go. Leave. Run.* Lead flooded my veins and weighed down my ankles like I was sinking below the surface.

Tears stung my eyes. I watched him disappear into the dining hall behind the reflective glass that bounced back what I could already see and hid what was inside. I slid the back of my hand under my eyelids and wiped it on my jeans.

"Hey, hey, hold up a sec." I felt my shoulders raise up like I was ducking into a tortoiseshell. I jerked away when a hand softly touched my elbow. I glanced up at the boy from the bike rack. His sandy blond hair seemed to be made of down and it fluttered in the breeze. "Sorry about him. Tate can be kind of an asshole." *Tate.* "Okay, I don't know why I said kind of. Totally an asshole." Why was this guy talking to me? "We got paired together for an econ project. Otherwise, no affiliation." He swiped his hand through the air for emphasis. "Swear. Can I walk you to your dorm or something?"

The boy's eyes were green and mossy like the woods. There was a freckle on his left temple and matching dimples on both cheeks. There were no hard edges to his voice, no inside jokes lurking underneath the surface of his words waiting to come out and bite me.

But when I looked up at him, I could find nothing to say to him—to anyone—but no.

That night I got dressed in my pajamas. I washed my face, braided my hair, and slathered lotion on my hands and feet. Standing in front of my vanity mirror, I selected a lipstick from one of my many makeup bags. I removed the cap and twisted the base until the dark red hue was exposed. My hand hovered over the glass.

And then I wrote a message.

TWENTY

Marcy

came into consciousness to find words on a mirror. Pleading, pathetic words. Only their color—red—made them appear angry. Otherwise they were as weak as skim milk and watered-down coffee.

They read: *You have to stop this. You're going to destroy us both. Please!!*

I saw them and laughed. I didn't know where I went during the times when I wasn't *here*, only that I would eventually return.

Besides, my time was getting longer, I'd noticed, and this was good.

I hated Cassidy. She was spineless. A joke. She knew nothing but how to be a nice girl. That above all else was why I despised her.

When I spotted her feeble attempt to stop me I ran the side of my fist through it and smeared the words until the glass looked like it'd been covered in fresh blood.

I then chose my own color—pink. Maybe Cassidy would understand pink. It was a nice girl color, after all. And I wrote my own message for her to find, words written across the mirror.

A warning? No, more like a promise.

When I was finished, the violent pink read in all caps: HIDE AND SEEK, HIDE AND SEEK, IN THE DARK, THEY ALL WILL SHRIEK.

I stood back, studied the words, and smiled just for a moment before leaving. *Try to stop me, Cassidy. I dare you.*

— — —

I MADE ONE pit stop into the shed that sat on the side of the house. I rummaged through it until I found what I was looking for. A couple cans of spray paint. One orange. One white. I shook each and tested them on a workbench cluttered with toolboxes and spare fishing lures.

Once out front, the exhaust pipe coming from the Blue Beetle parked two houses over burped ghostly fumes into the night air. The metallic clang of the door rang out like a gunshot. "How long have you been waiting?" I asked as I climbed into the passenger seat.

Lena twisted the cap on an empty can of Dr Pepper and dropped it into the open hole. "Only thirty minutes," she said.

I nodded. "Not bad. Getting better." I checked the clock on the dash. It was only 9:40. A breeze dusted the trees that ringed the cul-de-sac, bending them sideways.

I drummed my fingers easily on the armrest. "Do you have them?"

"Backseat." Lena turned onto Main Street. "A couple packages arrived at my house, too. I had to get them from the porch before my dad found them."

"Perfect." The rest should be there by tomorrow. I twisted to retrieve the "invitations" that Lena had copied for each boy. On the backseat were three manila envelopes. I pulled them into my lap and slipped my hand into the top one. It was labeled *Jessup Franklin* and underneath Lena had neatly printed his address at Graves Hall. Inside there was a flash drive. I cradled it in the palm of my hand. "Where to first?" I asked.

"Sperry Street," she said.

"Alex and Tate?"

"Do we have to use their names?"

"Sorry. Thing One and Thing Two?"

She nodded.

The climate shifted as we drove across the city line from Hollow Pines into Dearborn. We drove the length of fraternity row, but didn't stop at any of the large colonial houses. For a Sunday night, the mood was dampened. We passed police cars parked at nearly every block. Where were they when I'd needed them or when Lena had? Or what about the dozen other girls?

Probably eating doughnuts.

I stared out the window at a policeman leaning against his cruiser, sipping from a mug of coffee.

"Safety first," Lena muttered.

As she drove, fraternity row gave way to the town center, which was sparser still. Students walked in twos or threes—none of them traveled alone. Fear glued them to one another like a pack of animals. One boy was dead. One boy was missing. I rubbed the lines tattooed on my wrist and marveled—just a bit—at the shock waves

I'd left rippling along the surface of Corbin College's campus. They were lucky I didn't burn this town to the ground.

Lena concentrated on her phone to navigate.

"You know you don't have to do this," I said. "Any of it."

She rested her phone in her lap. "I'm not. I'm not doing it, I mean. I'm just opening the doors, laying the groundwork. What you do with that is your business."

"But you know what will happen when I walk through them, Lena. And I *will* walk through them."

"I only know what they did and what you did for me," she said. "You're a good person, Marcy."

"Then you're a terrible judge of character."

We took a right at a stop sign onto Sperry Street. The houses here were mostly one story, made from yellowing brick. Bicycles were chained to posts. Trash cans overflowed with red cups. There was virtually no such thing as landscaping on this stretch. All dead giveaways that this was a street for off-campus housing. Music floated out from a few of the homes.

"It's this one on the left," she said. We rolled past a nondescript house. Closed shutters blocked out all signs of life inside.

"They're probably not home, right?" I said. "It's a Sunday night."

"But look at all the cars parked on the street." I did and she was right. Cars lined the avenues bumper to bumper. The county curfew was having its effect. "We could leave it on the doorstep," she suggested.

I watched the horizon grow in the side view mirror next to me. "No. We can't risk anyone else finding it. We have to make sure the message gets to them and only them. Park over there."

I pointed at the end of the street where a fire hydrant marked the corner. Lena edged around it and parked a safe distance away. She cut the lights and the cabin faded into darkness.

"Coming or going?" I asked through the blackness that divided us.

She took a deep breath. "I'm coming. No reason to quit now." I could think of plenty of reasons, but it wasn't my job to explain them to her. She followed me out into the night where laughter came from one of the backyards. I handed the two envelopes to Lena and clutched the bottles of spray paint under one arm, then walked decisively to the address on Sperry Street.

There, Lena and I stood side by side on the front lawn as I tried to guess what was waiting behind the brick. At least from here, there were no signs of life. "Let's check the other windows." I kept my voice low.

Our feet swished through the grass as we walked single file. The first window was dark but the blinds were up. "Bedroom," I whispered, peering in at the rumpled sheets I could just make out.

I moved toward the back of the house and located a bathroom— I could just make out the top of the showerhead—followed by what looked to be another bedroom. Lena kept glancing over her shoulder every minute. As we got closer to the backyard, I could hear voices drifting through the windows. Then I could smell cigarette smoke. At the very back of the house, I motioned for Lena to stay put. I flattened my back to the wall and peeped around the side. A shaft of light spilled from an open window onto the grass, spotlighting several cigarette butts littered on the ground. Thin fumes still spiraled into the air from one of them.

I stood frozen, listening to the din of male voices coming from inside the house. Slowly, carefully, I inched my heels closer. The rough brick at my back pulled on the fabric of my hoodie. Finally, I was perched beneath the sill with the light cascading over me so that it cast a long, precarious shadow on the lawn. I turned and raised up on my toes until my nose was even with the window ledge and I could look inside. I didn't even dare breathe for fear of drawing attention.

Four boys sat around a table off the kitchen, each with a fan of cards in hand. Blue, black, and red chips scattered across the center of the table. Beer glasses sweat beaded droplets onto the wood laminate. I dropped back down and skittered away from the light so that my shadow disappeared and blended into the shaded grass. I felt half predator and half prey crouched in enemy territory. Above me a chair shrieked across the floor. I bit my fist and tried to go as motionless as the dead. I counted out seconds in my head.

One . . . Two . . .

Seconds passed. Footsteps, then the chair screeched again. No one came to look out the window. I let out the breath I was holding. I tried to remind myself that it wasn't the window or the walls of the house separating me from them. It was one more night. That was all I had to wait.

Keeping my back hunched, I moved swiftly back to the safety of the house's side where Lena waited, eyes wide and glowing like a feline's. I wrapped my fingers around her wrist and pulled her farther away from the open kitchen window.

"They're playing poker," I said. "Circus Master and Lucky Strike—I mean Tate and Alex, plus two other boys."

"Jessup?" she asked. I shook my head. She chewed a hangnail and glanced again over her shoulder. "Should we come back tomorrow then?"

I shook my head again. "No. We can do it now."

"But—" Her protest was a hiss in the dark.

I was already skirting the side of the house, looking for my way in. I tried nudging open the first window. It stuck in place. Moving briskly, I shuffled over to the second bedroom window. Locked, too. I grunted in frustration as I tried to pry the two ends apart. Nothing. I considered breaking the glass, but couldn't trust that the boys inside wouldn't hear. In fact, I couldn't even trust that those four boys were the only ones in the house.

I rounded back to the bathroom window. The opening was a little higher than the rest—presumably for privacy. I stood on my tiptoes and pushed the glass. It lifted with a rusty shudder.

I could smell Lena's fruity lotion near me. "Give me a hand up?" I asked, staring up into the fluorescent light.

She hesitated. "I'm not a cheerleader like—" She stopped herself. "Okay, sure, I can try." She laced her fingers together. I put my foot in the makeshift hold and used my grip on the sill to hoist my chest through the open window. From there, I shimmied through the gaping mouth and used the side of a bathtub to catch myself from face planting into the moldy tile. I popped my face over the ledge and stared out at Lena. Her lines were murky in the dark of night. *One second*, I mouthed.

The bathroom was a small, narrow room with a stained shower curtain and a puddled floor. My ears strained for any signs of life nearby, but all I could make out was the distant clink of poker chips and voices coming from the kitchen.

I poked my head out from the bathroom and glanced down either side of the hall before choosing left. The bottom of my boots stuck slightly to the floor and I wondered about the last time anyone had bothered cleaning it. At the first bedroom I pressed my ear to the door. When I heard nothing coming from the other side, I pushed it open. The hinges made a long groan that sent goose bumps prickling up the knobs of my spine. I pulled the door closed behind me and flicked the lock.

Crossing the room, I unlatched the window and slid it open. "Lena?" I stuck my head out.

Her voice was close and quiet, sticking near to the brick wall of the house. "Here."

I reached out a hand. Her milky skin stood out in the darkness. Her skin pressed against mine and I helped her into the room. Our shoulders touched as we took in our surroundings.

A twin bed, rumpled pillow shoved between the wall and mattress. Stuffed dresser. Fancy speakers. Desk. Bookshelves, the bottom rows of which were stacked with *Maxim* magazines. I thumbed through some of the papers on the desk, searching for a name. Lena found it first.

"Wallet," she called softly from her spot near the dresser. I came to stand next to her. She slid out a license. My instinctive response was a grimace when I saw the picture of Alex. The one that I called Lucky Strike.

Sure enough a carton of cigarettes was stashed on his nightstand.

Like a surgical assistant, she handed me the envelope with the flash drive and Alex's name on it. I balanced the featherweight of it between my hands. It didn't feel like enough. Nothing felt like enough.

Send a message. Get him to the location. And then I could make good on everything. One more night.

The smell of his cigarette breath hot on my neck as he held me in place lingered in my memory. He enjoyed my pain and I'll enjoy his. Fair was fair. I shook the can of spray paint and, above his bed, I sprayed angry orange letters: *Peekaboo. I see you.* The envelope dropped on his pillow, complete with the flash drive inside and the scratchy message I'd scrawled that told him to meet me at midnight sharp tomorrow. Or else.

I turned to Lena, who was staring at the violent letters scrawled and dripping down the wall. Her mouth hung open. "I can't . . . believe . . . you did that," she said just before her mouth stretched into a bemused grin. "Crazy. Totally off the wall, crazy."

She was right, of course. I felt beautifully crazy. Like I was balancing on a ledge and any second I might tip over into complete and utter insanity. "Your turn." I went for the door.

"We're going out *there*?"

I raised my eyebrows. "Scared?"

She rolled her eyes and snatched the spray can from my hand. "Give me that."

I held out my palm and motioned for her to wait. I cracked the door and listened. A great guffaw of laughter sprang out from the other end of the house. Lena jerked to attention beside me. I waited another beat. Then two before gesturing for her to follow. Together, we crept through the narrow hallway, past the bathroom, and all the way to the next bedroom door. Again, I listened from the other side, and again, when I heard nothing, I entered and turned the lock, shutting both Lena and me inside.

I wondered how they'd feel tonight when they came in and found that someone had been inside their home. Would they feel violated? Would they think they had a right to feel that way?

Probably.

This room was tidy. A clean plaid comforter covered a double bed at the center. A series of Tarantino posters were pinned neatly to one wall—*Pulp Fiction, Django, Kill Bill.*

I picked up a framed picture and studied the faces in the photograph of a family on a girl's graduation day. A sister perhaps? I set it down, unable to tell whether one of the boys in the picture was Circus Master. The meanest of them all. I opened a file cabinet and rifled through papers until I found a term paper. "The Effect of the Kemp-Kasten Amendment in Modern-Day Mongolia" by Tate Guffrey. My insides gurgled like molten lava.

I showed the name on the paper to Lena. "You're up."

She stared at the can of paint, took a step forward, and then looked back at me. I waited, not sure what she'd do. But she turned back and she aimed and fired. Instead of at the wall, Lena pointed the can at the made bed and scrawled a message identical to the one I'd left for Alex. She spun, one hand clapped over her mouth, her eyes all lit up. "I did it," she half squealed before catching herself and dropping the volume of her voice. "Oh my god, I can't believe I did that."

"Welcome to the dark side," I said.

But we had no time to celebrate because from somewhere on the other side of the door came a voice.

"Jesus Christ." Lena's sparkling eyes went cartoon-round.

I pressed a finger to my lips and listened. The voice was talking. I couldn't make out words. I couldn't tell if it was getting closer or farther or neither. Then a toilet flushed. My posture softened. A few short moments passed with the sound of running water.

"Marcy!" Lena's voice was strained.

Footsteps. A laugh. Words. I glanced around the room. Trapped. The doorknob jiggled.

"Hey, the door's stuck," said the voice. Tate. The poker game must be over. It jiggled again. I watched it like a grenade without the pin. "I think it's locked." He pushed against it and I watched as the thin wood bowed. "What the hell? Who locked this?"

"We've got to go." I dropped the envelope with the flash drive onto his pillow. Lena stood paralyzed, staring at the door. "Now," I said.

I struggled with the latches on the window. I got the first one unhooked. I thrust my weight behind the second, which seemed as if it must not have been opened for ages. Finally, it budged. My hand hit the glass with a loud clap.

"Is someone in there?" A fist pounded. "Screw you, guys. Who's in there? Is this some kind of prank?"

Lena's joints had come unlocked as soon as the window did and she helped me pry it open.

"I'm coming around," Tate yelled. "Don't be bastards."

"Go, go, go." I practically pushed Lena out the window. She landed softly on the grass below. I jumped down next to her. I took a final glance back. Together, we sprinted around the side of the house, disappearing into the next-door neighbor's lawn just as I heard the front door open and shouting spill out into the night.

I followed Lena, my arms flailing and hoodie fanning out from behind me like a cape. She twisted the key and jumped into the driver's side. I bobbed on my toes while I waited for her to pop the door on the passenger's side. I climbed in and let out a whoop of triumph.

Lena fumbled with the ignition and it sprang to life with a roar.

Her forehead dropped to the steering wheel. Her breathing heavy. Her back rose and fell. I watched the ridges of her back arch, my own chest heaving.

"Two . . . down . . . ," Lena wheezed. She turned her head and looked at me across the dark cabin.

I let my own head loll to the side. Lena's bangs swept sideways and I wondered if I was about to kiss her again.

"One to go," I said.

TWENTY-ONE

Cassidy

There was a soft knock on my bedroom door. "Cassidy?" came Honor's voice. This morning's sun was already blasting through my window. I closed my eyes and buried my head into the pillow. It was a school holiday, although even as I thought it, I realized that I probably wouldn't go to school, holiday or not.

A few seconds later, I listened to muffled footsteps on the carpet and then the covers were pulled back just enough for Honor to slide in. I felt the warmth of her body next to mine. She shuffled closer like she used to do when she was a kid.

"Are you sick?" she asked with concern. "You're soaked."

I felt the length of my sticky body to where my tank top clung to my ribs like Saran Wrap. Moisture glued strands of hair to my forehead. I rolled over to stare up at the ceiling, feeling weak and twisted but impossibly heavy all at once.

"I don't know," I said. "Maybe."

She turned into me, her freckled face inches from my cheek. She took a deep breath. "I'm sorry, Cassidy. About what I did, what I said, all of it. I was an idiot."

I sighed. "No, you weren't. You were just . . . I don't know . . . young."

She tilted her head and rested it on my shoulder. "Thanks," she said. And that was all she had to say because we were sisters and I would love her from now until eternity no matter what she did or who she became. I wanted to be someone that Honor could be proud to call her older sister, the way she used to be, but it seemed that every single thing that I tried failed. I was losing hope and options.

The only sliver of optimism available to me was the fact that another line had not appeared on my wrist. There were still only two. That was something.

"Do you want to know something crazy?" she asked.

I doubted anything that she could tell me would top any of the crazy confessions I could make, but "sure," I told her.

"My friend Meghan said that Teddy Marks was rushed to the hospital yesterday." If I wasn't mistaken, there was a waver of something that sounded suspiciously like a giggle in her voice.

"Yeah?" I tried to keep my voice neutral, but my mind raced. The pictures. The poison. These memories, unlike the ones that had been played back to me, felt more like my own. Bright and real. And yet what had come over me? Had I really poisoned a sophomore?

"People are saying I cast a voodoo curse on him. I know they're kind of kidding, but can you believe that? *Me?* It's funny. Sort of.

I mean, don't you think?" She reached for my clammy hand, laced her fingers between mine, and squeezed.

"Probably not to Teddy," I said.

Honor let out a soft one-note laugh. "No kidding."

I lifted my chin. "Is he going to be okay?"

She wriggled free of me. She sat up and flipped her hair back behind her shoulders. "Yeah, he's fine. Just some abdominal cramping, vomiting, you know that kind of thing. Meghan said he's supposed to come home from the hospital later today."

I exhaled a long breath of relief. That was good news. I was lucky. Teddy was fine. Maybe it hadn't been such a bad thing that I'd done then after all. My sister saved some face. Teddy believed he'd gotten a karmic smackdown. He didn't have to know that karma actually came in the form of a junior at his high school.

It wasn't so bad. At least not this part.

I cracked a sort-of smile. "Well, at least he won't try that again."

I rubbed my temples with my knuckles.

Honor laughed but quickly stifled it with the back of her hand. "Sorry, I shouldn't."

But then we both laughed, only when I laughed it felt like something was stuck in my throat. There was no joy behind it, either. It was as paper-thin as I was. As though I even knew who I was anymore.

"You better wash that stuff off your mirror before Mom sees," Honor says. "She'll think you've gone off the deep end or joined some weird emo cult."

I followed her gaze to the mirror above the vanity. My breath seemed to metastasize in my chest. There it was. A warning. HIDE

AND SEEK, HIDE AND SEEK, IN THE DARK, THEY ALL WILL SHRIEK. Straight from her. It was like she was there preparing to reach through the glass and strangle me. Three more tally marks, and she was going to make sure she was the one to put them there.

My mouth felt dry, my tongue coated in dust. "I—I—was just messing around. Some . . . song I—"

But Honor cut me off. "Hey, when did you get that?" She slid her ankles off the bed. She reached toward the music box, and for a second I worried she'd open it up and find the tablet of Sunshine hidden inside. But her hand passed over it and she reached to the other side. She cradled a camcorder in her palms.

I jerked upright, quickly unsnarling my toes from the contorted blankets. "Um, hold on there—" I didn't own a camcorder. I had no recollection of ever seeing this one before. So far things I didn't remember didn't have a great track record.

But my sister was already opening up the viewfinder, pushing the power button. There was a little chime to indicate that it was working. I made a grab for it and she snatched it away. "What is it?" she squealed. "Is it a sex tape?"

"No! God, of course not." Or I hoped not.

"Whoa, Cassidy! Was . . . when *was* this?" Her nose wrinkled and she peered closer.

"Give it back." I yanked just as she released the camcorder and I rolled backward so that my skull knocked against the head-board. *"Oof!"*

"Okay, okay." She dusted her hands together to show that she'd let go first. "Geez."

The effort left me panting.

"Was that Lena Leroux?" she asked.

The footage was already playing. I fumbled for the "stop" button while the video played and I was caught, mesmerized. It was shot at my school—worse—my school at night.

A shaky frame of the Hollow Pines auditorium where I recognized the barnlike set pieces. The clothesline. The wheelbarrow. There was someone moving on stage amid the eerie, yellow-green tint the camera used to catch movement at night. Two eyes peered back at the camera. The pupils glowed like a cat's. I recognized the dark bangs that brushed the eyebrows of the girl on-screen.

Honor was right. It was the sophomore Lena. Then, before I could stop it, there was a voice behind the camera. More tense and clipped than I was used to. "Say hello," it said. ". . . Do something," it commanded.

The voice behind the camera was mine.

I appeared on-screen, shooting middle fingers to an audience that wasn't there.

I jammed my finger into the "off" button and the screen went black. I stared wide-eyed at the blank viewfinder. Up until now I'd thought there might be some other explanation for the gaps in memory and for the strange things that I'd seemed to be involved in. I'd thought that maybe somehow I had nothing to do with them. But I had. The evidence was there. Whoever was doing these things to me . . . was me.

"How do you know Lena?" The skin between Honor's eyebrows puckered. She seemed almost hurt. Like if I was going to give attention to an unpopular underclassman it should have been her.

The room stopped playing at being a Tilt-A-Whirl and after a few false starts I was able to answer. "I—I don't." I squeezed my eyes shut as a wellspring of nausea started in the base of my stomach and pushed up against my throat. "She was filming practice for us." I thought fast. I lied. I never used to lie. "So we could see our mistakes. She forgot her camera. I just brought it home for her. That's all." Honor looked skeptical. "Thanks for reminding me. You know her?"

Honor's eyes brightened. I rarely asked her about her friends. Was Lena a friend? I hoped not. "Yeah, she's in drama with me. She does lights and edits the stage production videos and stuff, I think."

This was different from what Honor did. Honor wanted to be an actress and loved to sing, a gift that was otherwise at odds with her soft-spoken personality. Currently, she had a part with only one solo line, but from what I understood, even that was pretty good for a freshman.

"Oh, okay. Well, what's she like?"

Honor scratched a spot next to her eye. "I don't know. She's okay, I guess. Kind of weird." I raised my eyebrows, questioning. "Like dark, you know? She likes creepy music and sometimes colors her hair red and purple and blue."

"You know where she lives? I actually keep forgetting to return this thing." I gestured with the camcorder. My heart thumped in my neck and I tried not to look too hopeful. But I recalled how Liam found my number in the athletic directory. Maybe drama geeks had their own directory. I felt a spark of hope.

"She lives like five blocks over next to Kara on Oleander, near those apartments. Lena's dad never mows their lawn and Kara's mom is always complaining." I had no idea who Kara was. I should probably pay attention to my sister more. "But I can just give it back to her for you tomorrow, if you want."

I got to my feet. "That's okay. I need to get out to run a few errands anyway and I could use some fresh air."

I was jittery with something that felt equal parts excitement and panic. I would go to Lena. I would get answers. I would find out what was going on.

I used to be someone at Hollow Pines. Surely that ought to still carry some weight with someone like Lena.

One problem at a time. From a dresser, I grabbed an oversized sweatshirt that I'd stolen from one of the Billys back when I used to flirt. Back when I was happy. I threw it on over my sweaty tank.

"You're going like that?" I pulled on a pair of sweats and flip-flops. "Cass, it's still only, like, eight thirty."

I checked the alarm clock on my vanity. "Yeah," I said with a shrug. "I mean, I don't think it matters what I look like."

Honor stood blinking at me like I must be involved in some *Freaky Friday* moment, but she couldn't figure out with whom I'd switched.

"Later." I waved and grabbed my keys and left.

- - -

HOLLOW PINES WAS a small town, which meant there wasn't much room to separate the good from the bad and the bad from the ugly. We lived in one of the nice neighborhoods with stone mailboxes and automated sprinkler systems, but five blocks from our home, the scenery changed. The houses shrank and grew closer together. I got Kara's address from Honor. Her friend's house was quaint but pleasant. It had a Texas flag hanging out front. It didn't take me long to figure out which house was Lena's.

Instead of picketed wood, the fence was made of chain link.

Weeds crawled up the metal lattice. Grass grew ankle high and the white heads of dandelions speckled the yard. The closer I'd gotten to Oleander Avenue, the more restless my arms and legs had grown, like they were literally itching to get away from me.

I pulled into Lena's driveway and parked behind an old truck with a rusted tailpipe. I could still turn back and pretend that nothing ever happened—or at least pretend that I didn't know anything ever happened. But Lena was the last possible thread of a plan. Like a puzzle piece I hadn't turned over yet because I was saving it, hoping that it would fit. I was desperate. And I was edging closer and closer to my Hail Mary.

I found myself unbuckling my seat belt and stepping out into the fresh morning sun. At the stoop, I rang the doorbell and waited. A dog barked from somewhere within the house. When no one answered, I knocked. This time I heard shuffling and then someone yell for the dog to can it.

I stepped a couple inches back. There was no welcome mat at 1120 Oleander Avenue. Just bare concrete. Someone fumbled with the lock on the other side of the door and I stood up straighter. The latch clicked and a man, still guarded by a screen door between us, appeared in front of me.

"No solicitors," he said. "Unless you're selling Girl Scout cookies." His jowls were unshaven and he had swollen pouches under his eyes. "Are you selling Girl Scout cookies?"

My mouth dropped open and there was a pause before words came out. He must know I was too old for Girl Scouts. "No, sir. I'm looking for Lena," I said. "Is she home?"

He scratched a spot behind his ear. "She do something wrong?" The man's eyes weren't unkind, just beaten down like those of an overworked carriage horse. I didn't know what kind of trouble Lena would be in for which the authorities would send a teenage girl to reprimand her.

"No, sir," I said again. "Just some questions for . . . yearbook. At school. That's all." This lie came even easier.

"Oh, okay then." He didn't quite smile, but I thought there was something close to one lurking under the surface of his features. "Lena!" he called over his shoulder. "Lena, come out here. Someone's here to see you. She'll be right here. Probably still sleeping. She's like a vampire on the weekend, that one." He shook his head, then disappeared into the dim house.

I clasped my hands behind my back and rocked onto my heels. The screen door still blocked me from entering. It was a minute or two before Lena came to the door. Her dark hair was pinned into a messy bun using two pencils. Her face was even paler without makeup. She stood blinking at me through the mesh.

"Hi," I said. "Can I come in?"

Lena glanced behind her. She didn't answer right away. "Why?"

That wasn't the response I was expecting. Over the last week Lena had seemed intent on intruding into my life, but her mannerisms were now stiff and guarded. It felt like there was more than just a screen door between us. It felt like there was a wall.

"I . . . just have some questions." She didn't say anything. "I think we know each other better than I thought. But, I'm trying to figure out how. . . ."

"I don't know," she mumbled.

"I think you do, Lena." Desperation was seizing me. "The video. I found the video of you . . . and me. In the auditorium. I know we were there . . . together."

A flicker of interest. Her eyelashes fluttered.

"What were we doing there? Why—"

"I don't know anything," she said abruptly. "I'm sorry, but I can't help you."

A sharp gasp shot out of my chest. She stepped back. Her hand was reaching for the wood door behind her.

"Wait!" I grabbed the handle of the screen door and pulled it toward me. She quickly shook her chin. "Please, I need answers. I have to know what's going on. Please, Lena. How do I know you?"

A half a beat. "You don't," she said. "*You* would never spend a second trying to get to know me. Trust me." The door swung shut with a loud and final clatter before the lock slid into place.

I clamped down on my tongue until it bled. I tugged at the roots of my hair. Why on earth was this happening to me?

I had worked hard to transform myself into someone that people wanted to be friends with and sometimes just flat-out wanted to be, but it was starting to feel like maybe somewhere along the way, without even knowing it, I'd sold my soul to the devil.

— — —

ONCE HOME, I paced the rug at the foot of my bed. Back and forth I went, gnawing the tough skin at the base of my thumb. Lena wouldn't talk to me. Tate didn't know me. So why should I care about either of them?

When I reached my window, I turned and began down the same worn line that I'd already trod.

But I did care.

I thought of the boys.

If I didn't care, they may be dead soon.

Yet if Lena wasn't a willing link, I had no way into my other life, the one that took place after nightfall.

And with that, I kept circling around the same two points. Every few minutes I'd glance around the room as I walked. I'd see the photographs pinned on a corkboard. Friends sporting high pony-tails, our cheeks pressed together, giant red lollipop smiles. The orange and black pom-poms discarded next to a pair of overworked tennis shoes. SAT prep booklets. And my heart throbbed in pain. I missed it all. Even if popularity in Hollow Pines had wound up being less than a rags-to-riches fairy tale, I still missed it. *Please let me keep it*, I pleaded, as though she might somehow be able to hear me.

I sank onto the mattress and curled my thighs to my chest so that I could rest my forehead on my knees. Like grains of sand on a windy beach, I felt myself slipping away in pieces. Hot tears slipped down the hills of my cheekbones and crossed the bridge of my nose. My own mind was eating away at me, destroying me like a cancer.

I tried to breathe deeply only to have tears clog my nostrils. After several minutes, I finally wiped my nose and took several shaky breaths in and out of my mouth.

I didn't know when and I didn't know how, but I knew that if I didn't figure this out and stop her it'd be as though Cassidy Hyde never existed.

I slid my fingers again over the last slimy tears on my face until my skin was dry and chapped; then I sat up straight. I needed to channel the old Cassidy—both of them. The one that could solve math puzzles in her sleep and the one that could save Home-coming when the caterer backed out at the last minute.

Think, Cassidy. She is no smarter than you. You are literally the same person.

I had already tried to go around her, to head off her plans, to beg her to stop. None of that had worked. So, if I couldn't go around her, what would I do?

I must go through her.

My attention spiked like when I'd drunk too many Red Bulls before an exam. When I was younger, my mother used to tell me the story of *Hansel and Gretel* and the trail of bread crumbs. It was just a stupid fairy tale. It wasn't real. No fairy tale was. I knew that now. But if I was going into the mad forest, what I needed was a way out.

The hypnotist had given it to me.

I bounded down the stairs, out onto the driveway, and yanked open my car door. I found the black hoodie lying in the backseat, the one that I'd woken up wearing that day when I'd been late to school. It'd been stuffed in my car each day, taunting me. I slipped it on now, half expecting it to smell like someone else, the way other people's clothes tended to do. But that was stupid. The jacket was mine. I zipped it to my collarbone and went back inside because if I was going to bring bread crumbs with me into the night, I would need a place to store them, one I was fairly positive the other version of me would bring with her. Now I had one on.

"A way back," I repeated, this time under my breath, as I walked more slowly up the stairs.

Have you ever smelled something and been flooded with a memory? Dr. Crispin had asked. At the top of the stairs I tried to think about a smell that would force me to remember, when what I was trying so hard to remember was myself. My eyes snapped open.

Honor.

She was the only piece of me—Cassidy—untouched by the other *thing* that was lurking around inside my head.

I tiptoed to her door and listened. Usually when she was inside, I could catch her singing along to the soundtracks of Broadway musicals, but the room was quiet. I knocked just in case. Downstairs I could hear the television on and my mom banging around in the kitchen.

I let myself into Honor's room. She was a freshman, but her room hadn't made the leap to high school yet. I walked over a giant rug in the shape of a flower. Stuffed animals lined the window seat. I ran my hand over the tops of their heads, trying to remember some of their names.

Turning, I spotted Honor's blanket still scrunched half underneath her pillow. I crossed to reach it. The inside square of the blanket was knitted and it had a silky lavender border. I pressed it to my nose. It smelled as it always had, like laundry detergent, strawberry shampoo, and, okay, maybe a hint of drool. How many times had I made fun of my sister for keeping a stupid blanket? Mom said she'd grow out of sleeping with it when she was ready. Now part of me hoped that she never would.

In her nightstand, I found a pair of scissors. She would kill me once she found out. But I took the shears and cut a corner off the blanket and stuffed it into my pocket.

TWENTY-TWO

Marcy

The clock on the dash read nine o'clock when I pulled beneath the flickering fluorescent light of the gas station awning and parked beside the Dumpster next to Lena's VW Bug. I found her sitting on the hood of her car, back leaned up against the windshield, staring up at the stars. I thought about the stars on her wrist and wondered what it is that she would wish for.

I had only one wish now and it was about to come true.

"Why haven't you started already?" I asked.

She peeled herself off the glass. I'd been "waking up" earlier and earlier and tonight had set a record. But midnight was pressing in on us with an urgency so sharp that we couldn't dare waste a minute.

"I'm not going in without you." Her shoes squeaked across the hood. I held her hands to help her down. "The mill gives me the creeps."

"*I* should give you the creeps. The mill's just a mill. I'll be the scariest thing in there."

She looked seriously at me. "I wish you wouldn't say things like that, you know." The fringe of her bangs caught in her lashes. I brushed them free. She blinked at me for a second, then turned to rummage around in her backseat. She pulled out a heaping cardboard box and handed it to me, then pulled out another to balance in her own arms.

"Is this everything?" I asked, enjoying the weight of the box in my arms because it made things real.

"Everything that you ordered plus the theater department equipment you asked for. I need all this stuff back, though, Marcy. If it doesn't get returned to school, they could figure out it was me."

"Duly noted," I said, and made sure that nobody saw two girls disappearing into the field behind the station. The night consumed us as we walked into the high grass and picked our way over uneven terrain and torn-up roots to the shadowy silhouette of the old grain mill.

The hulk of metal and mortar twisted into the night sky, and I stared straight into its hollow, glassless eyes for windows. The darkness inside seemed to be deep and without a soul, and the presence of the mill worked chills up the back of my neck.

"Shall we?" I said with the same rush of excitement of a little kid on Christmas Eve.

I thought I heard the sticky sound of saliva sliding down Lena's throat beside me. We stepped over the broken threshold and into the mill, where sawdust made a sound like sandpaper underneath our boots. Lena clicked a flashlight on and then fished around for a couple of battery-operated lanterns that she pulled from her box.

The lanterns cast circles of soft glowing light on the cement floor. I paced the surrounding area, thinking, exploring, scheming.

How long would it take for stories to be told about this place? I imagined the future legends of the massacre in the old grain mill, forever haunted by the spirits of three college students. The idea was delightful.

Fingers of light stretched into the cavernous corners, revealing sharp objects and treacherous tilling equipment. A metal auger, a machine used to empty grain on the bin floor, was a razor-edged spiral that stretched horizontally along the length of one stretch of open space. A dormant conveyor belt ran along the perimeter, at the end of it a giant cogged wheel. Tattered burlap bags of grain piled up six feet high. Ladder rungs stretched into holes in the ceiling.

"How long will it take you?" I asked, hardly able to stand the anticipation. Seconds ticked by fast and slow all at once. My heart and soul were ready.

Lena rotated in place, peering around the room. "Not long if I focus," she said. The light from the lanterns played on the angles of her face.

She set up a series of three smaller cameras throughout the mill's bottom floor, checking in a handheld monitor to make sure she caught the expanse of the room on camera. Single red lights blinked on and began to watch us.

Lena worked with skill and precision. It was easy to imagine her directing the lights, the camera, the action from behind stage. Someday maybe I'd see for myself.

But not tonight.

She'd brought the stagehands' walkie-talkies. I changed the dials to matching stations and tested them. Then, I read through my list, checking items off as I completed a task. Lena showed me how to operate the monitor.

Minutes sank into hours and it was just after eleven thirty when I looked at my cell phone, wiped the sweat from my forehead, and realized that my honored guests would be arriving any minute.

"It's all working? Did you check the microphones to make sure they're picking up sound?"

Lena was adjusting a lens. She turned to me without a word, and through the nighttime dust-ridden air, I could make out the sparkle of tears in her eyes. "We don't have to do this," she said.

"Yes, we do." My voice went flat.

She closed the distance between us. Her hands were icy as they picked mine up and held them. "No, we don't. We could run away. Go somewhere, anywhere. Together. We understand each other and as of right now, nobody knows what you've done. We could stop this right here, right now. Please, Marcy. I know what they did to you, but it doesn't have to be this way." Her body reeked of desperation.

I examined her coolly. Finger by finger I removed my hands from her grasp, separating us. "You're wrong," I said. "This is the *only* way it can be."

Her breath caught. She looked down at the bare space between us where there was now nothing linking us together. "Then I—I don't think I can—"

"You can go," I said, and I wondered if she had banked on the fact that she'd need my permission. "This is probably the part in the horror movie where you'd want to cover your eyes."

She opened her mouth to say something, but there wasn't a good response to what I'd said because in this direction, there would be only suffering, death, and ugliness not for the faint of heart.

As she turned to leave, I wondered if she expected me to run after her, to make some grand romantic gesture. I wondered if she expected to be enough on her own. But I watched her go without feeling or regret.

Twenty minutes later, they were here and I was ready: *lights, camera, action.*

There was a knock, a creak, and then footsteps. If these boys had any imagination at all, they might have guessed what waited for them behind the walls of the abandoned grain mill—broken bones, flayed skin, and boiled blood sacrifices at the altar of justice. An eye for an eye. A tooth for a tooth. A life for a life.

The second they walked in, it was already too late for them. I wish they appreciated that, but then again, I loved a good surprise.

I perched on a crate on the second level, monitor in hand, ready to let the games begin.

I used the grain mill to design a maze of sorts that would separate the boys and bring them back together in turns.

A kinked cord attached a pair of headphones to the monitor so that I could hear what was going on downstairs. I'd have to ditch them as soon as the games began in earnest, though.

Shoot, popcorn, I thought with a snap of my fingers. I knew I forgot something. Popcorn would have been perfect.

I watched as three figures entered the shadowy ground floor. I could hear the shuffle of their shoes below.

Like mosquitoes to a zapper, the three boys gravitated to the lone battery-operated lantern that I'd left for them. I watched as they turned around, peered up, walked backward, and tugged at their hair, taking in their surroundings.

"What the hell?" The long-haired Jessup said this as if he'd been seriously inconvenienced. His voice echoed up to the second story. "Where are we?"

And, see, I would have thought that part was obvious.

Cruel, shark-eyed Tate with his cavalier, rumpled rich boy looks cupped his hands over his eyes as a visor and peered up into the rafters. "Is this some kind of joke?"

For the first time, I picked up the walkie-talkie and pressed down on the "talk" button. Three matching sets waited for them in a ring next to the lantern. "I'm afraid not." My voice crackled over their speakers.

All three boys flinched. Alex's arms flew up to the side of his skeleton face, half boxer, half refugee, preparing to get bombed.

"Who's there?" Tate yelled. His voice bounced off the walls and skipped back down, landing at his feet.

I smirked and spoke into the handheld device that contained so much power in this moment. "Why don't you read and find out?"

The sound was muffled, but I could just make out what Jessup said. "Look, there's a note."

"Oh goodie, I love notes," I said through the speakers. "Don't you? Read it for us, will you?"

Tate snatched it away from Jessup, then smoothed the sheet of paper. He picked up one of the walkie-talkies and held it up to his mouth.

His voice was gravelly as it came through, playing close to my ear. "Rules of the House." He scoffed as if he were the one in control instead of me. "Number One. Smile, you're on camera." Tate spun in place, held his arms out wide as though to say *come and get it*, and plastered a big grin on his face. "Eat your heart out, sugar. You can film me all night long." Of course, I would. Just like he'd filmed me. Fair was fair. After a full rotation, he returned to the list. "Number Two. There is no leaving the game. If you play the game from start to finish, the video invitation provided to you will not be made public. Ever." He glanced up at no one in particular. "It better not be," he said. "Number Three. If at any point you break the rules of the game, the video invitation provided to you will be released. Immediately." There was a low growling sound from Tate and he lifted his middle finger. He couldn't see, but I lifted mine right back. "Number Four. At your convenience, please deposit your cell phones in the storage box directly to your left. Any calls, texts, e-mails outside of these walls will be met with the same consequences as set forth in Rule Three above. Or worse. Number Five. Cheaters will be punished. Without exception. Number Six. Don't forget to have fun. You've earned it." Tate dusted off the knees of his jeans and shouted up at the ceiling. "So I guess you think you're funny, huh? You think you're clever with your little puzzle?"

"Ah, don't be a sourpuss," I said. "Next time you blackmail someone you can make the rules. Until then, though . . ."

Alex started to speak, then stopped himself, retrieving his walkie-talkie from the ground. "But what's the game? We can't play a game if we don't know what the hell it is," he said. "She mentioned a game, didn't she?" This he said more to the two boys at his side.

I smiled to myself. "That's the best part. You already know how to play. The game . . . is hide-and-seek."

"Are you serious?" Jessup said. The boys were exchanging looks.

"Deadly."

Nearby, there was a large, hulking generator. I flipped the three switches that were on the side. The insides of the mill groaned like the whole building had indigestion. The mill was coming to life. Below, I heard the auger begin to rotate, a sharp metal spiral. Cogs on various pieces of machinery lurched, noisy with rust.

"Dammit," Jessup yelped. The boys instinctively shuffled together. Tate shoved them away.

"And," I continued, "since I'm feeling generous, I'll give you to the count of twenty-five. No Mississippis, though, I'm not that nice. Are you ready?" I didn't wait for a response. "Okay, then, here we go. One . . . two . . . three . . ."

"We're not actually doing this," said Alex.

"Come on. We all saw the video." Tate was speaking through gritted teeth now. "If this gets out, my dad's career could be ruined. And if that happens, I'm ruined. You understand?"

"And I've got Anna, dude. She would freak out. It's just a little girl. What the hell are you afraid of?"

"Yeah." Tate pushed Alex in the chest. "Stop being such a pussy and play her little game."

Alex stumbled back. "But . . ." He dropped his voice lower. "What about Mick and Brody?"

"Ten . . . eleven . . . twelve . . . ," I counted.

"What about them? Brody was beaten to death with a bat. You think a girl did that?" Tate reached down and picked up the single remaining lantern. "Let's get this over with so we can move on and get out of here."

Jessup rubbed his bare arms. "How come *you* get the lantern?"

"Because I'm going to be the one to go find this bitch, unlike you two weenies. Now take your walkie-talkies and scram."

Alex didn't move. He looked to Jessup for help, but Jessup just shrugged. "Either we do what she says or we're screwed."

At last Alex caved. "Fine," he said, but it was to no one because Jessup and Tate had already gone their separate ways, wandering off into the bowels of the mill.

"Twenty-one . . . twenty-two . . . twenty-three . . ." I made sure I had what I needed. A new knife in my boot. A Taser stashed in the front pocket of my hoodie. A hammer clutched in my sweaty palm. I fitted a pair of night vision goggles over my eyes. My walkie-talkie. I wouldn't bring the spare lantern with me. It would be too much to carry. I took a second look at the monitor, then stuffed it into a thin backpack along with the two reams of rope and a roll of duct tape and slung it over both shoulders. "Twenty-four . . ." I took a deep breath and exhaled slowly. "Twenty-five. Ready or not, here I come."

Game on.

The sound of the churning machinery masked the sound of my footsteps as I spirited across a grain bridge and then down the rungs of a ladder fixed to the side of a silo. Last I'd seen, Alex had still been pacing indecisively near the entrance, unsure of which way to go. That was perfect. I'd make the decision for him.

"Do you see her?" came Jessup's voice over the walkie-talkie frequency.

Now on the same level, I could hear Alex click the button on his transmitter. "No. Do you? Over."

It was staticky when Tate's voice sounded. "She can hear you, you idiots."

"Right. Sorry. Roger that," said Jessup. "I've just always liked playing with these things."

Oh, don't you worry, California, you'll get to play soon enough.

Through the lenses of the goggles, the surrounding world was a wash of video-game green hues. I pressed my back to the curved surface of the grain silo. As I shimmied around the edge of it, using it to protect my backside, I scanned the area, landing at last on the form of Alex McClung. His cragged face showed up looking blotchy and pockmarked even in night vision. He hid behind the pile of burlap bags containing stores of grain like a coward.

I walked gently heel-to-toe so as not to be heard. Closer and closer I drew until I could see Alex's fingers turning an unlit cigarette over and over between them. My heart pounded in my ears. I stopped breathing. I was four feet, three feet, two feet. I thought he heard me. Or maybe he smelled me.

Whichever it was, there was a hammer to his temple before he could react. The sound it made was silenced by the grind of the machines. His head snapped back. Then, his knees buckled and he turned in at the waist and he was on the ground. I fought the urge to make a sound. Even a battle cry.

Instead, I stowed the handle of the hammer in the waistband of my jeans and hooked my hands underneath his damp armpits. I dragged him in short halting motions, checking behind my back every other step, until painstakingly, methodically, I pulled him over to the conveyor belt and up onto it.

He started coming to just as I was wrapping the duct tape all the way around his chest, pinning his arms tight to his sides. I twisted another quarter roll around his shins.

"Hey." His eyes fluttered open. "Hey, what do you think you're doing?" He scrunched his chin to his chest and tried to stare down in the direction of his feet. "Hey, watch it!"

I took a small strip and pressed it over his mouth.

At the end of the conveyor belt was one of the large, spiral augers, a perfect bit of machinery made from curved, metal blades that rotated in a lethal corkscrew motion. It was already twisting, making long scraping noises across the cement floor. I doubted that Alex could make out what lay ahead at the end of the runway, but I knew he could hear it.

A few feet above his head was a lever the size of my forearm. I wrapped my hand over the bulb at the top. I used the full force of my weight and I pulled it down toward me. The conveyor belt lurched, sputtered, and then began to move.

Alex tossed his head. Muffled screams came from behind the duct tape. I strode to his side, following him as his body traveled down the length of the conveyor belt. I stooped down close to his ear. "How does it feel not to be able to run?" I whispered, and his eyes widened.

He fought with his chest and waist against the tape. It didn't loosen. The belt chugged along. Closer. Closer. Closer.

His head was again lifted off the belt. I wondered if he could see what was ahead now. That was when the muffled screams reached a new pitch and I was sure that he could.

I counted down in my head. *Three. Two. One.*

His feet hit the auger and the sound was of shredded leather first. It was like a bird caught in a plane propeller. I could hear when the sharp, twisted metal found the bone, chewing it methodically.

At the same time, his limbs must have jammed the machine because it stopped working. I didn't have time to fix it because Alex had managed to yell so hard that the duct tape broke free of his mouth and he was now shouting and cursing and crying.

The air smelled like sweat and blood. I ran my tongue over my lips, tasting the sharp flavor that clung there. I made a quick promise to come back later before silently disappearing around the bend.

There was a rush of movement. I saw the bulb of light from the lantern bouncing. A cough and a sputter.

From Alex an "Oh god! Man! No! Don't—is it—don't look—god—are they? Help me."

"What the hell, you psycho bitch!" Tate hollered.

Over the walkie-talkies, Jessup came on the line. "Everything okay over there?"

"Alex lost his foot, man." Cue: Alex screaming. "Where are you?"

"Shit, I'm not saying now," Jessup said. "Not on here."

Tate cussed. *Hide and seek, hide and seek, in the dark, they all will shriek.* I hummed the notes to my little ditty.

Crouching down, I pulled out the monitor and scanned the frames for Jessup. I saw him climbing a ladder, up and up, to the third story. I grinned, returned the monitor to the backpack, and began scaling a different set of rungs, beginning to fancy myself a bit of a ninja.

I could already feel the sting of the tattoo needle on my arm. Two more tally marks, then a diagonal cross over the top to make five. And then and *only* then would I deserve her. Keres. With her tattered faerie wings and blood-soaked scythe.

The closer to the top I got, the slower I made my approach,

careful not to let the cold metal under my hands and boots creak. I heard a clang from above.

"Oof!" a voice said. Once on solid flooring, I jerked my head to see Jessup, both arms out, feeling his way around in the dark. The sound of the machinery was more muted here. "Who's there?" Jessup hissed, sensing my presence.

I didn't respond. I moved in a wide arc around him, circling, beginning to close in.

"I know you're in here. I can see you." But he kept whipping his head back and forth. His long hair kept getting stuck to his lips and his eyes were wide as saucers. "Don't try anything. I'm trained in karate."

Doubted it.

I tapped my fingernails against metal siding. He jumped and turned in the direction of the sound. He was standing precariously close to one of the open silos. I circled back the other way, then I sprinted the last few steps to him. His hands flew up protectively. I came to a hard stop an inch away from him. "Boo," I whispered. He lowered his hands from in front of his face, a look of surprise. Then I pushed him.

He fell without a scream. At least until he landed on a pile of grain.

"What—what is this stuff?" He was beginning to fight it. He was swishing his hands and feet through the grain in the silo like a swimmer and as he did so, the grain began to swallow him.

He thrashed harder.

"Did you know," I said, "that eighty percent of workers buried in grain up to their knees are unable to get free without assistance?" I peered down the barrel at him. The grain was already up to his waist and rising. He stared down at the grain creeping up his body.

He began to jerk, trying to wrench himself free. "That's not true," he shouted. "That can't be true!" But he pushed at the grain, trying to sweep it away from him. But that only opened up a larger hole for him to sink into. "*Relax*, Jessup. Chill out. It's not a big deal. Besides, don't you know that grain is like quicksand? The more you struggle, the faster you'll suffocate."

"Wait!" he screamed. He punched at the grain that was pushing against him on all sides. He struggled to yank out a leg at a time. "Wait! Don't leave me here! Where are you going? Help!"

I brushed my hands together, enjoying the show. He was tossing his head. He was pushing his elbows out, fighting against an opponent that was too strong for him. His chest and neck were already disappearing beneath the collapsing surface. He twisted. His long hair fell into his eyes. Within a few seconds, I couldn't hear him at all.

Back down the ladder I went. *Come out, come out, wherever you are*, I thought, while at the same time telling myself to be cautious, to be careful. I was so close to perfection. I couldn't get sloppy now.

"Jessup?" Tate's voice crackled. "Jessup, are you there?" No answer. Jessup was gone. "*Shit.*" A pause. "I'm going to kill you, little girl," Tate said. "Just you wait. I'm going to kill you."

Not when I kill you first.

The sound of Alex's intermittent screams rose and fell through the mill. I didn't know if he was still bleeding out freely or if Tate had managed to tie a tourniquet. On the second story, I knelt and fished through the remaining supplies in my bag, finally pulling out the rope. I stretched it out between my hands and gave it a sharp tug. The rope snapped with tension. The perfect strings for the group's puppet master. Now look who was in control.

I pulled out the monitor, checked for his whereabouts. I didn't see him the first several glances. And then I did. Back pinned into a corner. His chest rose and fell. With fidgety fingers, he was unfurling his belt from his waistband. He was looping the end through the buckle, testing its strength.

Points for improvisation, I thought drily.

Tate picked the lantern back up and began treading his way through the maze of grain bags and silver silos on the ground floor.

I pressed the button on the side of the walkie-talkie and sang to him, "Hide and seek, hide and seek, in the dark, they all will shriek; seek and hide, seek and hide, count the nights until they've died."

"Shut up, shut up, shut up," Tate shouted. He held his hands to his ears.

I went down to join him.

The grain dust floating in the air smelled sweet and old and tickled my nose when I breathed it in. Tate was easy to spot by the light of the lantern he was carrying like it was the thing that could keep him safe. That and his belt, apparently.

I bent down and scooped up a pebble that I'd stepped on. I threw it and it pinged against one of the silos. Tate spun and the lantern bobbed wildly.

"Show yourself," he demanded. Because he was used to being the type of person who could make demands and people would listen. I wasn't listening.

A system of cables and pulleys with steel hooks hung from floor to ceiling. Puppet master on a string. I ran my fingers up the length of one of the taut cables as I glided past. I picked up another pebble from the floor and chucked it at another silo, enjoying how he jumped at the clang.

I remembered how he'd laughed, how he'd encouraged the other ones, told them what to do. I remembered how he wore a smug look on his face like he was untouchable. I remembered it and I hated him.

Slowly, I reached into the front pocket of my hoodie until my hand closed around a thick, solid object. I pulled the Taser gun out and flipped it over. *Can you believe you don't need a license for one of these?* I mused.

I would hang Tate high until the last breath was squeezed from his neck and his eyes bulged and his tongue fell out of his mouth.

Tate turned just in time. We were both bathed in the glow of the lantern. I shot the Taser at him. The lantern banged against the cement floor. He hit his knees, muscles convulsing. It was a good look for him.

I wasted no time, though. I stuffed the Taser back into my pocket. Then I wrapped the rope twice around his throat, twisted the ends together, and hooked it onto one of the iron claws hanging on a cable cord. He squirmed like a worm on a hook. I wrapped my hands around the cable and pulled with all my might.

There was a crank and the hook moved up. The rope tightened around Tate's neck. His feet dragged on the ground. He wriggled to try to get them underneath his weight for support. His time was short and the flashes in his eyes told me that he knew it.

"Pop quiz," I said, keeping my hands gripped around the metal pulley system.

"Go . . ." He struggled. ". . . Screw . . . yourself."

"Wrong answer," I said, and pulled the cable again. He lost his balance and struggled against the rope to right himself. "Let's try this again. First question. What was the date on which you assaulted a high school girl named Cassidy Hyde?"

The pupils of Tate's eyes flitted from one side to the other. I tapped my toe on the floor.

"Aw, come on, Tate. You can do it. Here, I'll offer a reminder. She was about this tall." I held my hand even with my scalp. "She had brown hair." I slipped my hood off and flipped my hair over my shoulders. "Pretty. Very pretty, if I do say so myself."

Tate's Adam's apple bobbed against the rope.

I frowned. "No? Well, that's a shame." I tugged on the pulley cable and the rope tightened again.

He worked his fingers into the rope at his neck and tried to loosen it. A bead of sweat rolled down his temple.

"Are you ready for the next question?"

He twisted and fought against the rope. It began to creak. He had his fingers in between his skin and the rope. "You're not giving me much of a choice here, Tate." His eyes bugged. I reached into my pocket for the Taser gun again.

But out of the corner of my eye, I saw a scrap fall from my pocket and land on the toe of my boot. I blinked and glanced down. I bent and picked it up. For a second, I was lost in the satin texture. It felt familiar. Instinctively, I brought it to my cheek and rubbed it against my skin. Soft.

I took a deep breath and touched it to my nose. "Mmmmm . . ." I closed my eyes for just a moment.

Strawberry shampoo. Laundry detergent. Maybe a hint of something else . . .

TWENTY-THREE

Cassidy

I came to like a person breaking the ocean surface having held her breath for too long. My lungs welled up and I gasped. My first thought was of Honor. I looked down at the scrap of blanket clutched between my fingers and clasped it to my chest. I was back. But where was I back to?

"What . . ." I startled at the anger in a voice so close by. ". . . question?"

And then I saw him. *Him.* The boy from the dining hall. The boy from Dearborn. Tate.

Or at least it was a version of him.

I took two steps back.

He was dangling from a noose. Sweat bubbled at his brow line. Fury raged in his eyes.

"W-W-What question . . . ?" I stuttered. My fingers worked in the swatch of blanket.

My gaze skirted the strange factorylike place in which I found myself. I whimpered at the sound of soft moaning coming from a distance.

The contents of my stomach surged up my windpipe, choking me before I vomited.

"What's going on?" I pointed to Tate.

He gurgled. Tears were leaking from his eyes. "You . . . are . . . insane." His cheeks puffed out and sucked back in. "You know that?"

I felt my lower lip begin to tremble. I covered my mouth. "I—I tried to warn you."

Tate struggled to keep his feet underneath him. "Warn me? What *kind* . . . of warning was . . . that? You said *nothing*." His words were a growl. "Nothing!"

"I—I—I—you didn't even see me!" I shrieked. Hair flew in my eyes. I peeled it off. "You didn't know who I was!"

He sees you now.

I felt feverish. "Please . . ." I pushed my palm against my fore-head. "I didn't want this."

You wanted all of it.

"I just need to think." *Coward.* I shook my head.

Kill them. End it.

"No!" I shouted.

"You will pay for this. You hear me? My father is a congressman."

This is what you want. Justice. Make him pay.

I plugged my ears. "Shut up. Shut up. Shut up!"

They've ruined your life.

I screamed. "You're ruining my life!"

The Taser gun was a dead weight in my hand. All around me was terror. "This isn't me," I muttered. "This isn't me." *This is you. This is us. We are.* "No, no, no, I'm good."

Kill them. Do it.

She was taking over, strangling the Cassidy out of me like a boa constrictor. I took a final look around the horror she'd created. I couldn't fight evil with evil without being consumed in the flames. There was only one way to stop her. I pulled out the cell phone in my back pocket—*Disgusting, weak, spineless, he laughed at you—* and hit three numbers.

I had to if I wanted to preserve anything of myself. Time seemed to freeze over. When I could no longer convince the demented alternate being that was living inside me to stand still, I turned the Taser on myself, pressed it against my thigh, and pulled the trigger.

I collapsed to the floor and writhed there. The wait for sirens to approach stretched infinitely long until suddenly the blare of them was roaring in my head and panic warred in my chest.

It's too late.

Too . . . late.

The voice said.

TWENTY-FOUR

White walls. White mattress. No sheets.

   White elastic pants. No drawstring. White cloth shirt. Scratchy.

A metal door. Glass, submarine window set into the thick door. An untouched tray. On it, a whole apple and a peanut butter and jelly sandwich that had been sitting out since last night.

I wasn't allowed shoes . . . or socks. My toes were cold enough to be miserable but not cold enough to feel numb. I sat on the squeaky mattress that felt like it was made from flimsy foam poster board and tucked my feet underneath my knees. My back pressed into the bare cinder blocks behind me. I didn't know what time it was. There were no windows to the outside and I'd lost track . . . hours, days, weeks ago?

Down the hall there were clangs of doors and the uneven roll of wheels down tiled floors. I estimated that it was morning and didn't think I'd slept at all.

If I was right, my breakfast would arrive soon. Three strips of bacon, dry toast with a fried egg served on top. Since I'd left my dinner untouched, they'd make me eat it. Hold my mouth open. Force me to swallow.

They'd be here soon. They were coming for me.

Two knocks sounded at the door. Never three. Why not three? Two was unnatural.

"Go away," I said. "I'm not hungry." I pulled my knees into my chest and buried my face in them. Stringy hair fell in straight curtains around me. I didn't know how much weight I'd lost since I'd been in here, but my ribs poked through the skin on my torso.

A lock slid. I felt the cool manufactured air flow into the room without looking. "Cassidy?" The woman's voice was melodic. "Cassidy, your parents are here to visit."

I pulled my knees tighter and rocked.

"Cassidy, we're going to take you to see them. Okay? They're very much looking forward to it. We're coming in now."

I drew my chin out of the hollow between my knees and forearms. Dr. Blanche was a slender woman with a slick ponytail parted down the middle and red-framed glasses. She took out a pen from her lab coat and jotted something down on my chart.

An orderly filtered past her, pushing a wheelchair.

"I can walk," I said to the man whose hand was stretched out to help me into the chair.

"Standard procedure, miss."

I rolled my eyes and scooted off the mattress without taking his hand. I planted myself roughly in the leather sling of the wheel-chair and lifted my feet onto the stirrups.

"I'll be back this evening with a new prescription," said Dr. Blanche. "But you'll need to eat something. It's important to your recovery, Cassidy."

I glowered at her as the orderly wheeled me past. The halls of Maven Brown Psychological Treatment Facility were a labyrinth of bleached color and gave me an instant headache. I stared down at my lap as the orderly whisked me through a series of right turns.

"Patient for the visitor center," he said, pulling us to a stop at a sliding glass window. Something was exchanged. The orderly then lifted my limp wrist and buttoned a plastic hospital bracelet around it.

The window slid shut again and I was greeted with the whoosh of automatic doors that split down the middle to let me through.

"Enjoy your visit, Miss Hyde." The orderly parked me in front of a square table where pieces of a jigsaw puzzle were scattered.

"Hi, honey." My mother smiled wanly from across the table. A few pieces of the jigsaw puzzle were stuck together. They formed the eye of a kitten. The tip of a tail. Half of an ear.

"You look . . ." My father laced his fingers through my mother's and their hands disappeared under the table. ". . . good."

I scoffed.

"You know, we've been checking in more than once a day, Cassidy. This is the first time they would let us in to see you. You've had a friend here, too, from school. Lena, I think?" My eyes flitted into focus. "She keeps insisting she should be let in to see you, but it's only family for now, I'm afraid." I offered a curt nod. "Sweet of her to care so much." Mom tilted her head, the crow's-feet around her eyes stretching clear to her temples. "Are they treating you well? Are you getting enough to eat? No one's being mean to you, are they?"

"It's a regular Disneyland," I replied.

My father frowned. His face was exhausted, but I could still spot our resemblance. "I'm afraid they're only giving us a short time together so early . . . in your treatment. So we'll have to get right down to the reason they allowed us to talk in the first place."

My father reached underneath his seat and slid out a manila envelope. From it, he pulled a stack of papers and pushed them across the table, spinning the stack around so that the pages would face me right side up.

My mother reached across the table and laid her hand over the stack. "First, your lawyer assures us that this is the scariest part. After this, it'll be our turn to start piecing together a case, Cassidy, and I can promise you we've hired the best. They believe your actions, given the circumstances, were completely justifiable."

"Mom's right. The lawyers said it's not too much to expect very little, if any, hard time. There are precedents for things like this. Battered wife syndrome. Self-defense. That sort. Really, your mom's becoming quite the expert."

My mother retracted her hand and sat back. "So . . . just keep that in mind."

I tucked my hair behind my ear and pulled the papers closer. A tremor of impatience passed through me as I felt them focusing on all the wrong things.

My father shifted in his chair and it made a loud screech. "Sorry," he said nervously. "It's just that it does seem bad at the moment. Facing four charges of first-degree murder. And—" He coughed into his fist. "And the case of assault with intent to maim, kill, or dismember."

My eyebrows shot up. *"Four* charges of murder?"

My father's chin dropped. "Yes, I'm afraid one of the other boys died at the hospital . . . after. It's all in there." He waved at the papers. "Alex . . . McClung."

I sucked in a sharp take of air and dug my fingernails into my palms. I teetered on the verge of losing it. So Tate had survived. Tate Guffrey was still breathing. I jiggled my leg in the stirrup.

"Only four?" I said, unable to mask the strain tugging at my vocal cords. "That's *all?*"

My parents jerked and snatched each other's hands again. It was so annoying how they did that.

"Cassidy, we know it's a lot to take in. But yes, that's all the information we have now," said my mother.

No, that's not what I meant, I wanted to say.

"The lawyers say you'll testify, though, that you were frightened of them after the assault. That you didn't mean to hurt them but you had no other recourse." *Wrong.* They had it all wrong. I saw my knuckles turn white. "They think this will play well with the jury." Their voices sounded distorted like they were coming out of a faraway megaphone. What was wrong with them? How could any of this matter to them? I went still. "You're a star student. Homecoming queen. Captain of the Oilerettes. Paisley and Ava have both been over to ask about you, by the way." I felt my back rising and falling, seething like a cornered animal. "They're very concerned."

I waited for them to finish. My eyes bored into my mother's forehead. Then I swiped my hand across the table, and papers and puzzle pieces flew. "I am none of those things," I screamed, leaning forward and pressing my chest into the table.

"Cassidy, please," my father murmured. "We're all stressed here. If you just say—"

I scratched the wood table. Saliva gathered at the corners of my mouth. "For the last time, my name . . . is not . . . *Cassidy.*"

"Cassidy, honey." Tears sparkled in her eyes.

"My name's not Cassidy!" I pounded my fist and the remaining puzzle pieces jumped. "My name's not Cassidy. My name's not Cassidy!" My shrieks filled the hushed room where other visitors' heads swiveled to watch. "My name's not Cassidy!" A young girl nearby squished her hands to her ears. "Not Cassidy!"

The woman that was my mother slumped into the man that was my father. An openmouthed *o* of alarm was pinned to his lips.

"Do you hear me?" I screamed at them with such force that they pulled back like I'd literally blown them there. "Do you hear what I'm saying? I'm not Cassidy! Stop calling me that!"

Out of nowhere orderlies arrived on either side of me, strapping my arms to the chair, unlocking the brakes, wheeling me backward.

"Marcy," I muttered. "My name, I told you, is Marcy."

AUTHOR'S NOTE

Dear Reader,

This book is about one character's fictionalized response to an assault. There are as many ways to react to the aftermath of sexual assault and survivor trauma as there are victims. Although this is a horror novel, the *true* horror is that the inciting incidents contained in these pages are not far off from true-life events that are happening across high school and college campuses right now.

For support or for more information, please visit the Rape, Abuse & Incest National Network at www.rainn.org or call their hotline at 1-800-656-HOPE.

Sincerely,
Chandler Baker

ACKNOWLEDGMENTS

SITTING DOWN TO write this book, I felt lucky to be able to return to the world of Hollow Pines. Thank you to the team at Feiwel and Friends who made it possible: Holly West and Jean Feiwel, you both pushed me to take this story in a difficult but more personal direction. Holly, you've been the champion of these books. Thank you for loving Cassidy, Marcy, and Lena along with me. Molly Brouillette and Kallam McKay, I appreciate your hard work in helping these books reach their audience. Veronica Ambrose and Melinda Ackell, you keep me from making embarrassing mistakes within these pages for which I'm particularly grateful. And Rich Deas, thank you for having a vision and for creating gorgeous books.

When writing a horror story, it's nice to have people who can make the process a little less scary: A huge virtual hug goes out to Tony DiSanto. You're always willing to throw your heart and support behind these books. And to the rest of the team at DiGa, especially Tommy Coriale, Michael Maniaci, and Hayley Brooks, it's a thrill to be able to work with you.

Shirine Coburn DiSanto and Meghan Holston, you didn't have to, but you've adopted this project as your own and continued to be so generous with your time. Thank you both.

To my agent, Dan Lazar, your career advice this year has been invaluable. I'm glad to have someone like you in my court. And to Torie, for chasing down everything that needs chasing down.

I had a number of smart readers and friends who offered thoughts and motivation. Jeff and Maggie Langevin for clutch brainstorming. To Lori Goldstein, Kelly Loy Gilbert, Shana Silver, and Lee Kelly, thank you for providing a community of writers that understand. Charlotte Huang, as you know, I strongly believe that our e-mails are a little bit magic.

To my book club—Emily O'Brien, Kelley Flores, Lisa McQueen, Wendy Pursch, Julia Teague, Amy Morehouse, Kristen Largent, Kandice Karla, Whitney Waters, Kate Stein, and Susan Hobbs— for your cheerleading but also for years' worth of lively conversations about books I might never have picked up on my own. Also the wine.

Lastly, big thanks to my family. My parents, Coni and Mike, you understand my crazy schedule and love to pitch in. To my daughter, thank you for your patience in letting me finish this book prior to your arrival and then for your promptness immediately thereafter. To my husband, Rob, hell hath no fury like a woman who is nine months pregnant and on deadline. Thank you for your patience and for your supply of chocolate milk, peaches, and boxed mac 'n' cheese, among other things.